Moon and Back

Jelvia: Not Human, Volume 4

T.E Kessler

Published by Wise Publishing, 2022.

MOON AND BACK

First edition. October 8, 2022.

Copyright © 2022 T.E Kessler.

ISBN: 979-8215027615

Written by T.E Kessler.

PROLOGUE

James leaned in towards the computer screen, so close his nose almost touched it. He watched as the Jelvia used his claws to cut through the electrified barrier. The current sparked, and grey smoke puffed into the air, but the Jelvia remained unfazed. He clambered through the fence, keeping to the edges of the concrete grounds, and moved towards the building. As the security camera's red eye swept the yard, he jumped behind wooden pallets.

James had top-range protection, however, and this was not the only camera watching the Jelvia. The system—which James had built himself—did as he asked, and he had reduced the electric current to allow the Jelvia access.

The Jelvia moved from his hiding place and stopped behind a forklift. He looked up at the disused warehouse that James called home. The camera caught the Jelvia's illuminated eyes, and James recognised him instantly. He smiled. He had expected Calder, but Narcifer's presence made his flimsy plan rock solid.

Almost six years ago, James and his wife, Leigh, worked with Professor Jon Johnsen to uncover the Jelvian secrets. The project had ended in tragedy. His memories of that day were murky, but the horror he'd felt when the Jelvian spacecraft had been shot down under Johnsen's orders was still clear. Only two Jelvias had survived: Aldarn and Scasone.

James hadn't been directly involved, but his association with the project was enough to put him on Aldarn's revenge list. He'd been hiding ever since—until he'd chosen to reveal his whereabouts to save Harry and his girlfriend.

James flicked a switch and watched the screen as Narcifer turned towards the click of an unlocking door.

James pressed the intercom button.

'Come on up, Narcifer.'

1

He watched as the Jelvia circled the pallet-riddled yard and headed towards the door. His shape disappeared momentarily as he entered the building. The Jelvia's response had revealed no hesitation or surprise, and James felt the first tickle of apprehension up his spine. On the screen, Narcifer could be seen climbing the stairs, his throat expanded, ready to spit venom.

James swivelled his chair to face the open doorway, keeping the image of Narcifer in his peripheral vision. He glanced at the portrait of Leigh hanging in the centre of the wall. Her gaze was accusatory; he could hear her voice telling him he was being foolhardy, but he wasn't going down without a fight.

Narcifer's light tread interrupted the brooding silence, and James focused on the doorway. The Jelvia's bulk filled the entrance. His black eyes glittered as he saw James.

'One thing you need to know before you kill me,' James said, 'Macy's had a... well, let's call it "insurance".' James paused, watching Narcifer's face. There was no emotion: no panic, no flicker of uncertainty at the mention of the woman he professed to love, and James' confidence in his plan to use Narcifer's girlfriend as insurance wavered. 'If my heart stops beating, so will hers.'

This time there was a flicker. It was gone instantly, but relief flooded James.

'I was expecting Calder.' James stood and came forwards with his hand outstretched. 'I haven't had the pleasure.'

Narcifer ignored the gesture.

The Jelvia stepped into the room and closed the door. Snubbing James, he moved around the space, looking at objects, picking things up, and putting them down. He wasn't doing it to unnerve James; he was giving himself time to think things through. This pleased James, and he was even more certain his blackmail could work.

James sat down.

'Narcifer, do you know why you've been ordered to kill me?'

Narcifer swivelled. The speed alarmed James, and he jumped, then clenched his fists. He needed to keep it together. All of humanity depended on it.

Suddenly, Narcifer's hands were around his throat, jerking him from his chair, which crashed to the floor. Narcifer pushed him against the wall; his head banged painfully. James felt the cold hardness of the Jelvia's claws against his throat as his own hands circled Narcifer's wrists, trying to pull them off.

James knew it was futile, but panic made him struggle as his air cut off. He wheezed, clawing at air and raised his gaze to meet Narcifer's soulless black glare. Narcifer's claws bit into his skin, drawing blood. Then, just as suddenly, the claws relaxed, and Narcifer's arms fell to his sides. James slid down the wall, dragging painful breaths into his lungs. His eyes were watering, and he brushed the tears away with the back of his hand.

Finally, he straightened and looked up at Narcifer. The Jelvia's dead, soulless eyes stared back. James pointed towards a chair.

'Please sit,' he said, his voice croaking.

Narcifer crossed the room and sat down. Not trusting his own legs to carry him to his chair, James leaned against the wall.

'I'm sorry it's come to this, Narcifer,' James said, 'but since my wife died, I see no reason to live. However, I feel obliged to do so if only to give meaning to her death.' He cleared his throat delicately. His windpipe felt crushed. 'So, this is your real mission. Listen carefully.'

The burly Jelvia remained motionless.

'First, you're to tell Calder that you've been successful and that I'm dead. Second, you're going to bring Aldarn to me. Third, you will now be my protector—because if I die, so does Macy.'

ONE

Jayden's thumbs battled with the PlayStation controller as it jerked and spasmed in his hands. He was almost there—just one more to kill. His avatar, a muscular ex-army soldier called Monster, was weary and bleeding heavily. His energy was only five per cent.

Nearly there.

A crash from downstairs disrupted his concentration for a millisecond, making Monster fall. 'Fuck!' Jayden yelled. Monster's target had seen him fall. 'Get *up*,' Jayden yelled, jabbing at the controller as Monster struggled to his feet. The target-turned-predator was two metres away and taking aim.

There was another crash from downstairs. Then Jayden's bedroom door burst open, and a real monster stood in the doorway. Jayden didn't even have time to yell before his body was splattered all over the bedroom walls.

Macy and Courtney screamed. Lisa looked up from her book, pulled a face of disgust, and returned to her story.

'Those are awesome,' Narcifer said. 'I've seen them before on TV. What did the boy call them? Play-something?'

'A PlayStation,' Macy said. 'This was the most brutal ending of any movie ever, and all you're interested in is the video game?'

'They need to invent PlayStation for real. They look awesome,' Narcifer repeated.

'Wait, what?' Courtney said. 'They *have* already been invented in real life. Are you saying you've never seen one outside the TV before?'

Narcifer shook his head, his eyes on the TV as the credits played. 'I've never seen them on my island,' he said.

'I'll buy you one for your birthday,' Macy said, picking up the TV remote and turning the volume down.

'Birthdays only happen to humans,' he said.

'No birthdays, either?' Courtney stared at him. 'I don't get it. Everyone has a birthday. Everyone. How old are you?' she asked suddenly.

He looked thoughtful. 'I've been twenty-nine for a while.'

'You have Christmas, though?' Macy asked.

He shook his head and explained that the word 'Christmas' had never been in his vocabulary before coming inland to England. Even Mumma Lisa put her book down to listen as Narcifer explained that such traditions didn't exist where he came from. Macy loved Narcifer as an individual, but sometimes his Jelvian ancestry seemed one-dimensional.

'On that note, I'm off to bed,' Mumma Lisa said.

'Me too,' said Macy. She looked at Narcifer. 'Coming?'

'Soon,' he said.

Hiding her disappointment, Macy faked a smile and stood up. Her movements were slow and stiff, and Narcifer jumped up to help. It should have been sweet, but it made her feel like an old maiden aunt.

It was a miracle she survived when she was pushed from the car. Her injuries had been horrific, but she'd recovered relatively well, considering she'd been left with a shattered right side and fractures to her leg and three ribs, her arm and collarbone, and the front right lobe of her skull. Her left side hadn't fared too badly—just a broken wrist and a shattered kneecap. They had inserted a metal plate in her right leg; the scar, running from her ankle to her thigh, was like a seam inside her leg.

The incident happened several months ago when Courtney's ex tracked her down and tried to convince her Aldarn was stalking her. At one point, Courtney didn't know who to trust and unfortunately turned to Greg, who revealed his true colours when he tried to kill Macy and kidnap Courtney.

Worse for Macy was the psychological impact—the memory of the wind dragging at her when Greg opened the car door, his hand as he shoved her, her fingers clutching at air before she fell out, and the split-second knowledge that she would probably die when she hit the rushing ground. And then hearing the *thump* of her body on the tarmac before everything went dark.

She didn't think she'd ever get over that, but everyone assured her it was early days. And it was, she guessed. She'd only been released from the hospital two weeks ago.

On the other hand, Courtney had to deal with her guilt for letting Greg back into her life.

'It's okay, I can manage,' Macy said when Narcifer looked like he was about to scoop her up and carry her up the stairs. She didn't want to draw any more pity from him. She walked stiffly, feeling his gaze on her back.

Her room was directly above the kitchen. The sound was faint and muffled, but she could hear Courtney washing up their cups and wine glasses. Macy undressed, listening for sounds of Narcifer coming upstairs, but there was nothing. After a short time, she heard Courtney heading to her room, but Narcifer was silent downstairs.

Straining her ears, Macy heard the front door opening and closing. She forced her uncooperative body out of bed. She got to the window. Narcifer was already climbing onto a neighbouring house's roof. He scaled it quickly, his speed and agile movements a testament to his Jelvian genes. He could twist his body in ways that were alien to a human. Macy watched him jump from roof to roof, then disappear from view.

Letting the curtain fall, Macy turned from the window, her shoulders slumped. It was difficult to describe—Narcifer was as loving as always, but at the same time, he was distant. Macy climbed into bed, pulling the duvet up to her chin.

For much of her stay in the hospital, she had been encased almost head to toe in a cast; she'd been on a morphine drip, making October and most of November a blur. Then, just as she felt better, she developed septicaemia, which set her recovery back.

The cast on her right leg had come off in early December, and now, with many physical therapy appointments behind her, she could walk almost normally. Her leg tired quickly, and her gait was quick to turn into a limp, but she accepted that. What she found hard to take was that Narcifer found her scars repulsive.

And because it had been Courtney's ex-boyfriend who'd caused Macy's injuries, their friendship was under undue strain. Macy had shown restraint when Courtney had not only attended Greg's funeral, but also the wake, made her realise their friendship would never be the same again.

To be fair to Courtney, it must have been hard on her. She respected Macy's feelings despite her anxiety about Aldarn's recovery, who'd been injured trying to save her from Greg. She'd also been brilliant in supporting Macy's recuperation and well-being—brilliant and very professional.

If Mumma Lisa sensed the tension between them, she said nothing.

Macy sat up, flicked on the bedside light, and reached for her iPad. She couldn't sleep, and she *wouldn't* sleep until Narcifer was back. She opened the iPad, its glare blinding her momentarily. She had an alert set for any Jelvia or Wake Up Movement—or WUM as it was also known—activity. Thanks to the new bill in the House of Commons—which was debated throughout her stay in the hospital and finally legislated before Christmas—the media could no longer write negatively or broadcast stories about Jelvian activity, so most of her alerts were about the WUM.

Macy didn't know why the government had devised the new law. She didn't think it was to appease Jelvias. It was more than likely to stop the growing panic among the people. Although, there seemed to be no panic surrounding WUM, just pure hatred of Jelvias.

Their motto was *Wake up!* and their cause was steadfastly gaining support. The number of people claiming to be 'waking up' was worrying. It was like a type of madness spreading across the globe.

A knock on her bedroom door caused her to look up. Then the door opened and Courtney looked in.

'I saw the light on,' she said. 'Are you okay?' She came over and sat on Macy's bed. She was in her PJs. 'You've been quiet today. Worrying about going home next week?'

It wasn't going home that worried her. It was learning that Narcifer no longer wanted her as a partner and that it was only a matter of days before he would tell her. He wasn't a cruel man. He was probably battling with the correct words, so he didn't hurt her too much.

'A little,' she said. She'd already told Courtney her worries. 'I need to get back, though,' she added, knowing Courtney and Lisa wanted her to stay. They thought she was rushing her recovery. 'The Wake Up Movement has upped the pace since I've been in the hospital. I want to investigate them. Apparently, they've sent me letters and messages, and they're all sitting on my desk.'

'You're not going back to work?' Courtney asked, dismayed. 'I thought you wanted to concentrate on, you know, Narcifer? Your job should be the last thing you want to return to. It almost killed you in the summer.'

Macy snorted. 'That was Jon Johnsen, and he's dead. I've a new boss whom I've not met yet. Paul said he's great.' Paul was her line manager at *London Echo*, where she worked as a journalist. Macy had taken up the role of investigative journalist under Jon Johnsen to gain insight into Jelvian activity. That's how Macy met Narcifer and how Courtney met Aldarn. She hadn't reckoned on Johnsen having an ulterior motive and using her as bait, though. 'I *do* want to concentrate on Narcifer,' she added. 'But that means getting back to normal and going back to work.'

Courtney grabbed her hand. 'Macy,' she said. 'Forget about work. You need to concentrate on getting better, and for goodness' sake, tell Narcifer your worries about your scars.'

She shook her head. 'I couldn't cope with the confirmation that he doesn't fancy me anymore.'

'Aw, Mace! Of course, he does. He probably thinks it's too soon to do any more than kiss you.'

'He doesn't want to do that either!' She forced a light-hearted laugh. She hated people fussing around her. 'I'm fine. *We're* fine. How's you? You look tired.'

'I am. It was a long and arduous shift today.' Courtney stood up, yawning. 'Christ, I'm knackered. Don't let Mum wake me up in the morning.'

'I'll try, but you know what she's like.'

'She's putting the house back up for sale,' Courtney said, going to the door. Lisa put her house on the market in the autumn but had taken it off since Macy's accident. 'I know she wants to do a big clean before the valuers come again.'

'Like that'd make a difference.'

Macy smiled, and after a cheery wave, Courtney left her alone. Macy flipped her iPad closed and reached for the light. A noise outside made her stop, and she pushed back the duvet and padded over to the window. She pulled back the curtain to see Narcifer jump from the roof to land in the front garden. She watched from the window as he walked up the garden path towards the front door. He stopped and glanced up as if sensing her there. His face immediately lit up. He grinned, his dimples deeply indenting his cheeks, and raised a hand to wave at her.

Macy waved back, smiling just as widely. All her doubts about him vanished. He was the perfect boyfriend—except that he was a Jelvia.

And he killed people.

TWO

The house smelled stale. Macy had left it tidy, but it had been locked up for months. She scooped up the post from the mat, needing two hands to get it all, and plonked the pile on the dining room. Narcifer followed her in with their bags as Macy began opening windows.

It was almost February, and the air was sharp with the promise of snow.

'Are you sure about that?' Narcifer asked, watching her.

'Just for a while,' she said. 'The house needs airing.' She peeked at him over her shoulder. 'We could cuddle up in bed while the house airs?'

They'd made love since her accident, and it had been sweet, but it was always over too quickly and lacked the intensity Macy had become accustomed to. It was just lovemaking; there was no kinky fuckery or passionate sex.

He smiled, coming towards her and looping his hands around her waist. He pulled her in for a kiss. 'I wouldn't do that to you,' he said, drawing back and letting her go almost immediately. 'It was a long drive, and you're bound to be tired.'

She smiled, trying to keep the sting of his rejection from showing on her face. 'I am a little tired,' she said, and relief spread over Narcifer's face. She tried to ignore the hurt, but it cut her deeply.

Their love affair had been fast-moving and intense, and it'd happened in a few months. They'd hardly known one another before her hospitalisation. She worried their love would burn out while she'd been stuck in the hospital, but Narcifer treated her tenderly like she was a precious jewel.

'You have got a lot of letters,' he said, his voice breaking into her thoughts.

Macy glanced at him, then looked at the mail she'd dumped on the table. He picked up a handful of magazines—*Stunning Planet*, a subscription she thought she'd cancelled while away.

'Mostly junk, I bet,' she said. Then, leaving Narcifer to sort through her mail, she went into the kitchen. They'd come home with a few days' worth of home-cooked food courtesy of Lisa, including her signature lemon drizzle cake. She picked up the tin that housed the cake and lifted the lid. She breathed in the lemony smell.

'I'll have some of Mumma Lisa's cake,' Narcifer said, and Macy smiled.

She popped her head around the kitchen door. 'You couldn't have seen me open the cake from there, even with your Jelvian senses. You must have heard the tin pop or something,' she said.

He was looking at the front cover of *Stunning Planet* magazine. The headline read: **Rainbow Eucalyptus—Multi-Coloured Trees**. A photo of beautiful trees with bright stripes running through their bark graced the cover. She'd signed up for it on the promise that she'd travel around the world and see some of the wonders from the magazine in person.

He tossed her a grin and then pulled the polythene wrapper off the magazine to flip through it. Macy leaned against the doorjamb.

'Will you take me to visit your island?' she asked.

'It might be tricky, but I'll try,' he said, closing the magazine and dropping it back on the table. 'It's lovely there,' he said as he picked up a handful of the post. Most of it looked like junk mail. 'Beautiful rainbow trees, mountains, lakes—'

'Rainbow trees?'

'Yeah. Coloured tree trunks, like they've been painted on.'

Frowning, Macy's eyes flicked to the magazine he'd discarded.

'Hmm, this one's unusual. It's handwritten,' Narcifer said, and Macy looked up, forgetting the rainbow trees. He held a letter with her name on it.

She took it from him and opened the letter.

Macy Shaw,

I hope this finds you well. I mean you no harm, and I only wish to wake you up. But, like most of the world, you're asleep. I know you have a Jelvian boyfriend, and I know you think you love him. But how can you love someone who isn't what he thinks he is? He is asleep and has his memories fed to him.

This isn't real!!

WAKE UP!!!!

Please, Macy, don't regard this letter as a crank. Investigate the Wake Up Movement.

Yours,

WUM

'Ah,' Macy said. 'It's from WUM. I've been getting lots of these letters sent to my office at work—probably because I've not been answering my emails. They're protesters rallying against Jelvias, and I suppose they think I have inside knowledge.'

'WUM?' asked Narcifer.

'Hardly a fitting name for an apocalyptic movement, is it?' she said. 'They're just cranks marching through the city, telling us to "wake up". They have a bizarre website proclaiming that you're aliens who arrived on Earth in spaceships. This is why I wanted to come home. I want to expose them.'

'Aliens?' Narcifer chuckled. He sifted through her mail and found another handwritten envelope. It was quickly joined by another and then another. He looked at her in alarm. 'They are more than cranks, Macy,' he said. He opened one and handed it to her. 'Read it,' he said. Narcifer's reading ability was poor.

Macy took the letter and began reading.

Dear Miss Shaw,

WUM needs a member like you. Please investigate WUM and become a member. You will be contacted once you do.

WUM.

She looked up at Narcifer. 'Doesn't sound any more menacing than crank level to me,' she said as Narcifer opened another letter and passed it to her to read. That letter was much the same.

'I'm surprised you haven't seen them or been ordered to sort them out by the committee,' she said.

'The committee doesn't bother itself with protesters, and as for me not noticing them, I've had other things on my mind.' He raked his hair. 'I will investigate them and—'

'I want to work with you on this,' Macy interjected. 'I don't think they are anything to worry about, but their presence affects Jelvias wanting to live here. They are nothing short of bigoted Nazis.'

Narcifer's face softened. 'What's your other reason?' he asked.

She frowned up at him. 'Other reason?'

'You always said you had two reasons for returning home.'

'I want us to get back to where we were,' she said, her eyes searching his face.

'We are back,' he said, not meeting her eyes.

Macy sighed. Short of asking him if he found her repulsive—something she wasn't brave enough to do—she didn't know how else to get through to him. Instead, she watched him pick up another letter and open it. Then, predictably, he handed it to her.

She took it and scanned it. 'It says the same as the others. They're just begging letters.' She scrunched it up and tossed it onto the table with the others. 'I don't see anything threatening about them at all.'

'You don't? Mace, they know your home address.'

'They are *total* cranks who've gathered momentum in the last month. While in the hospital, I watched their so-called movement grow and kept track of their silly protests. According to Angela from work, they've been trying to contact me there. They're harmless.'

'Why didn't you tell me?'

'Because I had more important things to consider—like getting well.'

'And who's Angela?'

'A colleague from work. Narcifer, stop with the overprotective boyfriend crap. It's all okay, okay?' She rubbed her forehead in frustration. The last thing she needed was Narcifer using WUM to stay away from her.

'You look tired. Let's get you to bed—no hidden agenda,' he added at her raised eyebrows.

'I'm tired of being in bed,' she said. 'I'm okay. Anyway, if I sleep now, I won't tonight.'

He took her arm and led her into the lounge. 'Then at least sit down. I'll empty your case and sort out the house.'

She sank down on the settee, and tenderly Narcifer bent to lift her legs to make them rest on the sofa. 'Want some of Lisa's cake?' he asked.

'Yes, that'll be lovely.'

He smiled, dropped a kiss on her head, and disappeared into her kitchen.

She was lucky. She had a boyfriend who adored her; not everyone had that.

He just doesn't want to rip my clothes off anymore.

THREE

By early evening her eyelids were drooping, and despite her protests, Narcifer scooped Macy up and took her upstairs. He laid her on the bed, and as she stared into his eyes, her hands still around his neck, smiling seductively, he kissed her.

Macy melted into him, but he untangled her hands and stood up, leaving her gaping at him in horror that he'd rejected her again.

'If you need anything, just shout,' he said at the door.

She sat up. She wasn't imagining it—he *did* find her unattractive.

Swinging her legs out of bed, she stood up and undressed in front of the full-length mirror, torturing herself as her scars became visible. Along with the criss-cross mutilations on her legs and the long one on her inner left leg, she had ugly scars on her arms and one on her chin. Hiding the mark on her forehead with her hair was easy, but it reached her eye, making the lid droop and stopping her eyebrow from growing.

She'd never been particularly body-confident, anyway. Courtney was always the pretty one. She got all the male attention and, annoyingly, never seemed to realise. Then, when Macy was seventeen, she'd fallen in love and had been sure her love was returned—until she'd introduced him to Courtney. He'd made his move on Courtney, and although Courtney had been horrified and rallied around Macy with all the usual 'more fish in the sea' clichés, the damage had been done.

Macy got into her pyjamas and then climbed into bed, feeling miserable. Despite her mood, she must have fallen asleep quickly. She awoke in the morning to Narcifer lying beside her, one hand across his face and the other resting on his chest. Macy studied him as he slept. Even in sleep, he was beautiful.

She sat up carefully and slipped from the bed. She grabbed her robe and used the main bathroom on the landing so as not to wake Narcifer, then tiptoed down the stairs to make a strong coffee.

There wasn't much in the fridge by way of breakfast. They'd picked up a few provisions before coming home yesterday, plus the homemade food Lisa had given them, but Macy knew she needed to head to the supermarket. She wondered if she could send Narcifer with a list, but it was obvious he'd never shopped for anything other than small items in his life. He had everything done for him—wash his clothes, choose his clothes, his cooking, all of it. Even his shopping.

She finished making coffee and was just stirring in the milk when Narcifer came in, looking and smelling fabulous.

Ignoring the coffee, he came over to kiss her. Then, letting her go, he said, 'What have I said about leaving our bed without waking me?'

Narcifer didn't like sleeping. He'd admitted once that his dreams were very dark, and the only thing that could banish them was seeing her upon waking. He loved to just hold her, which usually led to making love—but lately, that hadn't happened.

'Sorry, but I was dying for a coffee. Want one?'

'That'll be great. Any plans for today?' he asked. Macy opened her mouth to suggest they could just spend the day together, but he continued, 'Because I do.'

'Oh?'

'Yeah, sorry, babe. I need to catch up with the others at Keats.'

Keats was Narcifer's house on Keats Avenue, where he used to live with a group of other Jelvias who'd moved off the islands.

'They can't phone you?' she asked, knowing she sounded ridiculous.

'Not really,' he said. 'It'll be boring, uninteresting stuff, like where the latest paedophile gang is hiding. We can't discuss that sort of thing over the phone. I'll need to check in regularly,' he added as if to warn her. 'I hate leaving you alone when we've only just got back, but I'm afraid it's out of my hands.'

Hurt made her turn from him, and she made a big production of looking through the fridge. 'No problem. I need to do a proper shop for the house, anyway. There's hardly anything in here.'

Large hands slipped around her stomach and pulled her back, so she was forced to let the fridge door fall close and rest against him. She thought he was about to say something apologetic, so she was taken aback to hear him say, 'Maybe you should've stayed at Mumma Lisa's.'

She pulled away and glared at him, unable to hide her hurt this time. 'This is *my home*! Why shouldn't I stay here?'

'Hey, I only meant so you're not on your own. Especially with WUM knowing where you live.' Fingers lifted her chin. 'Mace?'

'Your coffee is getting cold,' she said and began to sidestep him, but his bulk prevented her from moving away again. Instead, he lifted her for a bone-crunching cuddle. His delicious scent filled her sinuses, and her body reacted in its typical way, but her mind knew it was futile. Small kisses peppered her cheeks, nose, and chin, but they avoided her scarred eyebrow.

'It's going to take time until you're better,' he said, his words soft against her ear, 'but we've all the time in the world, haven't we, eh?'

She nodded, and he put her down. He smiled down at her. 'Don't worry about the coffee; I'll grab something at Keats. The sooner I get there, the sooner I'll be able to come back.' He winked, turned, and then was gone.

Macy stared at his coffee cup, then picked it up and tipped it down the sink.

She wouldn't cry—she *wouldn't*. But, like Narcifer said, this was going to take time. Her scars were a big deal to him, but that was okay. Sometimes people react to things in ways that surprise even themselves.

But the hurt cut deep no matter how she soothed herself.

~

She was surprised but pleased to see Narcifer's car in the driveway as she pulled into her street after her trip to the supermarket. But, unfortunately, a Rolls-Royce was parked directly behind, blocking Narcifer's car and preventing Macy from pulling up next to it on the driveway.

Macy knew the Rolls was the favoured car of the Jelvian community. She hoped their visitor wasn't Yash. She didn't know how she'd react. He and Aldarn had been involved in her kidnap last year, and although Aldarn had been remorseful, Yash wasn't. In fact, she hadn't seen Yash since. And then a skinny woman called Beth Roberts had come into the hospital asking for Macy's help because Yash was blackmailing her or something.

Macy parked on the road and climbed out of her car. Eyeing the Rolls nervously, she circled her Mini to the rear and opened the boot to get her groceries. Grabbing the bags, Macy heaved them out and carried them into the hall. As soon as she stepped inside, she heard raised voices and knew she'd walked in on an argument. Such was their argument, they hadn't heard her enter.

'Doing what the committee wants won't make them more controllable, Narcifer. You have to do it our way or theirs. There *is* no middle ground.' It was Calder talking earnestly, and despite his tone, Macy relaxed. He was one of the good guys. 'Your activities are making the Keats House unsafe for us all.'

Macy put the groceries on the floor and considered sitting in her car until Calder left. She didn't want to listen in—the last time she had done that, she'd got the wrong end of the stick. But neither did she want to sit in her car or walk into the room mid-shout, either.

'You're worried about the police now?' Narcifer said as Macy stood uncertain in the hallway. 'I'm sure you can handle them!' His tone dripped sarcasm. 'Or is it because you don't like your authority questioned?'

'You're not questioning my authority,' Calder said. 'We all have ways of keeping the committee at bay but you're going rogue.'

The argument sounded serious, but Macy had made up her mind. She banged the front door closed as loud as she could, yelling, 'I'm home!'

Then she opened the hallway door, stepped inside, pretending she was unaware of their argument.

FOUR

Calder enveloped Macy in a hug. 'Good to see you looking so well,' he said, letting her go and tipping his head to one side as if he'd practised the concerned look in the mirror. 'Are you fully recovered?'

'Getting there,' she said. She looked at Narcifer, then back at Calder. 'You two arguing?'

'No,' they both said at once.

'Want me to leave you to your, er, discussion?' she asked, looking at Narcifer.

'There's no need,' Narcifer said. He looked pointedly at Calder. 'He's leaving.'

Calder raised his eyebrows. 'You know,' he said to Narcifer, 'I don't mind having this conversation in front of Macy.' Then, he looked at Macy and said, 'Lately, Narcifer's been acting—how do you say it?—ah, out of character.'

'Are you surprised? We've had a stressful year,' Macy said.

'Undoubtedly. Unfortunately, Narcifer is handling it all wrong.' His gaze swung back towards Narcifer. 'I'll ask you again: Why were you searching my office?'

Narcifer glanced at Macy, but he quickly looked away again. 'I came to find you,' he said to Calder.

Calder's stare made Narcifer anxious, judging by how he ran a hand through his hair.

'That's a simple explanation, isn't it?' she said, standing closer to Narcifer in a gesture of solidarity. 'And he told me this morning he wanted to find you.' That was a lie—he had said no such thing.

'I'm sure he did,' Calder said, 'but why go to the effort to find out how long I'm going to be away before "searching" my office?'

'I...' She looked at Narcifer. Suddenly, she felt like a schoolgirl being reprimanded. It made her giggle, but his face was grave. Her giggles evaporated. 'Is this really serious?' she asked, swinging her

21

face back to Calder. 'I mean, I always go through Courtney's wardrobe.'

'But are you searching for evidence that she's covering something up? Narcifer, I've been lenient with you because of family connections, but I can't keep making excuses. It isn't fair to the others who live in Keats.'

'Oh, for fuck's sake, Cal,' Narcifer said. 'I went into your office to see you about the, er, assignment. I wasn't searching for anything. Christ, you're paranoid.'

'About that assignment...' Calder said.

Narcifer turned abruptly to Macy. 'Hey, babe, why don't you go upstairs? Put some music on or something.'

'You keep your work and your relationship with Macy separate?' asked Calder. He looked surprised.

'You know I do,' Narcifer said.

'He does,' Macy affirmed.

Calder flicked his gaze from Narcifer to Macy and back again. 'Well, that's something, at least.'

'I have no interest in your work,' she said.

'You're a journalist. Of course, you're interested,' Calder snapped. He turned away and faced the window, his hands clasped behind his head. He was angry. Macy could see the tension running through his powerfully built body.

Macy looked at Narcifer, who avoided her curious glance. But without another word, she left them to their discussion. She closed the door firmly behind herself and went upstairs. In her office, her iPod was already slotted into the speaker. She turned it on, picked up her headphones, and put them over her ears. She switched on her computer as Katy Perry's warm voice washed over her, and she tried to ignore the fact that there were two angry Jelvias downstairs in her front room.

She needed to back up the notes she'd made while in the hospital, so she kept herself busy doing that. Some were written, some recorded. She first worked on the recorded ones and listened to them as they downloaded. In her earlier entries, when she'd relied on medication to control her pain, her recordings were rambles and difficult to decipher. The written notes would be even worse to untangle, but she'd work on them another day.

There was a long entry in mid-November; reviewing it, Macy remembered she had watched an audience-and-panel discussion about the WUMs. Several WUM members had been invited to answer questions from the panel, but the panellists had shut them down as nonconformist eccentrics, especially when they'd insisted the Jelvias were aliens. They claimed they had come to Earth in ten spaceships. Allegedly, nine had disappeared into the sea only to reappear as the Jelvian islands. The tenth ship, apparently, had been shot down over London.

Macy smiled as she remembered the ripple of laughter that had gathered momentum through the audience. The following day, the newspapers had a field day hinting that the Wake Up Movement was run by parochial and moronic people and memes about the WUM followed. They were, in essence, an organisation that Macy need not worry about. However, they stoked people's fears of Jelvias, and made their lives difficult.

When the download was complete, Macy filed the entries in date order on her computer. Then she thought she heard a door close downstairs and pulled off the headphones to listen and heard Calder say, 'You won't find Al in my office.' It seemed like he was in the hall at the base of the stairs. 'What I said earlier wasn't advice. It was an order. Despite it being the easy option, we do not give in to the committee.'

Then, finally, she heard the front door open.

Feeling it was safe to leave, she left her office and leaned over the balustrade on the landing in time to see Narcifer close the door after Calder. He didn't know she was watching, and he leaned against the door and tightly closed his eyes. He looked anguished.

'Hey,' she said, straightening and going to him in concern. 'Are you okay?'

He looked at her in surprise as she came down the stairs. 'Of course,' he said and smiled. But the smile was forced.

'You don't look it.' She stopped halfway down the stairs, almost at eye-level with him. 'Are you in trouble?'

'It's complicated,' he said.

'What did he mean about "giving in to the committee"?' she asked. Even though the media was no longer allowed to report any Jelvias killing human criminals, it didn't mean they weren't happening. The law hadn't been made to protect Jelvias; it was to stop public unrest.

'"Giving in" means killing people, doesn't it?' she asked, looking at him with suspicion.

Narcifer rubbed the back of his neck. 'Not necessarily,' he said.

'Why are you looking for Aldarn?' Ever since Aldarn had saved Courtney from her deranged ex, Greg, he hadn't been seen.

'I'm not.'

'But Calder said "You won't find Al in my office."'

Narcifer raised his eyebrows at her. 'Have you been listening?'

'No! I caught the end of the conversation, that's all,' she said, feeling indignant.

'Sometimes I forget how nosey you are,' he said with a teasing grin.

She put her hands on her hips. 'I think I have a right to know if Aldarn's in England,' she said. She didn't want to encounter the big Jelvia again and had always assumed he'd returned to the Jelvian islands.

Aldarn's life-changing injuries resulted from human experiments conducted on him by Jon Johnsen. And during a brain seizure, when he, Courtney, Macy and Narcifer were together, he somehow connected Macy back to that traumatic event. She was certain he'd have killed her. She rubbed her forehead, feeling stressed.

'You have nothing to worry about. You're completely safe,' Narcifer said. He reached over and pushed her fringe back into place over her droopy eye.

Macy stared at him in shock, but he turned towards the hallway and the grocery shopping.

'Calder coming here has nothing to do with you or what Aldarn did to you. I have something going on with the committee, that's all,' he said, taking the shopping into the kitchen.

Macy followed miserably. Narcifer put the bags on the countertop, then turned and cupped her face in his big hands. He leaned down and dropped a kiss on her mouth.

'There is no way I'd let Aldarn near you, but I do want to find him,' he said, straightening as her hands came up to hold him close. He clicked his fingers as Macy lowered her hands self-consciously. 'Got it!' he said. 'If I can't get into Calder's office, I know somebody who can.'

And then he headed out of the house, fumbling in his pocket for the car keys. Macy heard the door close, and milliseconds later, his car started as if he couldn't wait to escape her. Macy went into the hallway, where there was a wall mirror. She looked at her reflection and then pulled out her mobile phone. She didn't have many photos of her mum on her phone (mobile phones weren't that popular twelve years ago), but she kept one inside her phone case. She pulled it out and looked at it.

Macy shared her mum's red curly hair, and the older she got, the more she grew to look like her. She could remember the pain of her mum dying like it was yesterday. It still hurt, and she still dreamt of it.

'I'm clinging on to him with my fingertips, Mum. But what else can I do? I love him so much.'

The image of her mum in the photo blurred as Macy's eyes began to well up.

FIVE

Macy wasn't one for self-pity.

She shook it off and made plans to seduce Narcifer that night. So, while he was out, she texted him, telling him to keep the evening free, and then an hour before he was due to come home, she dressed carefully, wearing a figure-hugging dress that embraced her curves and emphasised her breasts.

She'd taken her time with her makeup and hair. And when she came downstairs, Narcifer looked her up and down with that lazy smile on his face, dimples accentuated. He pulled out the chair for her to sit at the dining room table.

Not wanting to be enslaved to the kitchen for the night, Macy had ordered an Indian takeaway. Narcifer hadn't eaten Indian food before, so she'd played it safe, ordering a chicken tikka masala for him and a lamb dhansak for herself.

All the food was set out nicely, and dinner started well, with Narcifer flirting and playing footsie with her under the table. Her previous conversation about Aldarn was deliberately left out, and it almost seemed like old times—until Narcifer's phone pinged with texts. Seeming unaware that he was being rude, Narcifer constantly checked it until Macy felt he'd forgotten her presence.

Macy ignored an urge to flounce upstairs in tears, and as they sat in the lounge idly watching *Dunkirk* on Netflix, she was glad she hadn't made it an issue.

'I've missed this—us just being together alone,' he said, putting his arm around her and pulling her close.

Macy snuggled against him as his fingers stroked her upper arm. His thumb 'slipped' to graze over her breast every now and then. And Narcifer's phone seemed to be forgotten at last. She flipped a button on her dress and snuggled closer to him on the settee.

'This movie is very violent,' he said, pulling her closer.

'It's a wartime movie; it's meant to be violent. It's hard to imagine it happened, isn't it?' she said. She gathered up her dress to rest on her thigh, showing Narcifer a glimpse of red, lacy underwear.

'Did it?'

She laughed. 'Yes. It's *Dunkirk*. You know, World War Two.'

'Right.'

'Didn't you study this at school? It's where soldiers from the UK, Belgium, and France tried to evacuate from the town of Dunkirk. Did the Jelvias fight in the war? I remember photos and old newsreels, but it's not concrete in my head.' Narcifer's fingers brushed over her breast again. Then, smiling, she said teasingly, 'We don't have to watch the film.'

'Right,' he said.

That was *not* the correct response.

She peeked at him and noticed the unusual dryness in his all-black eyes. She didn't see it often—usually only when he was in 'Jelvia' mode. When the committee spoke to him, his eyes sparkled as if they conducted electricity—and he had the same sparkle when they made love. Macy suspected it was an emotional response. The dryness indicated calm anger or intense concentration—at least, she was pretty sure it did. She was still learning to read the different emotions that played in Jelvia's eyes.

And right now, Macy had expected to see sparks.

'Narcifer! I'm suggesting we go to bed, and that's all you can say?'

'Sorry, babe, you go to bed if you want to. You look a bit tired.'

He may as well have slapped her. Macy's head jerked back towards the TV, feeling unbelievably wounded. The images on the screen blurred as it became apparent that his short answers had been an automatic response to her questioning. His mind hadn't been on *her*. Instead, it was on the texts he'd received, and his hands brushing against her had been an accident—a movement he'd not even noticed.

Narcifer's phone pinged again, and he moved forwards so fast he almost pulled Macy with him. Macy sat back, feeling flustered. She wanted to be the centre of his world, but at the moment, she felt second best.

Narcifer read his phone. 'Good girl,' he murmured, dropping it back on the coffee table.

Good girl?

Jealousy flared in Macy's heart.

'Who was that?' she snapped.

'Oh, just Bren,' Narcifer said. He hadn't noticed her tone.

'Who's Bren?'

'She drives us around and monitors our targets when we track them. She's a Jelvia. She lives at Keats,' he added.

Is she pretty? She wanted to ask. *Young? Scarless?*

Macy glanced down at her legs, where her scars were clearly visible. She'd thought she was being sexy, allowing her skirt to ride up, but it made her look desperate. She smoothed her dress over her knees.

'And why is she texting you?' she asked.

'It's just Jelvia stuff, nothing interesting,' he said, not noticing her icy tone.

She sighed. It came out more loudly than intended, but Narcifer was oblivious anyway. He carried on watching the movie, even though she knew he wasn't paying it any attention. His mind was on other things.

Probably Bren.

Macy couldn't pinpoint when she'd first noticed Narcifer's withdrawal from her. His excuses had gone from 'not under Mumma Lisa's roof' to 'not wanting to hurt her'. But she was healed now, and Narcifer was still avoiding her—though she didn't blame him. The thought of his flawless face and body against her scarred one sickened her too.

'Good night, then,' she said, moving to stand up.

'Night, my love.'

'Wow, you're really making it obvious.' She gave a hollow laugh and crossed the room to the door. 'Good night, Narcifer.'

'Macy—hey, what?'

At the door, she turned to look at him. The dryness in his eyes had gone, and she had his full attention, but she couldn't be bothered with false platitudes. 'Nothing. Good night.'

He frowned, looking concerned, but didn't move from his position on the settee.

'Good night,' he said, and Macy turned to head up the stairs.

Later, in bed, she flipped onto her side and turned off the bedside lamp, listening for the sounds of Narcifer coming to bed. Instead, she heard the front door open, close, and lock. His car started up a moment later.

Macy scrambled out of bed. She reached her bedroom window to see Narcifer reversing out of the driveway. She watched as the car disappeared up the road.

SIX

Macy tossed and turned, wondering where Narcifer was and convinced herself he'd gone to Bren. Thoughts circled in her head. She pictured Bren as being tall, beautiful, and unscarred. She even imagined Bren and Narcifer making love, which taunted her all night.

She must have fallen asleep because it was morning when she woke up, feeling groggy. She looked across at Narcifer's side of the bed. It was empty, and as she felt the coolness of the sheets, she knew he hadn't been there all night. She lay back, staring up at the ceiling. He'd always been secretive about his job and what it entailed but never dismissive of her affections. And he'd never mentioned Bren before.

Usually, it was her he came to when his job got to be too much.

She rolled over and grabbed her phone from the bedside table. She had a text from Narcifer:

I had to go out really busy sorry back lunchtime I love you

There was no punctuation. He'd used the text-to-speech function on his phone. But it was easier to read than his normal texting. She looked at the time he'd sent it, and it showed the early hours of the morning.

She imagined him sitting up in bed, a doe-eyed Jelvian woman next to him, and saying, 'I'd better text the missus.'

Flinging off her duvet, she headed into the shower. But the shower did nothing to dissolve her anger and hurt. Downstairs, she made a coffee and pushed two slices of bread into the toaster. While she waited, she called Courtney. She needed a friendly voice.

'Hi, love, how's you?' Macy said as soon as they connected. But, weirdly, as soon as she heard Courtney's voice, her throat constricted, and her voice wobbled. She expected Courtney to notice, but instead, she sounded aloof.

31

'Hey, Courts. Just thought I'd check in with you. What are you up to today?' Macy asked after Courtney had spoken.

'I'm busy and have a shift this afternoon,' Courtney said. 'I've an afternoon of screaming kids in the mother and baby well-being group. I can hardly wait.' She stopped talking. Macy expected a follow-up question about herself, but none came. The pause was awkward.

'I'm up to nothing,' Macy answered as if she'd been asked.

'You're *meant* to be up to nothing,' Courtney said. Her tone was brusque. 'You're still recovering. It's not just your physical injuries; you've the whole mental aspect to get over. I hope Narcifer's looking after you?' The pitch in her voice on mentioning Narcifer rose slightly.

'I know, and yes, he is. He's, er, in the shower.'

There was a moment's silence; then, as if it were a foreign concept, Courtney said, 'In the shower?'

'Nothing wrong with that, is there? Are you okay?' Macy asked. 'How's Aldarn? Spoken to him recently?' Macy asked, wondering if Courtney had heard bad news about him. Macy's toast pinged up, and she buttered it with one hand.

'He's fine. I speak to him on Zoom regularly,' Courtney snapped. 'Why the interest?'

Her words stung. 'Nothing! Just making conversation. You asked after Narce, and I returned the compliment. That's how conversations usually go. Sorry, I phoned.'

She was about to hang up when Courtney said, 'Oh, God, I'm sorry! Macy—Mace, don't hang up. I'm sorry. You've caught me at a low point. I'm really missing Aldarn, and I buried my ex a couple of months ago.'

Macy didn't bother reminding her that Greg had tried to kill them both. 'It's okay. These are trying times,' she said instead.

'They are. And believe it or not, I'm missing you,' Courtney added.

Good way of showing it! Macy wanted to say it aloud but held her tongue.

'Al's recovering well on the islands, but I don't know when I'll see him again,' Courtney continued. 'Can you, er, communicate that to Narcifer when he's... out of the shower?'

She frowned at Courtney's words. She'd spoken as if Narcifer being in the shower was an odd concept. Macy took a bite of her toast absently. 'You make it sound like he doesn't believe Aldarn's on the islands,' Macy said.

'Forget I asked. Look, I have to go.'

'Already?'

'I'm getting ready for work. I'll check on you later, okay?' Courtney said and hung up. Macy checked the time; Courtney said she had a shift this afternoon, so it was too early for her to get ready.

Macy put her phone down and chewed on her toast. Thanks to Calder's visit, she knew that Narcifer was keen to find Aldarn, but would he pester Courtney? Could that be what had made her snarky?

No, she wouldn't overthink her conversation with Courtney; neither would she sit waiting for Narcifer to come home. She wasn't the type to sit around moping after a guy. She needed to get her life back in order, and to do that, she had to get back to work—the sooner, the better. She grabbed her phone before changing her mind and texted Paul, her line manager, asking if she could come in for a return-to-work plan. Paul texted back a simple thumbs-up emoji.

Perfect.

She picked up the other slice of toast, scrolled to the text Narcifer had sent her in the early hours, and reread it. Her hurt and stubbornness wouldn't let her reply, nor did she want to be here when he returned from wherever he'd gone.

She could be 'busy' too.

SEVEN

'Macy!'

Macy turned to see the receptionist rise from behind her desk. She couldn't recall having a conversation with her before, but the woman was all smiles and teeth as she walked across the foyer of the *London Echo* office to greet her, heels clicking on the floor.

'Hi, how are you? So awful, just *awful* what happened to you,' she trilled.

'I—er, yes, it was,' Macy replied. She took her handbag off her shoulder and reached for her security pass to swipe through the main door.

'Paul said you'd texted him that you were dropping by. So glad you did. We've all missed you. Here, I'll get that for you,' she said, seeing the security pass in Macy's hand. She tried to grab it, but the card slipped from her hands. 'Oh, butterfingers,' the woman said. She sank to her knees to pick it up, taking several long seconds because of her long fingernails.

It felt like an age before Macy got away and headed towards the lift.

The familiarity of her surroundings was comforting in her uncertain world—although the corridor seemed longer and the lift smaller as she rode it up to her floor. Stepping out, she crossed the hall towards the open-plan office. The office was deserted, and the lights were off. The weak winter sun shining pathetically through the windows made the place look bleak.

Macy stopped on the threshold, looking around in puzzlement at the usually busy office. It seemed utterly empty, but then Macy thought she saw someone kneeling behind the photocopier. She was sure she heard a muffled giggle. She stood there, uncertain. Then there was a sudden yell of 'SURPRISE!' as the lights came on, and everyone stood up from their hiding positions and began clapping.

Macy jumped, clutching her chest.

'Macy! Welcome back!' someone shouted. It was followed by more shouts of 'Welcome back, Macy.'

She caught sight of Angela, clapping like crazy. 'Welcome home, Macy,' she shouted.

'Wow!' Macy said, then yelped as someone let off a party-popper too close to her ear.

Suddenly, Macy was enveloped in a bone-crushing hug. Others piled on, patting her on the shoulder or back, kissing her on the cheek and exclaiming how happy they were at her return. Emotional tears gathered in her eyes.

'Cake time!' someone yelled, and Macy turned to see her desk covered with cupcakes of all varieties.

'I'll make tea!' someone else declared.

Angela pulled Macy over to her desk and pushed her into her chair. Macy stammered her thanks, but everyone leaned in, firing questions at her, and it was impossible to hear. Then someone offered her a chocolate éclair and pushed a cup of tea into her hand.

'All this for me?' she asked when she could get a word in. She put the éclair and tea down.

'As soon as you texted me you were coming in, I sent out for cakes,' Paul said, appearing in the throng of people gathered around her desk.

'That's why reception kept me chatting downstairs, I suppose,' Macy said. 'To give you time to hide. But I saw you!' She laughed and pointed to Ralf, who chuckled. 'Oh, my gosh. Thank you, guys. I'm... I'm overwhelmed.' She blinked back tears, dazed at the trouble her colleagues had gone to.

'Aw, bless her,' said Karen, the office "mum", leaning her ample bosom over the desk to smother Macy in a hug.

Macy fought her way out, laughing. 'I'm astonished you've all gone to this trouble. I only texted Paul this morning.'

'You look so much better,' Angela said. 'You had us all worried for a while.'

'I *feel* a lot better,' Macy said.

People drifted away, clutching their cakes. Angela grabbed a chair and pulled it over to Macy's desk.

'Mind if I take two?' Ralf asked, eyeing the treats. 'They're only small.'

Macy laughed. 'Go ahead,' she said.

Paul came over and chose a cake. 'There's still a lot left,' he said. 'You'll have to take them home, or Ralf will eat them all.'

'I'll take a couple for Narcifer,' Macy said.

Paul shifted uncomfortably. 'I heard he'd moved in with you. How is... I mean, are you okay with that?'

'Absolutely fine,' she said. She glanced at Angela to see if she shared Paul's negativity, but Angela glared at Paul.

'Of course, she's fine! Why wouldn't she be? It's so romantic how you and Narcifer met,' she said. She took a piece of cake and picked at it, putting one morsel in her mouth at a time.

'Sorry, of course, you're fine with it. But...' Paul stopped to scratch the back of his neck. 'It's all changed here, Mace. As you know, the new bill passed just before Christmas, and we can't mention Jelvias in a negative light. The new editor-in-chief is extremely hot on that.'

'Well, that's excellent because I have nothing negative to say about them.'

'Actually, he doesn't want them mentioned at all.'

Macy rolled her eyes.

'He's an utter dinosaur!' said Angela. She looked at Macy. 'Don't worry, we'll sort him out, won't we?'

'Er... I guess so,' Macy said, amused by Angela's stance of solidarity. They'd only met a few times before Macy had been reeled in by Jon Johnsen, the initiator of the Jelvian experiments and the cause of Aldarn's injuries. 'Hey, how many of these have you had?' Macy asked, spotting a familiar handwritten envelope tucked under the clutter in her tray.

'Quite a few, unfortunately,' Paul said. 'Er, can I speak to you privately?'

'Sure,' she said absent-mindedly, pulling the WUM letter out. The space was tight, and it brought out several more with it. They all had a second-class stamp stuck haphazardly in the corner—not hand-delivered, then, as the letters she'd received at home had been. She stared at them, amazed. 'Why are they targeting me?' Macy was more annoyed than worried. She had enough to worry about without WUM harassing her.

'That's easy to answer, unfortunately,' Paul said.

'We had a visitor, September to October time. Someone asking for you,' a woman said approaching Macy's desk. She paused to grab a cake. 'Skinny woman with long blond hair. Fuck-awful black roots.'

'That would've been Beth Roberts. She isn't a member of WUM,' Macy said. 'Thanks anyway.'

The woman shrugged and went away with her cake. She wafted it under the nose of Ralf, who pretended to take a bite.

'You've been receiving letters since August or September, which is probably when WUM realised you were involved with Narcifer,' Paul said, 'though you weren't here to receive them. We thought you'd deal with them when you got back, but...'

'I ended up in the hospital,' she said as he trailed off.

'They stopped sending them some time in November. I suppose that's when they found out you weren't at work. It's all very juvenile, really.'

'Yeah, I had a load of their crap on my mat when I came home.'

'You need to check your work phone; my phone is full of messages from them. All insisting that I tell you to contact them. You're important to them,' said Paul.

Macy pulled a face.

'And I think that's what's worrying Jack,' Paul said. 'Er, want to come to my office for a private chat?'

'Let her finish her tea and cake, Paul,' Angela said before Macy could reply.

'No, it's okay, Angela. I'm done here,' Macy said. She collected up all the WUM letters and put them in her handbag.

'Christ, she's your little pit bull,' Paul said, nodding toward Angela as he and Macy walked away.

'Shh,' Macy said. She glanced back at Angela, hoping she hadn't heard. It didn't look as though she had. She'd sat back down at her desk and was jabbing at the keys of her computer. 'She has my back, that's all.'

'So do I, and believe it or not, Jack does as well.' When they reached his door, he opened it, waving her through to precede him inside.

'The new boss doesn't insist on "Mr Gonzalez" then?' she asked. Paul's office hadn't changed at all. She sank down on a chair. It was tempting to sit in his oversized chair, as she'd sometimes done in the past, just to annoy him.

'No, he's okay, actually,' he said. Of Spanish origin, Jack—or Jacob—Gonzalez was Jon Johnsen's successor. He owned various papers, including *The Journal, Express Daily,* and *London Echo.* 'He wants me to arrange a meeting with you, but I want to brief you first.'

'Brief me on what?'

Paul sat in his chair. He steepled his fingers together and leaned forwards in his "boss" posture. 'I'm afraid it's serious, Macy.'

'Is he going to sack me?' Macy asked, joking. But the crashing of Paul's steepled fingers and his high-pitched nervous laugh were a major giveaway. 'You're kidding! Because of my interview? It hasn't even gone live!'

'No... actually, it's more than that. Look, I don't know what Jack intends to do. He just asked me to call him if you contacted the rest of the team or me.'

'He's making it sound like I'm some kind of competitor.'

Paul sighed. 'Look, I know you've been working hard on the Jelvia interview, but Jack won't commission it. He thinks it's a dangerous idea. He doesn't want any *Echo* staff associated with it, including you.'

They both looked up as the door opened, and a man entered, seemingly breathless. He patted his chest and puffed out a breath. It looked like he'd been hurrying and wasn't used to exerting himself.

'Ah, Jack. We weren't expecting you in today,' Paul said, standing.

'I just dropped by, and someone told me Macy was here,' Jack said with shallow breaths. He was a short, tubby man in his middle years.

Paul moved away from his seat and indicated that Jack should sit, but Jack shook his head. He stepped forwards, looking at Macy. 'Nice to meet you at last,' he said, thrusting out his hand, which she reluctantly took.

'Likewise,' Macy said.

'I was just about to arrange that meeting between you,' Paul said weakly.

Macy looked from one man to the other. 'What's going on?' she asked.

'Could we have a quick chat in my office?' Jack asked, putting out a hand to indicate she should leave Paul's office and head to his.

'Absolutely,' she said, standing. 'After you,' she said, mimicking his gesture of waving a hand towards the door. She wouldn't be followed out as if she were being frog-marched off the premises.

Jack stared at her, then nodded and preceded her out of Paul's office. Macy glanced over her shoulder at Paul, who shrugged and mouthed the words, 'It's out of my hands.'

She turned back, tilted her chin, and continued to follow Jack.

EIGHT

Jack's office was at the end of the corridor on the top floor. His PA was busily pounding on a keyboard and looked up when they entered.

'Ah, Danny, could you bring a coffee for Macy and me? Thank you.'

'Certainly, sir,' Danny said, jumping up and moving towards an oak-panelled door. Jack took Macy in through a similar door on the other side of the room.

His office was airy, with one large desk, several bookcases, and a beautiful wide window seat overlooking the town below. 'Please, take a seat,' he said, gesturing towards the chair closest to his desk.

Macy ignored the chair and headed to the window seat. Sitting down, she turned her body to look out of the window. Her anger from this morning had returned, and she hung onto it—it was better than the emotional mess alternative. She turned to look at Jack expectantly as he closed the door.

'I wanted to speak to you privately and apologise for how William Springfield duped you into meeting Jelvias and beginning this sorry business.'

'Don't you mean Jon Johnsen?' she asked.

'Whatever name he went by, he was a charlatan. But I won't beat about the bush—Macy, is there any way we can help you?' he asked. And surprised her even more by taking the smaller chair he'd previously offered and sitting directly opposite her.

'Help me?'

'We could offer you a safe house away from the Jelvias. Give you a new identity, whatever you want.'

Macy's mouth dropped open. Whatever she might have expected, it wasn't that.

'Johnsen did dupe me, but I went along with his plan to interview Narcifer and Aldarn willingly. And I still want the interview to go ahead.'

'I'm sure you've heard of the new law regarding Jelvias. Unfortunately, the government believes they court negativity, so we can't feature them in our newspapers.'

'What I have to say isn't negative,' she said.

Jack closed his eyes momentarily and muttered something under his breath. 'I was afraid you'd say that,' he said. 'I can't lie, Macy, Jelvias scare me, and I don't want them featured in my newspaper.'

'They scare most people.'

'But most people don't have colleagues *living* with Jelvias!'

'I live with *one* Jelvia.'

There was an uncomfortable pause between them, which was finally broken when Jack stood up and crossed the room to a filing cabinet. He took out a plastic folder and then pulled out several sheets. He handed them to Macy, and she took them sceptically.

'What's this?'

'A liability document. It was drawn up by our solicitors. I'd like you to read it at your leisure, and if you still want to refuse our help with protection from Jelvias, you need to sign the declaration.'

'This is so I don't go after you for Johnsen's mistreatment?'

Jack shook his head. 'No, you've every right to seek legal advice over that. This,' he said, pointing to the forms in her hands, 'will protect *us* if you get yourself injured or killed at the hands of a Jelvia from here on. Without Johnsen's backing, this entire chain of events might not have happened—'

A knock on the door stopped their conversation. Jack permitted entry, and the PA came in carrying a tray with their coffees. He set it down carefully and left them alone.

'How do you like your coffee?' Jack asked.

'Just milk, thanks,' she said as she glanced through the documents. This time, she'd show them to a solicitor.

They fell silent as Jack stirred milk into Macy's coffee before bringing it over. Then, putting the paperwork aside, she sipped the coffee and watched as Jack took his cup and sat down in his own chair this time. She'd refused his offer of help, so he was back to being the boss, about to fire his employee—or so it seemed to Macy.

'William Springfield was a good friend of mine, and when he died—no, when he was *murdered*—I was devastated,' Jack continued. 'The Jelvias are brutal killing machines, and they go without punishment. They kill us because they can. Do you want to live in a world like that? You don't think they need to be stopped, or at the very least, controlled?'

'And we can do that by ignoring their existence?'

'I never said I ignore them. On the contrary: I find it hard *not* to think about them, to be honest.'

'You and I perceive Jelvias in two different ways. I've learned things that will reassure the population. The Jelvias don't *like* to kill, but they *have* to. There's a faceless committee that controls their actions—'

Jack threw up his hands. '*Tonto del culo!* Is that meant to make me feel better? A "faceless committee"?'

'Yes, because most Jelvias live away from the committee, they can ignore or modify those commands. If they feel forced to kill humans, they target criminals, and our streets are safer than ever.'

Jack stared at her in disbelief. 'Have you watched the news lately? Read the newspapers? The WUM organisation are demonstrating all over and—'

Macy snorted. 'They're just a crazy bunch of zealots.'

'This is getting us nowhere,' Jack said with a sigh. 'Look, I know all about your dealings with Jelvias and how William treated you. I promise you that I never knew about his plan, nor did the company.

Because of that, I must move the *Echo* away from him and all dealings with Jelvias. It's not going to survive if I don't. So, I'm sorry, Macy, but your Jelvia feature cannot go ahead. And let's be honest: It never *was* going to get the go-ahead.'

'Why don't you read it before you make up your mind?' she asked, knowing it was a waste of time.

He shook his head. 'You're biased, Macy. Biased and in serious need of psychological help.' He held up a hand as she flew to her feet. '*Echo* has someone speaking on behalf of Jelvias next Monday. It will run after the big interview on the BBC this weekend—if our legal team can get around the legalities. Your interview is not in the public interest. It never has been. It was a concept of William Springfield's to entice you, and it worked.'

'I had the idea for the interview long before Johnsen stuck his beak in.'

'Macy—'

'And it *is* in the public interest,' she said. 'It's people like you who have the problem.'

Jack shook his head in denial; Macy could sense his brewing anger, but hers was off the scale.

'Macy, it's the law,' Jack said. 'We can't write about Jelvias, good or bad. Whatever is written about them will cause friction amongst the public.'

'Well, it isn't fair! The Jelvias have been here as long as we have, and it's time we allowed them human status. We don't own the world, and they have every right to be part of it. What the government is doing to them is unlawful.'

Jack's cheeks tinged pink, but his voice sounded calm when he spoke. 'I have no control over the government, and neither do you. But, as I said, a spokesman will be featured next Monday to run after Fenovo's interview.'

'What interview?'

'Matt Fenovo's interview on the BBC. It's being aired on Saturday evening. There will be a studio audience and a Jelvia expert named Graham Barringham.'

Macy had heard of Matt Fenovo. He was a straight-talking journalist turned broadcaster and television presenter. His interviewees feared his challenging questions.

'By the look on your face, you didn't know,' Jack said.

'No one told me.' She picked up her coffee, urging herself to calm down. But she'd never felt so angry. She wanted to storm out, cry, throw the horrible coffee, and smack Jack's chubby little face.

'You've been out of the loop for some time.'

Macy almost spilt her coffee. 'No, I haven't!' she flared. 'I'm living *inside* the bloody loop. I have all the details about Jelvias you could possibly want. Why is Fenovo talking to this obscure Graham guy when he could be talking to *me*? A "Jelvia expert"—who could be more of an expert than *me*? But we both know why, don't we? It's because I'll say nice things about Jelvias. All anyone wants to hear is the bad—how dangerous they are, how deadly their venom is, how lethal their claws are, how fast they move, how—'

'Rose-tinted glasses.'

'*What?*'

He moved papers on his desk and put his coffee down. 'You are either seeing things through rose-tinted glasses, or you *do* have Stockholm syndrome.'

'How dare—'

His head shot up, and his eyes blazed. 'No, Macy, how dare *you*. How *dare* you propose such an idea when this building was seized and your colleagues terrified by Jelvias last summer. Have you no respect for the feelings of your fellow employees?'

'That was Johnsen's fault, not mine.'

'But the issue is, it *happened*, and it happened to *your* colleagues. You need to take a step back and see what others see.'

Macy slammed her coffee down and stood up. It slopped over the sides, but she didn't care.

But, unfortunately, Jack hadn't finished.

'You've had a rough year, Macy. I'm not going to deny that—but I'm sorry, I can't have any of my employees associating with Jelvias. I have to think of the rest of my staff.'

'I'm sacked?'

'Not exactly. If you don't accept our offer, I'm under instructions to ask for your resignation. We'll make it worth your while.'

'Bloody hell! You *are* sacking me! I *knew* Paul was acting oddly. He knew, didn't he?'

'I'm not sacking you,' Jack said.

With her hands on her hips, Macy scowled at him. 'So, if I leave Narcifer and agree to your ridiculous offer of help, my job is safe?'

'That's right.'

'But if I refuse to resign or sign that bloody form, I'm out, right?'

Jack raked his fingers through his hair. He was handling his anger better than she was. 'I'm sorry, Macy. I've spoken to the board, and we can offer you a handsome payout and get you all the necessary help—new identity, new country, new job—'

She clutched her head but brought her hands to her sides with a slap. 'I don't *need* help.'

'We're prepared to make you the fantastic offer of twenty thousand pounds if you want to go your own way,' he said, ignoring her. 'Macy, this is just the start for you. You could start your own paper. I'm sure it would be well-received, even if people read it furtively. The public still wants to know about Jelvias and what makes them tick. The offer is there. If you want our help, we are prepared to help you.'

Macy snorted her disgust.

'I'm sorry, Macy, but it's now gone to the top level. You'll be forced out with nothing if you don't accept our offer or help.'

She gave a short laugh. 'And then I really *will* have a story.'

He looked at her levelly. 'I doubt many newspapers will touch you if that happens. You took the side of the Jelvias, which was career suicide.'

Narcifer had warned her. He'd said her life would change once she 'came out' as his girlfriend. While she was with him in Cornwall, she'd been protected, and then there had been her time in the hospital—but now she was back in the real world. And the real world was where Narcifer found her scars repulsive, and she was on the verge of being fired from a job she loved.

She stood up, suddenly needing air. She grabbed her handbag and the documents Jack had given her and rushed towards the door.

'Macy?' Jack called.

'I'll be in touch,' she said, close to tears.

She couldn't get out of the building quickly enough and, luckily, she didn't encounter anyone as she flew through the reception area.

NINE

Macy arrived home to an empty house. She dropped her stuffed handbag on the dining table, kicked off her shoes, and flung her coat to the floor. Then she stomped into the kitchen and flicked on the kettle.

Narcifer had texted, saying he was on his way home. He'd phoned earlier, but Macy didn't pick up. She refused to be the jealous girlfriend who questioned her boyfriend, though she was quite upset.

Opening the fridge, Macy took out a half-empty bottle of wine and was almost tempted to drink straight from the bottle. But, instead, she grabbed a glass, filled it, and drank it in one hit. She might as well become an alcoholic. At least it'd blot out her miserable life. She swept the back of her hand across her eyes.

There were no tears. She was still too angry to cry.

Her life wasn't going the way she'd planned, and every time she tried to steer it back on course, events knocked it adrift. Macy was jealous of this unknown Bren, hating her without even knowing her. She was angry at the mugger who killed her mum, angry at the industrial accident that took her dad, at Greg and Aldarn, and at Jack and *London Echo*. She was even angry about being angry!

Refilling her glass, she set it down on the table, pulled her handbag towards her and took out the documents Jack had given her. The WUM letters came out, and she pushed them away irritably. Jack's documents were full of legal jargon. They seemed official, but then she had also thought Johnsen's papers were legitimate. She tossed them all onto the table, where they landed on the accumulated pile of *Stunning Planet* magazines.

Looking at them, she remembered how full of optimism she had felt when she came home.

Reaching, she pulled out the top magazine to look at it. It was the one with the picture of the beautiful rainbow trees—Mindanao gum tree being the official name. Macy stared at the cover as she recalled Narcifer telling her about the 'rainbow trees' on the Jelvian island in the Atlantic Sea between Cornwall and Cork. He'd gone from glancing at the coloured trees on the cover to stating they grew on his island a moment later. Macy knew he didn't live in a climate able to sustain such trees. She didn't think he was lying. Narcifer preferred to omit something rather than lie. This time, it was as if his subconscious had liked the idea and run with it.

She reached for her glass of wine and sipped. The alcohol had already dulled her anger.

She grabbed a WUM letter and tore it open.

Ms Shaw,

Your boyfriend is an alien.

WUM

Macy giggled and sat down to open another letter.

Macy Shaw,

Narcifer's thoughts aren't his own. He's just a puppet. Please, get in contact so we can discuss this.

WUM.

Macy's mobile burst into song, and she dropped the letter to grab it.

The ID was private and she hesitated on answering it. But after the fourth right, Macy answered. The caller identified himself as James Sullivan.

In the past, Sullivan had been a mediator between Jelvias and humans. He'd even gained the trust of Aldarn, and they became friends, but their friendship went sour after Johnsen's laboratory incident.

She and James had never met, but they'd spoken sporadically over the summer, via Zoom and over the phone. He'd phoned her once in hospital, enquiring after her health, but since then, nothing. However, since discovering she had been a pawn in the hands of

Johnsen and Aldarn, Macy had been cautious of James. She'd trusted Johnsen and didn't want to make the same mistake with another person who claimed they were friends.

With the pleasantries over, he finally got to his point.

'I've been trying to get hold of Courtney,' he said, 'but her number is constantly unavailable. I've left her a text to phone me, but she hasn't yet. Is everything okay with her?'

'Well, she's pining for Aldarn, but apart from that, she's fine. She got a new phone at Christmas, though. Anything I can help you with?'

'I'm trying to contact Al,' he admitted, 'that's why I need to speak to Courtney to see if she knows where I can find him.'

'You as well?' She ran a hand through her hair. As usual, her fingers became tangled, and she yanked her hand away, wincing as she tore out several hair strands from the root.

'And what did you mean by "you as well"?' he asked.

'Pardon?'

'When I said I was trying to get hold of Al, you asked, "you as well".' His voice had a smile, but Macy could've kicked herself for her reveal. 'It kind of alerted me that I wasn't the only one looking for him.'

'Because everyone seems to be looking for him!' she said, trying to be as vague as possible.

'*Everyone*?' He sounded perplexed.

'Well, not everyone; I'm being melodramatic. What's the appeal with Aldarn? He's dangerous. Everyone needs to stay away from him.'

'Yes, I agree, but it's urgent, and I feel Calder is protecting him for the wrong reasons.'

'What wrong reasons?'

'Nothing major,' he said. 'Calder just wants everything to tick along like it has been, with him as the leader, Aldarn, the dutiful second-in-command, and Narcifer, the devil-may-care little brother.'

'Cousin,' she amended.

James' pause told her he didn't know about Narcifer's and Calder's complicated family life. During the summer, long before she got to know Narcifer, he had told her how a family member had fallen pregnant too young. His mother had taken the child in and raised it as her own. That child was Calder, and he and Narcifer had been raised as brothers.

'Ah,' James said once she explained, '*that* family story.' His tone made it sound like he didn't believe what she was telling him.

'Why is that so hard to believe?' she asked.

'It's too neat.'

'It's far from neat. Neat is a mum and dad, two children of either sex in a three-bed house with a garden.'

'Neat as in nicely told, flaws and all.' He sighed. 'I'm not saying Narcifer is lying... ah, Macy, this is all so complicated. Narcifer has been duped just as you have.'

'Duped?' she asked. She glanced at the WUM letter still lying open on the table, and reread the words:

Narcifer's thoughts aren't his own. He's just a puppet.

'Macy, I'm not questioning Narcifer and Calder's relationship. None of that matters.'

'It matters to you.'

'No, actually, it doesn't,' James said as if he had been tolerating a question from a child.

Behind, in the hallway, the letter box jangled as mail was delivered. Macy glanced out the window to ensure it was the postman and not an ambiguous WUM member delivering another begging letter. It wasn't, and Narcifer was sitting in his car outside waiting for the postman to finish before climbing out in case he was recognised as a Jelvia.

Macy's anger was under control now, but she wanted complete composure before confronting Narcifer about Bren. 'I have to go,' she said to James.

'Before you do,' he said quickly, 'I don't suppose you have Aldarn's number?'

'Sorry, no,' she said, thinking she'd not give it to him anyway.

'I didn't think so. Calder's hiding him. I can't stress enough how important it is that I speak to him. Will you ask Courtney to phone me if I give you my number?'

The door banged behind her, and she felt a blast of cool air. She looked over her shoulder at Narcifer as he entered. He bent to pick up the envelope that had been dropped earlier.

'Sure,' she said.

'It will only be active for a short time,' he said.

Macy grabbed a pen as he reeled off a number.

'Thanks, Macy. Hopefully, one day this will all make sense.'

'What—' she said, but he'd gone. Pulling a face, Macy turned around and looked at Narcifer. He was looking at the letter in his hand. 'Not another WUM letter?' she asked.

Narcifer looked up. 'Hey, look at you. You look good enough to eat! In fact...' He tossed the letter, his sunglasses, and baseball cap away—his disguise—and stepped towards her. She found herself pressed against him as he enveloped her in a hug.

'You didn't answer my text,' he said, his breath fanning the top of her head.

She pushed away from him and smoothed her hair. 'I was *busy*,' she said and saw his eyes crinkle in laughter.

'You're angry with me,' he said.

His spade-like hands reached for her again, circling her waist. One slid down to cup her bottom while his fingers edged up her skirt.

'I'm sorry, my love. I deserve your anger,' he said as his cool fingers traced the elastic of her knickers. He lowered his head to nuzzle her neck.

'Narce, stop it,' she said, wriggling away. 'Where have you been all night?'

'Just Jelvia business. All boring, really. I love it when you struggle,' he added, his hands slipping beneath the material of her knickers to stroke her bare flesh. His strokes became stronger, and he pressed her against him. Macy was losing it, her anger forgotten as desire ignited.

'Narce...' she protested weakly. His hands moved over her arse, dragging his short nails across her skin.

'I'd love to turn your milky white skin rosy red,' he murmured.

'Milky *scarred* skin,' Macy said before she could stop herself.

Narcifer's hands stalled on her backside at her words, and then he let her go, allowing her skirt to fall back into place.

'Sorry, that just slipped out,' she said, offering him a weak smile. 'I've had a bad day—no, a bad week. I thought once we were back home together, things would be like they were before... you know.'

'You can say his name. It's Greg.'

'I don't want to. I hate him. This is all his fault. My scars, us, my job, being out of the loop of the WUM invasion. But Christ, they were nobodies back in September, and now they're doing interviews with bloody Matt Fenovo. That should be *me* with Fenovo.'

'I have no idea what you're talking about,' Narcifer said. He reached forwards and brushed her hair away from her droopy eye. 'And don't ever be sorry,' he said. He caught her hand as she tried to sweep her fringe back to cover her scar. 'If I could kill Greg again for what he did to us, I would,' he said.

As his words settled on her, she gaped up at him. 'Wait... what do you mean if you could kill him again? You weren't there when Greg died!'

The look of horror on Narcifer's face made it all clear to her.

'Oh, my God. He survived falling from the bridge, didn't he? He survived, and they took him to the same hospital I was in where *you* killed him!'

TEN

'I killed him,' Narcifer said. His face was expressionless. 'He probably wouldn't have survived anyway. Lisa and Courtney were terrified he'd come and kill you and come after Courtney again if he recovered.'

'Do they know you killed him?'

Narcifer nodded. 'We all agreed not to tell you.'

'But I'm glad you did! I only wish I'd been well enough to watch.'

Narcifer looked relieved that she'd taken the news so well. 'That's why they moved you to a separate wing, away from everyone—not because of Greg, but because of my visits after it became known that Greg had died by a Jelvia sting. And I had to be accompanied by Lisa or Courtney at all times.' He gave a low chuckle. 'No one said a word when I visited alone, but I was compliant, for Lisa's sake. Are you sure you're okay? This kind of thing separates a human from a Jelvia.'

'I'm fine. I can't imagine Courts being okay with it, though.'

'She came to terms with it eventually.'

'Now it makes sense why she felt the need to go to Greg's funeral, and it must have been guilt that made her want to see his family at the wake. But, Christ, Narce, why didn't *you* tell me? Is there anything else you're keeping from me?' *Like Bren?*

She ignored her jealous inner voice.

'Not keeping things from you, babe. A bit of good news, though,' he said, smiling at her. 'I had a breakthrough last night. Bren is Calder's driver, and she's promised to tell me when she takes him to Aldarn.'

'And it took all evening for you to convince her to do that?'

If Narcifer guessed how she felt, he didn't show it.

'I didn't spend the evening with Bren. I... er...' He floundered, then turned from her and headed into the kitchen, saying, 'I'm so hungry.'

'Do you still love me?'

He swivelled around at her blurted words, his face shocked. 'What kind of question is that? Of course, I love you!'

'I'm scarred now. I'm a nervous wreck, and I get tired easily. I'm not the Macy you met in the summer, and now another woman's name is on your lips.'

He looked startled, but then a slow smile spread over his face. 'You're jealous? Oh, Macy, Bren's not a woman. Well, she is, but I don't see her as a woman. She's just... Bren. She does odd jobs for us—chauffeuring and watching tracked people on our computer systems. She does all the crap jobs, basically.'

Feeling defensive, Macy said, 'How would you feel if I mentioned a strange man's name and then disappeared for the whole evening?'

'I'd track you both down. I'd kill him and make you promise never to do anything like that again.'

Macy stared at Narcifer, realising there was something different about him. He looked like a weight had been lifted.

'And I'm supposed to just accept your excuse?' she asked eventually.

'I texted you,' he said. 'I even tried to phone you.'

'I know. I didn't answer on purpose.'

Narcifer laughed. He came over and cupped her face with his hands. 'And I haven't helped lately, have I, babe?' He dropped a kiss on her mouth and then enveloped her in another bone-crushing hug. 'I just can't tell you how urgent it is that I find Al. But now that Bren has promised to help me, you have my undivided attention.'

Macy pushed him away and wrinkled her nose at him. 'Well, I'd like your undivided attention, but only after you've had a shower. You stink.'

His lips quirked in a smile. 'How about you join me? I've tried to be a good, sensitive boyfriend, but I can't keep it up. I need you, Macy.'

She looked at him in confusion. 'You've been avoiding me. How is that sensitive?'

'Huh?' He looked indignant. 'You pushed me away while we were staying at Mumma Lisa's. We only made love in the dark or under a damned bedcover. Courtney said you felt embarrassed by your scars,' he added, his gaze suddenly full of concern. 'The number of cold showers I've taken over these last few months—I must be the cleanest person in the world—and the coldest.'

She giggled.

She loved this Jelvia. The WUMs—and James—could go fuck themselves.

'You really think I was keeping away from you because *I* wanted to?' he asked. He sounded incredulous. 'It's been the hardest few months of my life.'

'And mine,' she said. 'I've missed the intensity of our lovemaking. Missed being kinky,' she added,

A lazy smile spread over his face. 'You're such an innocent,' he said, laughing. 'I'd only just started training you to my demands.'

The feminist in her bristled at his choice of words. 'Training?'

The grin hadn't left his face. 'Yeah, *training*,' he said, emphasising the word. He patted her on the head. 'Problem with that, human?'

'Actually, yes,' she said, her hands on her hips. She stared at him, but he continued to grin down at her.

'Now we've established that you've missed being kinky...' he said. Then, nonchalantly, he dragged a finger from her throat to the middle of her breasts, where he flicked open a button on her blouse. 'We've months to catch up on,' he continued.

Catching on slowly, Macy relaxed.

'I know you've had difficulties with Courtney, but she does care about you,' Narcifer said. His finger was against her skin, in the space of the popped button. He drew a small circle, touching the swell of each breast. His eyes lifted to meet her gaze. 'She said you didn't want me to see your scars in case they revolted me. But, babe, I don't mind your scars. You do know that, don't you?'

'I told Courts that in confidence,' Macy said, wanting to be annoyed but failing.

'She wanted to help.' He bent and kissed the tip of her nose. 'Her words were, "Look after her, or I'll come after you with a knife and cut off your balls with the blunt edge". And, "Macy's sensitive about her scars and will need time to adjust to them herself before she allows you to see them." That's all. We didn't talk about your deepest, darkest desires or anything—because, frankly, that's for me to find out. Now, shower,' he said. Holding her hand tightly, he pulled her behind him towards the stairs.

ELEVEN

Narcifer filled the bathroom with his bulk, but for his size, there was a gentleness, too—a sensitivity absent in most men. Macy undressed, waiting for the look of horror on Narcifer's face as her scars became visible, but his expression never faltered from one of hunger. He stared at her as if seeing her for the first time. Ordinarily, this would have sent Macy wild, but she had a thick scar on her right collarbone, and she was convinced the bone protruded beneath her skin. She was even more certain he was looking right at it.

He moved, causing Macy's eyes to rise to his. They were liquid black with a shimmer of diamonds, and firmly fixed on her. He looked incredible naked. His golden-brown body was hairless; he had a chiselled eight-pack; and his body looked like it had been sculpted. Macy felt her stomach flip-flop.

'Stop it,' he said.

'What?'

'Worrying. You're beautiful, Macy. This,' he said, holding her still as she tried to wriggle away from him and tracing a scar on her hip with his finger, 'is just a scar on the softest, creamiest skin I've ever touched. And this'—he bent and kissed her droopy eyelid—'is on the most beautiful eyes. Most human eyes are shades of blue, brown, or green. But yours are grey, and they darken when you're excited.' He gave her a slow smile. 'I love knowing I can make them dark.'

Narcifer's voice deepened when he was aroused, and the sound was mesmerising. She watched as his eyes wandered over her. Her skin prickled with the intensity of his gaze.

The shower was steaming when they stepped beneath it. Narcifer's hands were all over her body; there was no order to his touch. His mouth gently kissed her shoulder, moving up and nibbling her neck. Macy sighed, closing her eyes. She thought about how unbelievably good his lips felt when Narcifer took it up a level, kissing her with such force she felt her flesh drawn into his mouth.

She squealed a little.

'That's for believing small scars could stop me from loving you,' he said. His eyes, bright and glowing, roved over her lower body. 'You may hate your scars, but they're on the most beautiful, slim, long legs, and I think about them wrapped around me all of the time.' His hands gripped her hips, lifting her slightly. 'And your bum—I missed your naked bum. It wiggles when you walk as if inviting me to spank it.'

Narcifer moved down, somehow folding his body into the small space they occupied. His mouth tasted her skin. The water, hot and delicious, pounded their bodies. Macy gasped, feeling Narcifer's tongue in her navel. One hand was on her hip, pulling her against him; the other pushed her legs apart. She was happy to oblige.

She felt his eyes feasting on her before he lowered his head and kissed the insides of her thighs.

'I can...' he said between kisses, 'taste you already. Such sweetness... I missed that sweetness. You're nectar, Macy. You always will be.' He stopped kissing her and raised his head to look intently at her. Macy quivered beneath his glowing gaze. 'I'm going to hold you still while I fuck you with my tongue.'

Macy could barely breathe. She could only watch as Narcifer bent his dark head again to press his lips inside her. At first, the pressure was light, as was his tongue. Gentle flicks and nuzzles. But then his hands gripped her hips, pulling her, lifting her until she had to grasp the top of his head for balance. Then he plunged inside her—sucking, guzzling, *consuming* her. It didn't take long to bring her to climax, and she shuddered against him as she spasmed.

Macy was used to Narcifer's sudden movements and his strength, but they never ceased to amaze her. While she was still in the throes of climax, he'd risen, lifted her, and replaced his tongue with his cock, holding her with one hand while his other pressed against the wall for balance. Macy wrapped her legs around his body. She could hear him sigh his pleasure, and held him tight as he sank deeper and deeper inside her.

She squealed as another orgasm ripped through her, this one more intense than the first. She felt Narcifer's warmth splash inside her, but he continued to thrust until she quivered and shouted against him.

Exhausted, all her limbs seeming boneless, Macy allowed her legs to loosen from around Narcifer. He slowly lowered her to her feet without letting go of her.

Macy rested her head against his chest. She could feel his heart beating, and she suspected hers was racing just as fast.

Finally, she had her hero back.

TWELVE

'Aren't you going to tell me about your day?' Narcifer asked, picking up his knife and fork and vigorously attacking the omelette in front of him. She had made them a bacon and sausage omelette.

Macy was still bathed in the glow of their lovemaking, while Narcifer looked unruffled. They sat at the dining table amongst the clutter of the magazines, Jack's forms, and WUM letters, which still hadn't been put away.

'Where do I start? It does sound daft now, and you're going to think I'm overreacting, but I phoned Courts this morning, and she acted strangely. Things have been a struggle recently. We were getting on fine before we left, but she was definitely flat when I called her.'

A flash of unease crossed his face. 'What did she say?'

'Oh, she was polite and nice, just not *Courtney*.'

'Sorry,' he said.

'It isn't your fault.' He looked anxious, and not for the first time, Macy saw worry lines on his handsome face. She frowned. 'You really are worried about Aldarn, aren't you? But, you know, you can tell me anything. In England, we have a saying, "a problem shared is a problem halved".'

He appeared to give himself a mental shake. 'No problem could be bigger than keeping you happy, babe. I'm fine, and I don't think you're overreacting. Maybe you caught her at a bad time?'

'Maybe.' She frowned at him, cocking her head.

He flashed her a smile. 'I'm fine; now carry on. What else happened?'

'Well, I texted Paul, my line manager, and told him I'd come in to discuss my back-to-work plan, but the office was in darkness when I got there. It was so bizarre—the lights came on, and everyone jumped out from their hiding places shouting "Surprise" at me.' She smiled at the memory. 'They'd bought lots of cupcakes to welcome me back.'

'That sounds nice.'

'It was,' she said with a sigh. 'But then the new boss got wind I was there and ordered me to his office.' She pointed to the paperwork in front of her. 'That's some legal crap I need to sign, telling the company I don't hold them responsible for meeting you.'

'Me?'

'Jelvias in general. And then he fired me.'

'*Fired?* As in shot?'

'No, silly. Sacked. Made redundant. Asked to hand in my notice.' She could see he was struggling to understand her. She cut off a piece of omelette and popped it into her mouth. 'My new boss doesn't want me working for *Echo* anymore. He's offered me twenty grand if I accept, nothing if I don't. He thinks I have Stockholm syndrome.'

'Because of your injuries?'

She laughed. 'No, it's a condition where the hostage falls in love with their captor. Jack believes I'm a prisoner of Jelvias. Aside from all that, the WUMs have bombarded *London Echo* with their stupid propaganda. My email is all clogged up with this crap, too.' She pointed with her fork to the letters scattered over the table in front of them. 'I don't know what they want from me, but I think it's time I stopped seeing them as cranks and started taking them seriously. So, I'm going to meet with them—on *my* terms—and find out why they keep harassing me.'

'We have an interrogation room at Keats you could use,' he said.

She laughed. 'Can you imagine trying to get WUM members to Keats? They'd rather pull out their own eyes, I'm sure.'

He pulled a face. 'You're so gross.'

'The way you eat is gross,' she said, watching him devour the omelette as if he hadn't eaten in weeks.

He tapped her plate with his fork. 'And if you don't hurry and finish that, I will steal it from you.'

Smiling, Macy pushed it towards him. She'd eaten enough. Remembering the letter Narcifer had brought in with him and wanting to keep all the WUM letters together, she got up and went to fetch it.

But this one didn't look like a WUM letter. It was neatly typewritten and had a stamp.

'Who was that on the phone?' Narcifer asked as she came back into the dining room.

'Phone? Oh, you mean earlier? It was just James,' she said absently. She looked up with a start as Narcifer's knife and fork clattered onto his plate.

'Sorry,' he said, but his expression was anything but sorry. He looked annoyed. 'What did he want?'

'He was asking how I was feeling,' she said, eyeing him curiously. 'Is that all?' His voice was clipped.

'Yes.' A smile broke over her face. She sat down at the table and reached for her glass of wine. 'Jealous, Narcifer?'

He looked surprised but then laughed. 'Yes. Yes, I'm jealous. So that was all he wanted?'

'That was all,' she said, dropping her gaze to the letter. Then, putting her wine glass down, she opened it and pulled out a single sheet of paper. She scanned it quickly. 'This isn't a WUM letter. It's from my neighbours. They've figured out you're living here, and this is a warning that they're setting up a petition to force me to move.'

Narcifer snatched the letter from her fingers. Then, making a noise of disgust in his throat, he pushed it back at her.

'Read it all to me,' he said.

Knowing his reading abilities were poor, she read the letter aloud. 'I bet old Mrs Donald typed it,' she said after finishing. 'Look, two spaces after the full stop. No one does that these days.' She thrust the sheet under Narcifer's nose, but she could see he didn't understand.

'I don't understand your legal system. Can they make you leave?' Narcifer asked.

'No. No, I'm sure they can't.' Macy folded the letter and tucked it back into the envelope. She tossed it towards the pile of WUM letters and reached for her wine again. 'But you know what? I don't care.'

Her worries last night, her anxiety this morning, her fears about Narcifer having an affair with Bren, her being sacked at work, and finally, the neighbours' petition to get her to leave—] she didn't care about any of that now. She had Narcifer's love, so all was right in her world.

God, she was pathetic.

THIRTEEN

Macy awoke slowly, feeling unbelievably relaxed. The smell of coffee reached her nose, and she turned her head towards the bedside table to see a steaming cup. Narcifer's side of the bed was empty, but she was used to him waking before her. He didn't seem to need as much sleep as she did. She didn't know whether that was a Jelvia thing or just a Narcifer thing.

Pushing herself up, she reached for the cup.

She had a few bruises from last night's lovemaking. This was the second time since she'd come out of the hospital that she'd fully let herself go. But, unfortunately, her body was now paying for her lack of inhibitions.

She smiled. It was worth it.

The coffee wasn't strong enough, but Narcifer was getting better at making it. His tea-making had much improved, too. He'd stopped opening the teabag, anyway. Macy curled her toes under the duvet, enjoying the peace and the coffee despite its lack of kick.

The rattle of the letter box made her start a little. She groaned and hoped the letter was something ordinary, like a bill. Putting her coffee cup down, she swung her legs out of bed and reached for her robe. Tugging it on, she headed downstairs.

The house was quiet—too quiet. Her heart sank, knowing that Narcifer had left her to her own devices again. But that wasn't unlike him, and she couldn't expect to have him around 24/7.

There were a few letters on the floor in the hall, and Macy bent to scoop them up. No WUM letters, thankfully. It seemed her wish had been granted—all bills. She headed through the lounge to the dining room, where her phone was charging on the table. She picked it up and turned it on. She had several texts from Narcifer.

Back soooon xxxx

Love you lots xx

Xxxxxxxxx no idea wat these meen u use them a lot xxxxxxx

He obviously didn't want her to think he'd abandoned her again. She smiled. He was trying hard, and she would have to trust that his weird working hours had nothing to do with wanting to avoid her. Her obsession with her scars was making her insecure. Narcifer had always worked odd hours or left on sudden notice, which had never bothered her. And when he returned, he was usually subdued or needed Macy to teach him 'something human', as he called it.

She smiled as she remembered when she, Mumma Lisa, Courtney, and Narcifer had all played Monopoly over Christmas. Once he had the hang of it, they learned that Narcifer was very good at cheating. So, in return, Lisa taught him how to play poker using the Monopoly money and won all the money back to teach him a lesson. It'd been the funniest poker game ever.

Chuckling at the memory, Macy saw she had a missed call from an unknown number. She was cautious in giving out her personal number, and only her closest friends knew it, so she assumed it must be either a wrong number or James. She didn't want to talk to him again. Something about his call yesterday had pissed her off.

Leaving her phone on charge, she headed for the kitchen, searching for breakfast, but her phone rang. Turning back, Macy saw it was that same unknown number. She picked up the phone, ready to tell James she didn't know where Aldarn was.

'Macy Shaw?' a male voice asked. He didn't sound menacing. In fact, he seemed hesitant. 'My name's Oliver, and I'm from the Wake Up Movement. Have you heard of us?'

How could she not have! 'Just a little,' she said.

'We were about to approach you when you had the accident. Are you okay? All recovered?'

'How did you find this number?' Macy ignored his false concern. 'I've listened to your messages on my work phone and read all the unsolicited letters you've pushed through my door.'

'I apologise for the letters. Unfortunately, a few of our members were overzealous about getting you on board.'

'On board with what? You run a deranged crusade spouting "wake up" to those who won't conform to your beliefs. I don't want any part of that.'

Annoyingly, he gave a little laugh. 'We aren't deranged. Have you read our website? Listened to our podcast?'

'Oh yes. You're a laughingstock, don't you realise? And if,' she said, '*if* what you say is true, why aren't the Jelvias coming after you? Before you answer, Oliver—if that's your real name—I'll tell you: It's because they think you're crazy too. They can't be bothered with you.'

'They can't see us, Macy,' he said.

She snorted.

'Almost six years ago, every human saw them arrive. Immediately afterwards, we all had a collective mind-blank. Since then, humans have believed that the Jelvias have been here forever. Reality—*your* reality—has been distorted. We are victims of an alien attack.'

Macy gripped the phone. People like him had got her the sack and made her relationship with Narcifer difficult.

'I'm sorry, I've shocked you... Macy?'

'You haven't shocked me. You disgust me,' she said, finally. 'You're stirring up a frenzy against Jelvias. All they want is a normal life. Your defamatory remarks about them are dangerous. Don't you realise the damage you're doing to their lives?'

'They *don't* want a normal life, though, do they?' His voice was low and calm. He didn't sound mad. He sounded like a bleeding-heart counsellor. 'They kill criminals to stop themselves from killing innocents—that seems to be their protocol, doesn't it? But if that were the truth, there'd be more criminals dying, and they're not. There *are*, however, more innocent people dying at the hands of Jelvias than ever before. And what of our population? Have you ever wondered why we're being told we're in decline when babies are born every day? Macy, you may think we're mad—God knows, I've thought myself mad a million times—but when you begin to question something, and it only brings you more and more unanswered questions, you're forced to realise things aren't as they seem.'

Macy hung up. He was probably still rambling. She dropped Angela a curt text.

Hi Angela, please find me the leader/organiser of the WUM group ASAP.

She regretted it as soon as she sent it. Angela wasn't her PA. The phone call had got to her. She knew she shouldn't allow emotion to override her professionalism, but it was down to the Wake Up Movement that she and Narcifer couldn't live an everyday life together.

She received a reply from Angela almost immediately.

On it!

The entire WUM movement had been born of racism. It evolved to where it was today, terrifying people and instilling a hatred of Jelvias. She kicked the leg of the chair, making it topple to the floor. She kicked it again for daring to fall, then swivelled around to punch the wall.

Narcifer caught her wrist.

'Hey,' he said. 'What's happened?'

'I'm venting,' she said, releasing her arm from Narcifer's grip. She looked down at the shopping bag he was carrying. 'You've been to the shop?'

'There was no bacon in the fridge.' He pointed to the chair. 'The chair giving you a hard time?'

'I just had a phone call from a member of the WUM named Oliver. He made me angry.'

'Angry?' He pretended to look scared. 'Remind me never to make you angry!'

'Idiot,' she said affectionally as he moved into the kitchen.

He unpacked the bits of food he had bought. 'What did Oliver want?'

'I hung up.'

'Good.' He placed four packs of bacon on the kitchen counter, followed by a tin of cat food and a cake similar to Mumma Lisa's lemon drizzle.

'No, I wish I hadn't. I should have stayed to listen, but his voice was annoying, whiney.' She sighed. 'I just need to get the WUM thing out of my system. I'll phone this Oliver bloke back and arrange a meeting,' she said decisively.

'Whoa! No way. That could be dangerous.'

'They're cranks.'

'Cranks who know where you live, work, and your phone number.'

'People are listening to them, and before long, the government will, too. They need to be stopped.'

'But not by you, Mace.'

'I've interviewed worse people than them. They don't scare me.'

'That's what worries me.' Then, turning to her, he said, 'I'm glad you're getting back to being yourself, but while I think this WUM group is harmless, the individuals might not be. The handwritten letters tell me you're being watched.'

'I probably am.' Then, standing on tiptoe, she pressed a finger against Narcifer's lips. 'And maybe you can trace this Oliver person?'

'Me?'

She lowered her hand. 'What's the point in having a Jelvia if I can't get him to do my dirty work?'

Narcifer stared at her as if trying to see the logic in her mind. 'You want me to kidnap a member of the WUM group?'

'I didn't say "kidnap". I said *trace*. I'll find out the name of the organiser.' She stopped, holding up the can of cat food. 'What's this?'

'It looked interesting,' he said. 'I thought we could have it for dinner tonight.'

'It's cat food.'

'Yeah, and?'

'Food *for* cats.'

Narcifer took the can from her, looked at it, and then at her. 'It's not food?'

'No,' she said, amused.

Narcifer pointed to the pig on the packet of bacon. 'But that's food, right? And it's an animal?' He pointed to the picture of a cat on the tin. 'And so's that. I can't see the problem. Humans and Jelvias have been eating animals for years. I've never eaten a cat. I thought we'd try it.'

'Are you winding me up?'

The look he gave her showed her he wasn't. 'How often do you shop on your own?' she asked.

'Not often.' He picked up the tin of Whiskers. 'Should I put this in the fridge?'

'No,' she said with a sigh. Then, changing the subject, she said, 'Did people hide from you when you went into the shop?'

'Some did, and some pretended I didn't exist, as usual.' He pushed the bacon towards her. 'Show me how to make it crispy. Do you have any plans tomorrow?'

'Tomorrow?' she parroted.

'Yes, tomorrow. I've been neglecting my little human, and I want to make it up to her,' he said. He pointed to the bacon. 'Er, the bacon?'

Smiling, all anger gone, she moved to turn the grill on. Then grabbed the bacon and laid six rashers on the rack.

'Aren't you having any?' he asked.

She glanced at him, then turned and added two more rashers. Finally, she closed the grill door and turned to Narcifer, who opened the cake he'd bought.

'What's happening tomorrow?' she asked, standing before him, her hands on her hips. Narcifer regarded her leisurely, then putting the cake down, he came over and cupped her face, pulling her towards him. Macy was forced to grip his wrists to steady herself, her hands unable to even circle them halfway.

'Tonight, you'll pack a bag,' he said. She smiled at him, but he continued, 'And tomorrow, you'll service your Jelvia.'

FOURTEEN

'Ready?'

'Yes,' she said, and Narcifer took his hands away from her eyes.

He pointed her towards window-like doors and the stunning city view overlooking London. She gasped at the sight and moved towards the scenery. 'Wow, we're high.'

She turned to face Narcifer but then took in the rest of the vast space, from the enormous chandelier above a circular bed plumped with gold-and-red cushions, to the dining area at the other end of the room. There was also a red-and-gold striped settee and matching wing chairs facing the floor-to-ceiling window overlooking the city.

The room made the penthouse suite in Seagull Estate in Cornwall, where they'd stayed last summer, look underdeveloped.

'This is amazing,' she said, still trying to take everything in. 'You arranged this all for us?'

He smiled, looking pleased. 'I wanted to make up for neglecting you.'

'You didn't.' She was ready to forgive him for everything. 'It was a misunderstanding, that's all.'

Other than telling her they could 'recreate a memory', which made Macy think he'd booked a hotel by the coast, she hadn't known what Narcifer had planned. They'd driven into inner London after lunch, then exchanged the busy road for a curling driveway towards the front entrance of the Rose. Built in the 1920s, it was a notoriously expensive hotel. Macy had heard of it but never dreamt she'd stay here.

She sat on the edge of the bed and gave a little bounce, grinning at Narcifer. Then she moved to the dining area to the shiny worktops, state-of-the-art coffee and tea machines, and a bar with a filled chiller.

'This must have cost a fortune,' she said.

Several bottles were in the chiller, including white and rosé wines, champagne, bottled lagers, and soft drinks. From it, she handed Narcifer a can of cola and then took out a bottle of champagne. He took it from her automatically and used a thick claw to pop the cork before Macy could brandish the corkscrew.

She rolled her eyes and found a wineglass, and Narcifer filled it. She sipped the wine. It tasted so good. She didn't know why, but she felt nervous about what Narcifer had in store for her. She wanted it to be as good as before, if not better.

She needed this so much. She needed Narcifer's dominance, his hardness, his control. She clutched the wineglass as if it were a lifeline and watched as Narcifer opened the bifold doors until the entire wall was open to the balcony and the view of London.

It was late afternoon, and the city was growing dark. Twinkly lights were beginning to pop on, but the traffic noises and hubbub of human activity below were minimal. They were too high up for the sound to have much effect.

She followed him outside, noticing that the balcony had a partial roof with heaters that blasted down welcome heat towards the outside seating area. She looked over the balcony. From here, Macy could see the winding Thames and Tower Bridge.

'There's everything we could possibly want here. It's amazing,' Macy said, turning.

Narcifer had seated himself on the low patio sofa. He held a hand towards her, and Macy scooted over to sit beside him. She leaned her head against his shoulder and sipped her wine.

'I want to take your mind off your boss, the WUMs, and your neighbours,' he said. 'I want you back to the carefree days from last summer. Where you held no inhibitions.'

'You certainly took them from me.'

He chuckled, but she suspected there was a more serious reason he had brought her here. She waited for him to explain, watching as more London lights came on.

'This isn't just a room where we can indulge in one another. It's a place to escape our thoughts, worries, outside influences... We haven't been alone together since you came out of the hospital, and the job I'm currently on is complicated, so the time we have here is special.'

'I understand.' She didn't, but she said it anyway.

'The job's taking longer than I expected—mainly because of Calder's interference.'

'Want to talk about it?'

'No, I don't. We're here to forget, remember?'

'Agreed,' she said. 'For the duration of our stay here, we'll not mention Calder, Aldarn, WUMs, my job, or anything. I wish we could stay alone together always. How long are we here for?'

'We've three days. I must be back Saturday when Calder is meeting Aldarn.'

'Oh?' she said, trying to prompt him for more.

'Bren's driving him—remember I told you?' he said. 'But I will follow them to ensure she doesn't double-cross me. She's done that before. But hey, they don't exist, do they?'

Macy smiled at him as he slipped his arm around her shoulders. She finished her wine, feeling peaceful. She sighed, then felt Narcifer's gaze on her. She looked up.

'I don't think you realise how important you are to me.' Before she could answer, he reached out and brushed her fringe away from her droopy eyelid. 'If I ever lost you, I think I'd just cease to exist. Seeing you on the road, all broken like that... I can't forget it.'

'You're not going to lose me,' she said.

'I love you more than life itself.'

She didn't like this sudden sombre tension. She punched him lightly on the arm. 'I love you to the moon and back.'

Finally breaking into a smile, he said, 'And I love you to Itor and back.'

'Itor? Where's that?'

'It's a planet, isn't it?' he said.

'Never heard of it,' she said, resting her head against his shoulder on a happy sigh. She was just glad they were back to normal.

The world, everyone, could cease to exist.

FIFTEEN

Macy, feeling like a kid on Christmas morning, explored the rest of the flat. She found a steam room, and as she stepped inside, miniature lights, like hundreds of fairy lights in the ceiling, flicked on. She looked around in awe. The walls and ceiling were mosaic-tiled in browns and golds, which reflected the lights and made them twinkle. In the corner was a gold mosaic chair, which held a pile of neatly folded towels bearing the Rose logo.

A knock on the main door brought her out of her thoughts.

'Expecting someone?' Macy called, heading towards the door.

Narcifer had already beaten her to it. Pulling his sunglasses over his eyes, he opened the door, blocking Macy's view with his bulk.

She was always nervous when Narcifer interacted with other humans. It wasn't that she didn't trust him, but humans overreacted in Jelvian company, and his glasses provided minimal camouflage. The last time he'd been found out, it had caused a rampage at the hotel where they were staying.

She waited, ready to intervene, as Narcifer stepped back to let two uniformed women in. One was pushing a trolley, and they both looked anxious. Keeping their heads bowed, they headed straight over to the dining area. One unloaded the trolley onto the shiny worktops while the other set the dining table.

When they finished, they scuttled out of the door without a word.

Narcifer dropped his sunglasses on the bed and ambled into the dining area to fawn over the food. He stuffed several canapés in his mouth.

'Hey,' Macy said, jerking her thumb towards the door, 'don't you think that was strange?'

'I'm used to it,' he said, his mouth full.

'More and more people are noticing you're a Jelvia.'

He nodded absently, picking up another canapé.

Macy stared at him, wishing she had some of his recklessness. She cared what people thought. He didn't. He glanced around at her, a pastry halfway to his mouth.

'Come on,' he said, beckoning her over with an impatient hand. 'You'll need to eat to keep your strength up later. Or maybe it'll be tomorrow.' He pretended to contemplate. 'I haven't decided yet.'

She walked over, smiling. 'What have you got planned?'

He shook his head at her. 'You shouldn't question your dom.'

Her eyes widened, and a slow grin spread over his face.

She punched his arm. 'I'm not into that, as you well know.'

'We'll see,' he said, his eyes drifting from her face to the rest of her body. They lingered on her breasts, which were covered with a thick jumper—but that jumper suddenly felt tissue-thin. Her body thrummed in anticipation, but Macy tried not to rise to his teasing. Instead, she looked at the tiny morsels arranged neatly on serving plates. The food looked almost too good to eat. She lifted a silver cloche to reveal two steaming plates of various delights. 'Oh, wow.'

Narcifer didn't answer. His mouth was full. He mumbled something which she thought sounded like, 'Nice!'

As she watched, he picked up a cheese-topped biscuit. He was going through the canapés as if he hadn't a care, whereas she already felt foreplay was in full throttle. Trying to act nonchalant, she picked up a chocolate-covered pastry topped with a strawberry.

'Oh, God, that's to die for! How'd you book all this, Narce? The other day you mistook cat food for human food—then you do something like this?'

'Aren't you ever going to let me forget that?' he said.

Macy finished the chocolate pastry and sipped more of her wine. 'Never,' she said, smiling at him.

'We have the staff at Keats to arrange stuff like this. I wouldn't have a clue.' He bent to pick up a creamy pastry and held it towards her lips. 'Open.' Macy opened her mouth, and Narcifer popped it inside. 'Good girl,' he said, 'and remember to be that obliging later on.'

'One minute you're unbelievably romantic, the next crass!' she said, swallowing the pastry and then laughing. He had an incredible knack for knowing how she felt and being able to relax her.

'I've something for you,' he said.

'A present? All this is more than enough,' she said.

'I didn't say it was a present,' he said, soothing and energising her, keeping her in a state of high anticipation.

She gulped but trotted behind him towards their luggage. He picked both bags up from the rack where the porter had placed them, put hers on the bed, then dumped his on a high-backed chair and rummaged through it.

Macy peered to look, but he sidestepped to block her view. Sitting on the end of the bed instead, she unzipped her own bag and shook out her clothes. She hadn't known what to expect, so she'd packed a selection, including a pretty lingerie set she bought in the summer. She'd thought she would never wear it again because of her injuries.

'Here you go,' he said, turning and holding out a gift bag.

She took it curiously, peered inside, and looked at Narcifer in confusion. 'Ribbon ties? Ah...' she said, her tummy suddenly erupting in butterflies. 'Is this for your dom thing?'

Narcifer took the bag from her. He dipped his hand inside and pulled out a blindfold.

'This will give you confidence when you're naked in front of me,' he said. 'I think your feelings have nothing to do with me seeing your scars. It's *you* seeing them.'

Macy stared at him, dumbfounded.

'And this,' said Narcifer, holding up the ribbon, 'will stop you knocking my hands away every time I get too close to a scar.'

'I don't!'

'You don't *think* you do, but you do. Ah, and here we have my favourite.' He pulled out a black leather paddle and held it to the light to admire it. He caught Macy's shocked eyes and winked. 'There's nothing like a good spanking, now is there?' She felt herself flushing, and his grin widened, his dimples twinkling at her. 'I think I've been lax in keeping you in line, my love.'

'You're not using that on me—no way, José! Or the ribbon. I'm not into bondage, Narce,' she said, trying to gain some sort of control over the situation. Or pretending, at least. She sat on the edge of the bed, but suddenly she was tipped backwards. Narcifer straddled her and held her arms above her head.

'Say that again?' he said.

'I'm not into bondage,' she repeated.

'I know you enjoy bondage, and I aim to please my pet human,' he said, pretending to mishear her. It was all part of the game. He bent and gently touched her lips with his mouth.

'The paddle will hurt,' she protested weakly against his mouth.

His lips moved from her lips to nibble her ear. Then he whispered, 'It's meant to hurt.'

Tingles erupted all over her body, and she stared at him hungrily, but he lifted from her and climbed off the bed. She watched him head back to the kitchen to eat more canapés. She stared at his back. He really had no clue how he made her feel—or maybe he did, and this was part of tonight's experience.

She pushed herself up, trying to look calm, and pulled her luggage towards her. 'I hope I've brought the right clothes. It looks classy here,' she said, but was annoyed when her voice sounded breathless.

Narcifer looked round, a strawberry halfway to his mouth. He popped it in as he watched her sorting through her bag, and she noticed him smiling from the corner of her eye.

Yep, he knew.

'You'll look beautiful whatever you wear,' he said, coming over. He peered into her bag. 'Hey, what's this?' He pulled out a notebook. 'Not thinking of working, are you?'

'Believe it or not, that's the same notebook I used when we first met. It's been in the bag that whole time.' She sat up on her knees and took the book from him. 'See where I've written Springfield's old phone number on the front.'

Narcifer looked. 'That number caused us a lot of trouble.'

Still on her knees, Macy flicked through the book as Narcifer turned away and picked up a small remote control. He pointed it at the large fireplace, and the flames *whooshed* into life. Then, dropping the remote, he walked back to the kitchen area, collecting her empty wineglass en route.

'A glass of champagne, madam?' he asked.

'Lovely,' Macy said absently. She was staring at something she'd drawn—a doodle of three Jelvian islands between Ireland and England. She frowned. Why had she drawn three islands when there were clearly four? There was even a note beneath the drawing:

3 Jelvian islands.

She might have *written* a simple error, but to *draw* it as well? How had she missed the fourth island between Norway and Iceland in the Arctic Circle?

'What's up?' he asked.

She looked as Narcifer held out a glass of champagne towards her. Then, taking it, she said, 'I wrote something really bizarre here.'

He sat on the bed next to her. 'Like what?'

She sipped her wine, then tapped the notebook, saying, 'How many Jelvian islands are there?'

'Four,' he said.

She held up her notebook. 'Exactly. So why did I write that there were only three? I even *drew* them.'

He took the notebook from her fingers and tossed it back in her holdall. Next, he took the champagne flute from her and placed it on the side table.

'From here onwards,' he said, 'the outside world doesn't exist. It's just you and me.' He took her chin and pressed his lips against hers. 'Just me and you,' he said, slowly emphasising each word against her mouth.

SIXTEEN

After the canapés, Macy hadn't thought she'd be able to eat anything else, but dinner had been delicious.

The meal had been delivered to the room by two waiters. The service waiter had offered to stay and serve them, but they declined, so their chilled food was placed in the chiller, and the heated trolley was left for them to help themselves. She felt like a queen. Narcifer made every effort to impress. He teased her throughout dinner, giving her a running commentary of what he would do to her later.

But now that dinner was over—nothing.

It was all part of the game he wanted her to play. He pushed all her sensory buttons; making love with him always seemed like the first time. They had come outside to sit on the balcony, and she watched as he settled back, raising his face to the warmth of the heaters. London twinkled below them.

'Hey,' she said, giving him a nudge. 'Are you asleep?'

He opened his eyes and the intensity in the all-black gaze made goosebumps erupt over her skin. They slipped from her face and down to focus on her cleavage. He smiled lazily, and Macy didn't even see him move to flip open the top button of her blouse. Instead, his finger lingered and stroked the bulge of her breast. Macy leaned into him, but Narcifer took her by the shoulders and firmly eased her away just as smoothly.

Macy gaped at him, but his head was tipped towards the heaters again, and his eyes were closed. Her body burnt from his touch. How he could turn off like that was beyond her. He was making her wait on purpose.

The paddle he'd presented her with was lying on the low table in front of them. He'd brought it out, left it without speaking, and ignored her questioning gaze. He was playing with her, and it both annoyed and excited her. Although she knew she could never permanently lead a dom/sub life, she loved his dominance during love play. Outside of that, she was her own woman.

She leaned against him and placed her hand on his thigh. She drew a leisurely circle on his leg with her finger, but Narcifer's hand pressed firmly down on hers, stopping her.

'I'm in charge tonight,' he said. His eyes were still closed. '*I'm* the one to decide when, where, and how far we'll go. No more touching until I say. Is that clear?'

Macy's mouth hung open. She snapped it closed, pulling her hand away. She felt offended yet strangely thrilled, too. Her eyes fell on the paddle as she picked up her wine from the low table.

'See that?' he said, and Macy looked up to see his gaze on her face. He was pointing to the paddle. He must have seen her looking. 'That's going to connect with your arse so hard you'll scream.'

She snorted. 'You're not using that on me,' she said, but the thought of *Narcifer* using it made her entire body throb. She quivered at the image of Narcifer domineering her body over his lap, pulling her underwear down and turning her arse pink as she kicked and fought for her freedom. She coughed, taking the wine down the wrong way.

'Maybe you need to ease up on that,' he said. He took the glass from her and set it back on the table. 'I want you to remember this evening, after all.'

'I'm okay,' she said, patting her chest to ease the coughing. Then, unconsciously, her hand moved to fasten the button on her blouse.

'Hey, what are you doing? I never told you to do it up.'

She looked at him, and he raised his eyebrows at her. Then, without another word, she unfastened it. He was playing a game, and he might be playing it annoyingly slowly, but she'd play along. She glanced at the paddle again.

'Stop looking at it,' he said.

'It's making me nervous.'

'It's a state of anticipation.'

She stared at the paddle until Narcifer put his arm alongside her backrest. His fingers touched her cheek, and he gently pushed her head around to face him. Slowly, he lowered his head and kissed her mouth, then trailed hot but slow kisses down the side of her neck.

About fucking time.

Narcifer flicked open another button until her cleavage was fully exposed. He bent and kissed the mound of one breast beneath the lace of her bra. He tucked a finger into her bra and brushed a hardening nipple.

Macy sighed and closed her eyes. His lips followed his finger, trailing a fiery path across her breasts. A shiver danced along her skin, making her murmur. Narcifer lowered the lace and exposed her nipple to the air. Then, taking his time, he bent his head, took the puckered nipple in his mouth, and sucked. Macy clutched his shoulders as he greedily took from her. He kissed the hollow of her throat again before claiming her mouth.

Drawing away, he said, 'Open your eyes.'

Macy opened her eyes to find him looking at her. His breath was ragged, and his all-black eyes sparkled with desire.

'Go get the silk ties and the blindfold,' he said.

Macy stood up without any thought other than what Narcifer wanted of her. She knew she could stop anytime, but she didn't want to. She was a willing captive and fascinated to know what he would do to her.

She went to collect the items he'd requested. They were still in the gift bag, and she took them out and brought them out to Narcifer. He didn't look at them, nor at her.

'Put them on the table,' he said.

Macy did as asked.

'You've so much to learn, my little human.' Before she could do or say anything in return, he stood up. 'With you all tied up, I will hold all the power. You'll be at my mercy—I'll be able to do to you as I like. The ropes will allow you to surrender to me. Surrender utterly and completely.'

He cupped her chin and raised her head.

Macy looked into his eyes, no longer feeling agitated or slighted. She was massively turned on, but she felt safe and cosseted at the same time. She'd handed the responsibility of her body over to Narcifer. It felt wonderful.

'I want you to stand at the front of the balcony, away from the heaters and in full view of the city below. Then take off your clothes.'

Macy walked across the balcony and then turned around to face Narcifer. She unbuttoned her blouse the rest of the way. Nobody could see her from this height, but it was chilly, and the wind made goosebumps erupt on her skin.

Narcifer got up and went inside. Frowning, she clutched her blouse together and watched as Narcifer pulled off the black T-shirt he wore. His back was facing her, and the bulge of his muscles as he performed the simple act of removing his shirt made her belly flip-flop. He tossed the T-shirt onto the chair and strode further into the room's dimness. Squinting to watch, Macy saw him pull on his Jelvia coat. It was strange how clothes could change a person. In an instant, he'd gone from being Narcifer to a Jelvia.

A killing machine.

He turned towards the balcony, and Macy quickly dropped her blouse and wriggled out of her tailored trousers. In her underwear, she stood watching him as he moved near the door. In the dim light, his black eyes seemed like empty sockets in his face, and they travelled all over her body.

'All of your clothes,' he said.

Macy unclipped her bra and then stepped out of her knickers. She kicked them to one side and stood looking at Narcifer. Narcifer was watching her from inside and made no attempt to join her outside on the balcony.

It felt like a waiting game, but Macy stayed quiet and still. Waiting for her dom.

Finally, he moved, but he didn't acknowledge Macy. Instead, he came out, sat down, and raised his legs on the low table.

The movement knocked the paddle off the table. His eyes followed the paddle to the floor, and then he lifted them to look at Macy. Quickly, she moved to pick up the paddle. She placed it back on the table and then resumed her position. She was no longer cold. The heat was circling her bloodstream.

'Turn around,' he said.

Macy turned around. Her breasts were level with the top of the balcony railing, but it was made of transparent safety glass. Her naked body was bared to the world.

'Spread your legs and bend over.'

His words excited her, and the actions he was requesting were beyond thrilling. Keeping her hands on the railing, she stepped back to spread her legs and bend over. She heard him move, then felt him behind her. Warm fingers stroked her buttocks. Then his whole hand stroked her. He petted her behind with hands that became firmer with each stroke.

'Open more.'

She shifted and opened her legs to his command.

He pressed his warm mouth against her backside and trailed soft kisses up her spine. 'You're utterly beautiful, Macy,' he said between kisses. Then, moving up, he lifted her hair off her nape to get to the soft skin beneath and nibbled her neck. It tickled, and Macy bit her lip to stop herself from reacting.

But then, just as abruptly, he left her.

Still holding onto the top of the balcony rail, she turned her head to look at him, watching as he returned to the settee beneath the overhead heaters. He was watching her just as intently. Then, slowly, he leaned forwards and picked up the paddle. He turned it over in his hands, then raised it in one hand to smack it against the palm of the other.

The sound made Macy's insides quiver.

He stood up again and came towards her with the paddle. Macy watched his approach, feeling her pulse beat with each of his strides. When he put his hand on the top of her head and forcibly turned her face away, Macy sucked in her breath at his brutality, but she couldn't deny it thrilled her. Giving her little time to think, he pressed the paddle against her buttocks. He patted her gently with it, then raised his hand high, making her wince with expectation, but brought the paddle down gently on her flesh.

Then he stepped away.

'Come to me,' he said.

She turned around and did as he asked, standing before him with her head slightly bowed.

They'd ceased to be Narcifer and Macy.

They were now master and submissive.

SEVENTEEN

He swooped down, lifting her, and then carried her inside.

He sat her on a chair before the fire and closed the patio doors. The warmth of the fire stung her skin, and she realised how cold she had been, but the cold was just on her outer layers. Inside she was burning hot, burning for Narcifer.

He turned and stood watching her. She stared back, waiting for his command. Instead, he slipped his hand into his pocket and pulled out the blindfold.

'It is time, my little human,' he said.

His voice, his words, made her throb. She gripped the sides of the chair as he stepped towards her and bent to fix the blindfold over her eyes. She knew he was doing this for her benefit; he usually liked her to watch everything he did to her. But, with her sight restricted, her other senses intensified.

He took her hands and pulled her to stand. Narcifer led her forwards until she felt the rug's softness beneath her feet and knew she was standing in the centre of the room. He let her hands go, leaving her standing alone.

Macy listened for him but couldn't hear anything other than the mechanics of the gas fire.

'On your knees,' he said, his voice coming from behind her and making her jump.

Macy was getting into her role as a sub. She felt electrified and was almost ready to kiss his feet or do anything else he might ask her.

Narcifer took her hand as she knelt. She sat back on her heels.

'I said *knees*,' he said, giving her hand a squeeze.

Macy knelt upright, and he let her go.

'Put your hands behind your back.'

Macy did as asked, the movement jutting her breasts forwards. She hoped Narcifer was getting an eyeful. She could hear him circling her passive pose. His knee-length, black Jelvian coat rustled as he moved agonisingly slowly. He was taking his time. Finally, he stood behind her, and bound her hands together. It wasn't painfully tight, but they were definitely tied firmly.

The coat swished.

She jumped as he gently patted her breasts, making them jiggle. Then he tweaked her nipples. The movement was almost painful, but she remained upright on her knees. Narcifer fondled both breasts until she pressed into his palms, but he moved away. She followed the movement with her head until he disappeared entirely behind her. She thought she heard the chair squeak as he sat down, or it could have been the bed.

The silence was excruciating.

'Up,' he commanded after what seemed like an hour.

Macy moved one leg but struggled to raise herself without using her hands because of the injury to her other leg. She stumbled, but Narcifer was at her side and steadied her before she fell. He hadn't been sitting, after all, but was close by.

'Okay? Want to carry on?' he asked, both hands on her upper arms. His thumbs stroked her skin.

'Yep,' Macy said. She definitely wanted to continue with this game. She was so turned on, and her skin was on fire.

'Remember our safe word?'

'I do. And I'm not going to say it,' she added impatiently.

'You can. At any time.'

'I don't want to.'

He let her go, and his absence was startling. She heard him circling her. He was getting back into his dom role. It hadn't taken long. Firm fingers gripped her around the back of her neck, and then she was pushed to walk.

The carpet beneath Macy's bare feet became tiles, but Macy knew she wasn't in the kitchen. Instead, she was in the hallway, by the entrance to their flat. Macy couldn't see anything through the blindfold, but enough light penetrated to know it was dazzlingly bright.

Narcifer stopped her. She could feel him next to her, but he was silent. She knew every inch of her body was being scrutinised beneath the bright lights and squirmed. Macy was proud of her body—or had been before she'd been disfigured. Thinking of her scars and wondering which one Narcifer was looking at made her want to cover up, but there wasn't anything she could do with her hands bound. She stood still and submissive, enduring the silent appraisal.

She jumped as an unseen finger traced a line from the middle of her shoulder blades to the tip of her tailbone.

'Beautiful,' he murmured. He replaced the finger with his lips, stopping at her tailbone to nip gently at her bottom. He moved around her and kissed her throat. Macy raised her head, but he moved down her body, kissing between her breasts and down to her navel. She felt his breath on her pubic area but somehow wasn't prepared for his tongue to flick out and catch her clit. She hissed beneath her breath while trying to keep her body still. He flicked her clit again but didn't linger. He was just teasing her.

'And now, my little human,' he said, nipping at her again, 'I'm going to flog you.'

She gulped and bit down a nervous giggle. He was good. Terrifyingly good. She was actually feeling scared.

A door opened, and a wave of heat billowed over her. The steam room. Narcifer guided her inside, and then he manhandled her until she straddled a bench. With her arms still behind her back, he pushed her forwards until she lay flat on her front. He'd put down a few pillows and cushions, so it was comfortable.

Macy began to relax—until, suddenly, one end of the bench lifted, and her lower body was raised, leaving her legs to dangle down. She slipped forwards slightly, but Narcifer gripped her hips, pulling her back up the bench until she felt its end against her thighs.

Then something slipped between her bound wrists, locking her to the bench and stopping her from sliding forwards. She was naked, straddling a bench with her lower half raised as if that was the only part of her that mattered. It was a subservient pose. Narcifer gave her bottom two sharp swots before his fingers began touching her feet. It made her squirm and giggle, and then he moved to her calves and the backs of her knees. Macy had never realised she had erogenous zones in her legs. His fingers felt so good as they stroked and caressed her. Finally, his touch reached between her legs, cupping, fingering, and pressing against her until she whimpered.

Then nothing.

Macy raised her head to listen for a sound, but her head was roughly pushed back down on the cushion. At this point, she was ready to stop the play. She didn't think her body could take much more waiting. She thought she would explode, but then his hands were back, stroking her backside, becoming harder each time until she was pressed deep into the cushions on the bench. Each time his hand left her flesh, she thought she would receive a slap, but she was caressed each time. It was strange. She both wanted and dreaded the spanking.

Then it came. A slight, gasp-making smack on one cheek. Then the other side, until he was spanking her in earnest, alternating on each buttock with short, sharp slaps. She wanted to kick and squirm from his hand, but she was stuck to the bench. She both enjoyed his dominance over her and hated it all at once. She loved the strange sense of freedom the spanking made her feel. It just felt so good.

Narcifer stopped, and she lay panting into the pillows as the sting in her buttocks radiated over her flesh. He left her alone briefly to let her experience the spreading sting.

Macy whimpered into the pillows.

Then he was back, and his hands stroked and petted her burning behind. It felt good. Calming. Macy was coming down from her high and feeling relaxed when Narcifer's tempo changed again. He gripped her hips, lifting and yanking her until the restraints on her wrists pulled tight. Then he buried his head between her legs.

Macy gasped and grabbed a pillow between her teeth as he licked around her opening, pulling her clit into his hot mouth. He sucked hard, and Macy squealed into the pillows. He lapped at her, his hands holding her hips until her orgasm built.

She shouted as Narcifer's tongue continued to lick and lap. Finally, her climax consumed her, bursting from her, leaving her limp. Before she could collect herself, Narcifer released her bonds and hauled her upright. In her post-orgasmic fog of pleasure and pain, he spun her around and moved her to another part of the steam room.

He placed her hands against the wall. Then, placing one hand firmly on the centre of her back and another around her belly, he strong-armed her until her top half leaned forwards, her hips and buttocks protruded.

Narcifer moved her feet to part her legs, and her wrists were tied to something above her. Macy vaguely remembered seeing wooden beams embedded in the ceiling. She gripped the ties with her hands as she waited, listening to the sounds of Narcifer moving around her softly.

His hands circled her, pulling her back against his body. His warm tongue grazed her ear, and his mouth nibbled her neck as he pressed against her. He wasn't naked; she could still feel the abrasive material of his jeans. Something pressed against her bottom, then moved down, stroking each leg and inner thigh. The pressure was hard, and then she realised what it was.

The paddle. It patted her tender bottom.

'Are you ready for this, my little human?' Narcifer's voice in the quiet made her jump. 'I hope I don't have to gag you,' he added.

Macy shook her head almost violently. She didn't want to be gagged. The paddle caught her unawares, striking her on the centre of her bottom, another blow on the left cheek, then to the right. Macy yelped with each strike, but she didn't feel any pain. Her mind was languid, and her body was soft and warm. She was utterly at peace as the noise of the paddle striking her flesh ricocheted off the walls in the steam room.

Narcifer's breathing had thickened, and Macy heard him unzip his jeans. It was stifling hot in the steam room, and she was sweating. Perspiration and the moisture in the air mingled to drench her face, and her blindfold had slipped from one eye, and from that eye, Macy could see that Narcifer was totally naked. His body was glistening too, and he was highly aroused.

It felt like her mind was filled with fluff. She felt the strong length of him press against her flaming buttocks. His fingers bit into her flesh. He wasn't gentle. He mumbled something, his words almost a growl.

'Narcifer,' she said in a whisper. She was breathless, feeling like she was in between worlds. It was a strange sensation, and she couldn't pull herself back. She didn't *want* to pull herself back. Narcifer's hands moved around her stomach and gripped her between the legs, holding her tight against his body. She was in a high state of arousal, distantly aware that she was teetering on the edge of something primal.

'Narcifer,' she whispered again and felt all her muscles disintegrate. She would have fallen if it had not been for the ties around her wrists. Instead, she hung, her head lolling forwards.

Something warm splattered against her bottom and thighs. Narcifer stepped away from her, gripping his erection and marking her with his seed all over her body.

High on endorphins and enkephalins in her happy place, Macy sighed.

EIGHTEEN

Macy lay on a warm sandy beach as sunshine bathed her body and the ocean lapped at her feet. Sighing in contentment, she sat up on her elbows, but instead of seeing the sea, she was back in the hospital and staring at the window across from her bed.

Feeling bemused but still enveloped in warmth, she watched as Narcifer climbed through the window. He was in full Jelvian uniform, wearing the knee-length black, bullet-proof coat. He sat by her bed and took her hand.

'I'll always be your hero, Macy Shaw, whether you reciprocate my sentiments or not.'

Macy opened her eyes. She was naked in bed, and her buttocks were tender, but she also felt very relaxed. With Narcifer spooning her, she lay sleepily, not wanting to move. She thought about her dream, knowing it was a combination of real events. Narcifer had often climbed through the window to visit her in the hospital, and when they first met, he'd given her that cheesy line that had melted her heart.

She turned in Narcifer's arms to face him. He was awake and he smiled at her.

'Good morning, sleepyhead,' he said.

'I had the weirdest dream,' she said. 'One minute, I was on a beach, the next in the hospital. Then, you came through the window and sat by my bed.'

His grin widened. 'I often visited that way. I scared people coming in the ordinary route.'

Macy snuggled against him as the dream slipped away. 'Do you remember what you said to me after you saved me from the caves? You said you'd always be my hero.' His body stiffened. It was momentary, but Macy felt it. She looked up. 'What's up?'

But his smile was just as bright. 'Up? Nothing.' He dropped a kiss on her head. 'How do you feel after last night? Did I work my little submissive a little hard?' he asked.

Macy smiled, her dream forgotten. 'Watch it,' she warned playfully. 'What happened exactly, though? I felt drunk, but I only had two glasses of champagne.'

'You were in subspace. Apparently, it's a trance-like euphoria of overly intense emotions,' he said as if reciting something.

'Yeah, I've heard of it. I liked it.' She grinned. 'Can we do it again?'

He looked amused. 'Every day, if you like.'

She laughed. 'And there was me worried we'd be unable to top our time at the Seagull Estate. But this... it was on another level.' She rolled on her back and stared at the ceiling. She felt so at peace.

'It didn't hurt too much, then?' he asked.

The heat in her buttocks was already ebbing away. She shook her head, then looked at him. 'You were good at playing a dom. Pretty scary, in fact. But, hey, would you really have gagged me?'

'Oh, yeah. If you were too noisy.'

She punched his arm. He grinned at her and cupped one side of her face, brushing her lips with his fingers. Macy opened her mouth and took his finger inside. Narcifer watched in fascination as she sucked on his forefinger. Then, letting him go, she sat up and roughly thrust against his chest until he was forced onto his back. She straddled him.

'Okay,' said Narcifer. 'I guess breakfast will have to wait.'

He placed his hands on her hips as she teased his probing penis by brushing herself against it. But she didn't allow him to enter her. Narcifer shifted, lifting her to position himself, but Macy took his hands and held them above his head on the pillows.

'Uh-uh,' she said, shaking her head. 'My terms.'

Narcifer grinned at her, his all-black eyes sparking. Smiling, Macy leaned forwards and dragged her short nails down his chest. Her breasts wobbled with the movement, and his gaze flickered there. She lowered her face and trailed soft kisses over his upper body, gradually moving down, nipping and licking his skin.

Narcifer murmured nonsense. Sitting up, Macy guided him inside her and sank deep onto him. She moved up and down along the length of his shaft, slowly and purposefully, tilting her hips and pushing down so she could feel him inside her. He raised his hands but caught himself and put his hands down.

'Good Jelvia,' she said, and his grin widened.

Macy ground against him, watching as the expression on his face changed to rapture. She moved up and down, then switched to a rocking motion, her movements becoming harder and stronger as her need grew.

She slowed down and speeded up according to *her* needs. She tried to keep the tempo low-key, but as Narcifer's climax spiralled, he grabbed her hips and tipped her over until she was lying flat and he was above.

Macy yelped.

'Sorry,' he said, his voice husky. 'But you're teasing me, and I'm stronger than you.' And then he kissed her, his tongue plundering the softness of her mouth as he burst inside her. He kissed her, his lips moving from her mouth to the side of her neck, shoulder, and then her collarbone. Finally, his mouth fastened over one nipple, where he sucked greedily.

His hips continued to thrust against her until her climax made her cling to him and beg him to stop. But he didn't stop until they were both slick with sweat and collapsed on their backs.

NINETEEN

The three days spent at the Rose were magical, and neither was keen to return home. Macy felt that she and Narcifer had connected all over again. Her relaxed and sated state was only marred when she remembered Narcifer intended to follow Calder to Aldarn's whereabouts.

She didn't understand Narcifer's obsession with Aldarn. She hoped that once the two had spoken, any fears Narcifer held would be alleviated. Then they could carry on with their lives.

They checked out after a lazy lunch on Saturday and began the slow drive home. Then, speaking hesitantly, as if reluctant to return to their world, Narcifer forewarned her that he'd have to leave her straight away and would probably not be back until the following day.

Macy nodded and played the understanding girlfriend to perfection.

Narcifer was a Jelvia, not a human. So she couldn't expect him to act human. *'Alas, they aren't human and never doubt they can be, Macy.'* The words popped into her mind, but she couldn't remember who'd said them.

William Springfield, she told herself. He'd been the only one to say things like 'Alas' or 'my dear'. He treated her like an impressible young girl, but back then, she had been. She felt she'd grown a lot since then. She didn't readily accept everything Narcifer told her anymore, either.

Ah! How's that going for you?

Rolling her eyes at her own internal dialogue, Macy settled back into her seat. The radio was on low. She looked across at Narcifer as he drove them through London. He drove confidently and sometimes without regard for other drivers, but he didn't make Macy feel unsafe. She looked out the window and focused on how she could get her interview with Narcifer broadcast to the nation. She'd do it without *London Echo*.

Thinking about it reminded Macy that she'd asked Angela to find out who the key player of the WUM organisation was, and she bent to rummage in her handbag, bringing out her phone. She had turned it off for the duration of their stay at the Rose, and emails from WUM began flooding in when she turned it on. She glanced at Narcifer as they pinged into her inbox one after the other.

He looked back, raising his eyebrows.

'WUM,' she clarified. 'They're ridiculous. Why are they so desperate to speak to me?'

'You're high profile, I guess, and you have a Jelvia living with you.'

She snorted. Ignoring the emails, she checked her text messages. The first one was from Jack, her boss at *London Echo*. She must have made a noise of displeasure because Narcifer looked at her again.

'Everything okay?'

'Jack texted. He's saying I must decide to come back to work by Monday.'

'And have you?'

'I was going to get legal advice, but I'm not now. I've made my mind up. I'll give Jack what he wants and resign. If I stay, my interview will never see the light of day.'

'I'm sorry, babe.'

'It isn't your fault.'

He gave a hollow laugh. 'Yeah, it is. If I were a regular boyfriend, you'd still be employed.'

'And still chasing shallow celebrities for their boring life stories. Nah, you did me a favour.' She watched him smile. Then looked back at her phone and opened a text from Angela.

The organiser's name is Phil Oswald. He put the WUM together two years ago with Oliver Kennedy. At first, it was just

the two of them, but their numbers grew as various people claimed to 'wake up' and join them.

Angela sounded like a hopeful puppy looking for a pat on the head, even in text mode. Smiling, Macy tapped back:

That's great. Thank you, Angela.

It had been several days since Macy's initial text and this response, so it surprised her when Angela returned her text quickly:

It might be better to speak to Oliver before Phil. I got the impression that Phil's not as easy going as Oliver.

Macy: **Gotcha! Thanks, Angela. I owe you one.**

Macy clicked off and dropped her phone back in her handbag. Angela really was like that little dog, always trying to please.

Narcifer glanced at her as he navigated the car through traffic, turning it down a street towards the main road. 'More bad news?' he asked.

'No, not at all. I asked Angela for information on the WUM organisation. She came up with two names: Phil Oswald and Oliver Kennedy. I spoke to a man called Oliver on the phone a few days ago, so I'm going to presume he runs WUM jointly with Phil Oswald. Think you could entice him—or both—to that interrogation room you were talking about?'

'You're still sure about that?'

'Absolutely. They're the reason we can't have normal lives.'

'Nobody takes them seriously.'

'So, imagine how difficult life will become once they *are* being taken seriously.'

Narcifer reduced the speed as the traffic slowed ahead, and then finally, all cars came to a complete stop.

'What's going on?' Macy asked, peering to look.

'Just traffic,' he said, glancing in the rearview mirror. 'Ah.'

Macy turned to see a police car draw up behind them, closing the road to prevent the jam from getting worse. She spun to the front and noticed a traffic cop in Hi-Viz was already knocking on car windows from the line of stationary cars in front.

She turned the radio off and looked at Narcifer.

'Police?' she said. Her voice came out squeaky. Her heart thumped as memories of the night she was taken hostage in the bistro rushed back. All she could envision were the armed police, drones, strobing lights and an armed helicopter dragging a net as it pursued Narcifer. They hunted him down like an animal.

'I don't think they're stopping the traffic because of me,' he said. 'Can you hear that?'

Macy cocked her head. Not hearing anything, she buzzed down her window. Sounds of chanting immediately filled the car:

WAKE UP! WAKE UP! WAKE UP! WAKE UP!

She closed the window. 'WUM,' she said in relief. 'I never thought I'd be pleased to hear them.'

'It's just the police redirecting the traffic away from the protests,' Narcifer said. They watched as the policeman ordered the car at the head of the line to turn and go back the way it had come.

'Is he going to speak to each car in turn?' Macy said as the police officer moved to the next vehicle. 'We get it; we know we have to turn,' Macy said.

'I'm going to try and turn before the police get to us,' Narcifer said.

She looked over her shoulder at the car behind. Its nose was close to their rear. Narcifer edged forwards, but the vehicle behind moved too. Narcifer swore under his breath as he became sandwiched between two cars.

'Do you have my glasses?' he asked. His SUV had blacked-out windows, preventing anyone from looking in, but as soon as his window was down, his true identity would be revealed to the officer.

Macy rummaged in her handbag and opened the glove box to look inside. She looked at Narcifer. 'They aren't here. I think you put them in your holdall, and that's in the boot. I'll get them,' she said and reached to clip off her seatbelt.

'No time,' Narcifer said, and Macy looked up to see the officer coming towards them.

'You need to run,' Macy said, feeling panicked. It was almost as if she could hear the helicopters, the drones, and the wailing police sirens like when she had been taken hostage at the bistro.

'Head left to Keats Avenue,' he said, opening the door. Macy scrambled across the seat to the driver's side. She watched the traffic cop glance at Narcifer as he hurried away. Hopefully, the officer hadn't noticed he was a Jelvia. Macy lowered her window and shouted a greeting at the officer to draw his eyes away from Narcifer. It worked, and the policeman came over.

'Miss,' he said and began his commentary about how she needed to turn around because of the road blockage caused by the protesters. Macy nodded and pretended to listen while glancing at Narcifer's figure in the rearview mirror as he passed the second car. The officer there was waving traffic past the blocked road. But the officer gave Narcifer a double-take, and Macy's heart sank.

'Miss, are you okay?'

Macy looked back at the first officer and realised he'd expected an answer after his boring annotation. 'Eh? Oh, I need to turn?' she asked with a smile and tried to keep her eyes on him and not on the mirror at Narcifer. 'That's fine. I'll turn around and find another way home,' she said quickly, moving the car forwards but forgetting it was an automatic. Macy had only driven a manual car before. The SUV lurched to a stop when she put her foot on the brake, thinking it was the clutch.

Fuck!

She glanced in the rearview mirror. The second policeman had followed Narcifer, and Macy's breath caught in her throat. She released it when the other officer stopped as Narcifer rounded a corner but caught her breath again when she saw the officer raise his hand to his radio.

Macy's head whipped to the first officer as his radio crackled. He turned away to speak into it, then looked over his shoulder at Macy, giving her no doubt the radio conversation was about her and Narcifer. Macy turned the car's ignition on. But the officer, very smoothly, moved to the front of the car as he spoke into the radio using law enforcement jargon. Short of running him over, there was nothing she could do. She looked in the rearview mirror. Narcifer was nowhere in sight.

'Miss, can I ask you to step out of the vehicle?'

Macy looked up. The cop was now leaning in through her window. He reached in and switched off the ignition.

'For stalling a car?' she asked.

'I'm sorry for the intrusion, Miss, but I need to check whether you are okay.'

'Yes, I am. Is that all?' she said, making no attempt to exit the car. Instead, she glanced in the rearview mirror. The other policeman was walking briskly towards them. She tried to keep calm, but pinpricks of sweat appeared on her brow. The chanting of the WUMs was getting louder, adding to her agitation.

'Where are you heading?' the first said.

'Home.'

'Where is home?'

'In Richmond.'

'Nice area,' he said. 'So, where have you been?'

'I stayed at a hotel called the Rose for a few days.' His colleague had reached them, and he pulled the first officer to one side and whispered something to him.

'What's going on?' she asked, trying to keep her voice normal, but her lips were sticking to her teeth.

'Protesters have blocked the road,' said the first officer as the second walked away again to answer his radio.

Anger bubbled inside her. It was as if the officer was deliberately obtuse. 'I'm aware of that,' she snapped. But suddenly, the noise of a helicopter caused a wave of panic, and all fury disintegrated. She glanced at the sky, looking for the helicopter, but its noise was behind a building. She glanced again in the rearview mirror at the other officer, wondering if he was calling for reinforcements to capture Narcifer.

'You seem nervous, Miss?' the first officer said, and she looked back at him.

'We want to be on our way so we're not caught up in the protests,' she said.

'We?' he said.

Macy rubbed the back of her neck and stared at him, not knowing what to say. 'I meant me and the car,' she said weakly. She immediately cursed herself.

Keep talking, Macy. You won't need an opposition solicitor. You'll give yourself twenty years inside all by yourself!

The officer regarded her, and then leaned in through the window, his arms resting on the rim. 'Where did you say home was?'

'I told you. It's Richmond, but is that any of your business? Are you arresting me?'

'No, Miss Shaw, you're not under arrest. Can we call someone for you? Can we take you somewhere safe?'

Macy narrowed her eyes. 'You know my name?'

His radio crackled, and he moved his hand to silence it. 'Just say the word, and we'll take you somewhere safe,' he said.

'I've told you. I *am* safe.'

'You're not,' the police officer said, 'you think you are, but you're not safe.'

TWENTY

What did he mean?

The police officer let her go. He had to. She'd done nothing wrong even though she felt guilty by association. She turned the big car around, mulling over his words. Narcifer was nowhere to be seen. But Jelvias had an unconventional way of getting around. In towns and cities, they moved from rooftop to rooftop, dodging CCTV.

Trying to ignore the helicopter's drone until she was out of sight of the police, whose gazes she could feel burning her, she joined the diverted traffic. Macy had never driven an automatic before, and several times, she'd put her foot on the brake thinking it was the clutch, but luckily, the traffic was slow and allowed her time to get used to it.

Narcifer has said he'd meet her at Keats. He was probably worried the police would follow her home. From here, Keats Avenue was probably only an hour away. She realised she should have turned left instead of right and cursed. She was stuck in traffic and couldn't turn around until it moved.

The road was slow and crowded due to the diversion, and the helicopter didn't help as she was sure many commuters had slowed to watch the aircraft. And Macy couldn't pretend it had anything to do with the WUM protest.

It was following her.

She didn't understand the concern. Jelvias were dangerous to criminals, not ordinary people, and Narcifer certainly wasn't dangerous!

He was a pussy cat.

She lowered the window, looked out, and saw the helicopter directly above. It was closer than she thought, and its presence startled her. Other people were looking as well. She noticed a pedestrian pointing at something high up and flipped off her seatbelt to look out the other window.

Her eyes widened.

There was a dark-clad figure on the roof of a building.

'No...'

Not again!

The car rolled in her inactive state, and Macy stopped it with a jerk. She climbed out and stared up at the building. The figure was running on the edge of the roof. He was probably inches from the long drop down. Macy's heart was in her throat. She couldn't be sure if it was Narcifer, but who else could it be? The figure reached the end but didn't stop and jumped to the next building. He landed, still running.

Macy opened her eyes. She'd closed them automatically when he jumped.

The helicopter wasn't following *her*. It was following Narcifer—or Narcifer was following it. The aircraft was directly above him.

Panic settled on her, and she clutched her hair in fists as all sorts of scenarios filled her mind. The government hated Jelvias and had a shoot first, ask questions later policy. She felt ashamed when she remembered how excited and pumped she'd been when Narcifer's presence was discovered on the catamaran during the summer last year. Back then, she hadn't realised how much authorities feared Jelvias. And it wasn't until the incident in the bistro that she realised a fraudster and murderer was valued over any Jelvia.

The helicopter's drone penetrated her mind as it circled. No sniper was hanging out of the aircraft this time, and neither was anyone ready to cast a net to capture, but that didn't make it any less dangerous. People's voices drifted over her as others stopped to look. The traffic line became stationary while other cars' horns peeped, but Macy paid no attention. Her gaze was on Narcifer on the roof. He jumped from one building to the other, never stumbling or hesitating, and then he disappeared from view.

Macy glanced at the aircraft. It hovered, then moved over the building, coming down low as if to land. Macy lowered her hands. She could no longer see Narcifer. Her heart was rapid in her chest, and bile filled her throat.

The traffic moved again, and Macy dived for the car, hoping she could get ahead of the helicopter and catch Narcifer's attention to get in the car. She didn't want any heroics. She wanted him safe.

Macy was just about to close the door when she heard a scream of a bystander, followed by excited voices. She jumped out again and looked up. The helicopter was swaying. It rose up, and below it, on its landing skids, was Narcifer. As Macy watched with terrified eyes, Narcifer climbed up the undercarriage towards the door. He slid it open, only for someone inside to slide it back again.

The helicopter lurched to the side as if trying to dislodge him. But Narcifer hung on. He attempted to open the door again, but the craft rocked. Macy suspected Narcifer was fighting to hold on. He didn't look like he was struggling, though. Instead, he climbed higher up the underbelly, standing on the skids as if trying to gain entrance through the window.

Then the helicopter listed to one side, and Narcifer lost his footing and slid down. He grasped the landing skids and hung with one hand.

Macy closed her eyes.

'Are you all right, love?'

Macy looked around. An elderly man, leaning on his walking stick, stood looking down at her. She stood up. She hadn't realised she'd sunk to her haunches to hide from the eventuality of Narcifer falling. Macy risked a glance at the helicopter. Narcifer was still hanging on.

'They'll fling him off,' the old man said, clearly believing Macy was on the helicopter's side.

'He can't fall.' Macy breathed the words as Narcifer pulled himself up. He stood up on the skids and moved until he was beneath the door again. But he didn't try to open it. Instead, he moved sideways until he reached the end of the skids and faced the tail. Macy couldn't tell if he fired his venom at the rotors, but it seemed likely as the rotors missed a beat, and then the helicopter rocked.

Macy couldn't take her eyes off Narcifer. He dropped, and whether or not it was deliberate, Macy didn't know. He grabbed the skids and hung suspended again as the helicopter wobbled. Somehow, the pilot stabilised it, but Narcifer climbed up again. This time, he jumped on the skids, rocking the craft.

The aircraft tipped, and Narcifer jumped again.

He must have weighed nothing against the craft, but it was already unstable, flying low towards buildings. The vessel spun.

Macy's heart was in her throat, and she clutched the old man's arm in distress.

'What's he doing?' she asked, more to herself.

The old man didn't answer her. Sirens broke through the *chug-chugger-chug* of the distressed helicopter, and cars attempted to pull to the side to let an unmarked police van through. It stopped further up the road. Its siren was silent but still flashing, and several dark-clothed officers climbed out.

They all had guns.

The public scattered into nearby buildings, and the elderly man clutched Macy's arm.

'In here, love,' he said, trying to pull her into the safety of a shop. He was stopped as ordinary beat bobbies came tearing around the corner and instructed everyone to leave the area. The old guy let Macy go and shuffled to save his own skin.

Macy dropped to the ground and climbed into her car in a strange half crawl. She pulled the door shut and kept low as the police outside ushered people off the streets. She didn't want to get locked in a shop or a business. Officials overreacted around Jelvias; she'd be locked in for hours if she was seen.

She lay still, feeling uncomfortable as the handbrake dug into her ribs. It was nothing compared to how Narcifer must have been feeling. She tortured herself with visions of Narcifer falling and lying injured. Then she envisioned the armed police finding him and shooting him.

She whimpered, telling herself his Jelvian birth gave him an advantage by making him stronger and faster, but then remembered Aldarn's injuries when he was captured almost six years ago, and her whimper became choked. She couldn't see what was going on from her position, but the noise was extreme. She tried to drown out the helicopter's noise and focus on one voice, but there was much shouting. She couldn't differentiate one voice from the other.

Macy inched to the passenger seat and opened the door a crack. Through the gap, she looked up to see the helicopter's tail disappear behind a building. It was out of control, but worse, she couldn't see Narcifer.

Then, like a stone, the craft fell.

Macy closed her eyes as a cataclysmic bang followed by a ball of fire that lit the gloomy sky. She pulled her head back into her car and closed the door. She stared at the black smoke lifting from the building the helicopter crashed against. The silence after the noise was unnerving. It was shattered by more sirens. This time they belonged to fire engines and paramedics.

TWENTY-ONE

A knock on her window made her jump. Her door opened, and a WPC poked her head inside. 'You need to evacuate your car,' she said. Her face changed to one of concern. 'Miss, it's okay. No need to worry.'

Macy stared at her outstretched hand, then realised she was blubbering like a baby, which had caused the officer's concern. When Macy didn't move, the officer reached in and took Macy's arm.

'Come on, let's get you somewhere safe.'

Macy found herself inside a pub, and it was the night she was held hostage at the bistro all over again. Back then, when she was taken to 'a place of safety', it may have been Aldarn's fault, but her ex-boss, William Springfield, otherwise known as Jon Johnsen, was the ultimate cause. But unlike last time, when she had Courtney with her, Macy was alone.

The pub was a typical backstreet boozer. The ceiling was low, and the interior was dark. The smell of stale beer and sweat washed over her. Finally, the WPC left her inside and went back out. Macy found a table and plonked herself down, feeling numb.

'Here,' someone said. It was the old man. He shoved a tumbler of brandy into her hand, and then he wandered off back to the bar, his walking stick tapping on the floor.

The pub was filling up as the WPC led more people in. Excited voices washed over Macy, and she looked at them dumbly. She didn't want to connect with anyone. But then, her phone rang, and Macy put the shot of brandy on the table and rummaged inside her bag. Her heart thumped. It was as if she knew it was Narcifer.

It was.

On a sob, she answered.

'Oh, my God,' she said. Her voice was shaky. 'Narce?'

'Of course.' He sounded surprised but didn't voice why he thought she should be surprised that he'd called her. 'Are you still in London?'

'I... yes, I'm still here.' His voice warmed her, but her tears spilt over. Tears of relief. 'Still in London,' she added, brushing a shaky hand over her wet cheeks. She studied her fingers, seeing them tremble.

'Still?'

'Still,' she said. She picked up the brandy and took a small sip. It burnt her throat, but the warming effect was welcomed. 'Are y-you okay?' she asked, pushing the drink away. The taste wasn't worth its warmth.

'I'm okay. I'm watching for your car on the road towards Keats Avenue.'

'I'm still in London.'

'So you said,' he said, sounding puzzled. 'Why?'

Macy rubbed her eyes and gave a low, incredulous laugh. 'What did you expect when you pulled a stunt like that? What the hell, Narce? I thought you'd *died!*'

There was silence on the other end. Then, 'Died? Why would I die?'

'You were fighting a fucking *helicopter!*'

'Ah.'

'Yes, "ah". Narce, what were you thinking? They weren't after us. They were watching the WUM protesters.'

'Where are you now?' he asked, ignoring her wrath.

She was shaking. She was no longer overcome with grief. Anger fed her emotions instead. 'In a pub. No idea what it's called,' she snapped. 'I've been caught up in *Jelvian activity* and stuck here until police can *secure* the area. Some *mad* Jelvia took down a helicopter, apparently.'

'You didn't turn left to go to Keats, did you?' he said softly.

Macy was so angry that she didn't understand the question. 'It's gridlocked here. The helicopter *crashed*. People have died, Narce! You can't go around doing what you like because something or someone disagrees with you.'

She reached for the brandy, tempted to drink the lot but put it down instead. Anger wouldn't get her anywhere.

'Babe, no one died. The two in the helicopter bailed. I saw them fall to a building roof just before the craft went down. Both got up and ran away, and that's when I disappeared too. I had no intention of killing anyone. I won't get any demands to kill from the committee for a while.'

Only recently, Macy learned the 'demands' weren't words or orders. She once believed Jelvias wore an earpiece, but Narcifer explained the demands as a growing thirst until it became excruciating. She thought he was describing something more extrasensory, like a telepathic electrical charge straight to the brain. She'd never spoken much more to Narcifer about it. The bistro and then Greg trying to kill her last year halted her investigations of the Jelvian civilisation.

'I just wanted to stop the copter from following you,' he said, breaking into her thoughts.

'I was so scared,' she said. 'It felt like the bistro all over again.'

'I'm sorry, babe,' he said, sounding contrite. 'I promise you I'm okay. I wouldn't take risks knowing you're waiting for me somewhere. You've made my life precious.'

'Where'd you learn to be so smooth?' she asked, her anger dissipating as quickly as it began.

'Smooth school.'

Macy snorted. This was her Narcifer, not the venom-spitting, helicopter-fighting Jelvia on the roof. 'I'm sorry, too.'

'For what?'

'For being angry.'

'You were angry?'

'Ready to kill you,' she said. Then, feeling eyes on her, she looked around. A woman and a man holding half-empty pint glasses looked away quickly.

'I hope that's a figure of speech,' he said. There was a smile in his voice.

'It was,' she said. 'But I won't know whether to shake or hug you when I see you next.'

'Do both if you like. Either could get interesting,' he said.

Macy glanced over at the couple again. Something drew her to them, and it wasn't because she felt a connection. They were listening. Interested in her conversation. The woman didn't look much older than twenty, and she was of mixed-race. Her short dreadlocks were pulled high on the top of her head in a spikey-looking ponytail. The pale-skinned man had brown hair tied in a bun on the back of his head and an untidy, wispy beard. He downed his pint, giving Macy a side-glance.

Macy glared back, showing him she knew he was listening.

'Hang on,' she said to Narcifer and, standing, headed for the exit. It was still light outside, but it wouldn't be like that for long. The sun set in the late afternoon in England in the winter. A police officer was outside with his back to her. There was no sign of the WPC who brought her in. It was unnervingly quiet outside. 'Someone overheard our conversation,' she said, looking out at the road. She was tempted to run for her car, but the road was littered with abandoned vehicles, imprisoning hers. She'd never get away. A policeman nodded a smile to her, and she slipped back into the pub.

'Overheard what?' Narcifer said in her ear.

Back in the pub, Macy spotted a door to the ladies' toilet and made for that. Inside, she was pleased to see it was empty, but she checked the stalls just in case. 'I'm almost a hundred per cent certain the people who heard us talking were WUM members. They just looked protester-like. Especially the man. He had a manbun.' She rubbed the back of her neck as Narcifer chuckled down the phone.

'They don't matter, babe,' he said.

'They do! Christ, I'm inside a loo just to get away from them.'

'Have they approached you?' His tone changed, and she was quick to pacify him. She didn't want more panic if he turned up.

'No, and I'm sure it's a coincidence they're here.' She rubbed the back of her neck. 'I just wish you'd warned me what you planned. I'm stuck here now, and you're there.' She felt her bottom lip protrude. She didn't like to be parted from him at all. 'I'm not sure how long I'll have to stay here. Shall I meet you at home?' she asked.

'Remember, I'm following Calder tonight,' Narcifer said.

Macy pulled a face. She'd forgotten. 'I still don't understand why.'

'I need to find Al, babe,' he said.

The door to the toilet opened, and the girl with the spiky dreadlocks came in. She didn't look at Macy but put her oversized fabric bag in the sink and rummaged through it. She brought out eyeliner and lined her already made-up eyes.

'Okay,' Macy said to Narcifer, watching the girl. She knew she'd come in just to spy. 'I have to go. I'll see you tonight if you're there, tomorrow if not.'

'Yeah, sorry, sweetheart. I'd like to continue where we left off last night—or even from this morning. You have an irrefutable sexual appetite!'

Macy blushed. She turned her back on the woman. 'See you later, Narce. Love you.'

'Love you, too,' he said. 'To the moon and back,' he added.

Smiling, Macy dropped her phone in her bag and, completely ignoring the girl, shouldered open the door. As the loo door swung closed behind her, she caught the gaze of the man with the man bun. He'd obviously expected to see his accomplice. He looked away from Macy just as quickly and inspected his painted nails.

Macy was tempted to call him out but headed to the crowded bar instead. She wanted the leaders, not WUMs' minions. Keeping her eye on them, Macy saw the woman come out of the toilet a moment later and join the man. The man was definitely punching above his weight. Macy watched as they moved further up the bar and sat on barstools.

The little backstreet pub was busy because people were ushered inside. Finally, the bartender came over and eventually served Macy her Coke.

'Wish my trade was like this every day,' he said, putting her drink in front of her and almost snatching the fiver from her hand. He brought back her change and then went to serve someone else, offering the same line he'd said to her. Macy moved away from the crowded bar, keeping her eye on the WUM couple. She was sure they were part of that group.

Over the pub's noise, Macy hadn't heard a phone ring, but the man obviously did because he pulled out a mobile phone from his pocket. He looked at the screen and mouthed to his companion: 'Phil'.

In Macy's head, that confirmed it. The phone call could only be from Phil Oswald, the founder of WUM. Manbun held the phone between him and the woman so she could listen. They weren't paying Macy any attention, so she picked up her Coke and moved around the corner out of sight. They were so engrossed in the phone that they overlooked Macy listening to their call. Macy stuck one of her fingers in her ear to block the pub's noise as she tried to listen to their conversation. Two—or rather—three could play the listening-in game!

'You got my text? It's the perfect opportunity—no, okay. Keep your hair on, Phil. I won't approach her. Yeah, Dulcie's with me,' the man said. Macy wondered if the text he was talking about was about her. 'Are you still leading the march up to Westminster?' he continued into the phone. 'I think the Jelvia's gone now. Satisfied with destroying a helicopter.'

She had wondered if Manbun was Oliver Kennedy, the other half of Phil, but Manbun had an Eastern European accent, whereas Oliver had an English accent.

'You think it was a coincidence that the Jelvia was here? Right... maybe... yeah, it would've been more of them... But I suppose you're right. You want us to what? I suppose... Dulcie has a few in her bag. Yeah, was gonna grab the banners off Mark and Sylvie... leaflets... we'll hand a few out. I could do a speech!'

'It's a captive audience,' the woman called Dulcie said. She had an Essex accent. Macy peeped around the corner to see the man holding the phone to her ear and smiling as Dulcie said, 'They stand no chance!'

Oh, great! And now I have to listen to a WUM demonstration inside a backstreet pub.

Fearing she was about to be discovered listening in as they finished their call, Macy moved away, sipping her Coke. There weren't any spare seats or tables, and people were milling around in groups, still talking excitedly about the 'Jelvia attacking the helicopter'. Macy headed to the exit again, hoping to see people moving their cars so she could escape in hers, but the sound of someone banging an object against a glass tumbler quietened the room, and curious, she turned around.

Manbun was sitting on the bar while Dulcie pulled leaflets from her bag and handed them out. He was clinking a cigarette lighter against his empty pint glass.

'Can I have your attention,' Manbun shouted. 'On the ninth of March, six years ago, Earth was invaded by ten spaceships. Nine landed in the Arctic and Atlantic Oceans, but the tenth was shot down over London...'

'Shut the fuck up,' someone shouted, and laughter erupted in the pub.

More clinking. Manbun had responded to the interruption by moving to stand on the barstool. He made a funnel with his hands and bellowed, 'Six years ago, we were invaded by aliens!'

Putting her drink down, Macy continued to the pub's exit. She was glad of the throng of people to mask her movements, but she still expected Manbun or Dulcie to call her name and include her in their impromptu demo.

'...But the time the aliens landed were wiped from your memories, and you only know what you know today, that the Jelvias have been here forever. They haven't. They are aliens and arrived in ten space pods six years ago.' Manbun was in his element, oblivious to the uncaring faces of those looking up. Dulcie was pushing leaflets into people's hands, and those same leaflets were being trampled to the floor. It gave Macy some satisfaction that their movement was seen as inconsequential. 'You don't have to believe us, but keep an open mind. An open mind leads to you waking up. Then, when you've woken up, contact us.'

'Get off my bar!' yelled a voice, and Macy glanced around to see the barman flapping a tea towel at Manbun's feet.

Giggling, Macy got to the door and pushed it open. Dusk had fallen, and the street looked abnormally empty. Several police officers were outside, but none seemed to be patrolling the pub or the accompanying businesses. The restaurant across the road didn't look as crowded as earlier. Macy noticed some stationary cars on the road were occupied and realised people had vacated their 'place of safety' for their vehicles. It looked like normality was slowly resuming. Other than a few strobing emergency vehicles, there was no sign of anything happening.

Something made Macy look at the darkening sky, and didn't see, but *pictured* ten alien spaceships in the sky.

She stared, perplexed, feeling a sense of déjà vu. There was nothing there, but it was like she'd lived through a moment of seeing UFOs and could even feel the accompanying fear. She blinked; the image from her memory was gone. She gave a small laugh and blamed it on the unsolicited WUM demo in the pub playing on her mind. It'd been her imagination playing tricks, that's all.

But as she stared at the dimming sky, the strange sense that she'd been in this moment before, and had been a witness to those alien spaceships, remained. The image was no longer there, but the lingering feeling of terror remained.

Puzzled and disturbed, Macy climbed into her car.

TWENTY TW0

After thirty to forty minutes, traffic moved, and Macy continued home. The feeling of terror faded as if it'd never been there, and Macy brushed off the imagined alien spaceships for drones inspecting the airspace of the doomed helicopter.

Even so, her body was high on adrenaline, and her foot on the gas pedal was heavy. She got home faster than she had anticipated. The house was empty as she knew it'd be. And it looked like Narcifer had gone straight to follow Calder's journey to Aldarn. She hoped he was successful. If only to give him some peace.

The mail had accumulated from her three-day absence, and Macy scooped it up on her way into her house. She dropped it on the table, which was fast becoming a dumping ground. Then she grabbed her phone from her bag and texted Narcifer.

Home.

Milliseconds later, it rang.

'I told you to phone me. You know I can't read symbols,' Narcifer said.

Macy smiled. 'They're words, not symbols. It says I'm home.'

'Good. Sorry about earlier.'

'It's okay. You can make it up to me tomorrow.'

'Oh, I will. What do you fancy, my hand or the paddle?'

Macy flushed. Her body reacted to his words as heat filled her veins.

'Silence, Macy?' he said and then laughed softly.

Macy's flush deepened. 'Stop it, Narce,' she said. She twirled a curl around her finger. 'Hand,' she said, and his laughter deepened.

'After tonight, you'll have my undivided attention,' he said.

'Where are you now? It sounds quiet.'

'I'm in a car, outside Keats. I'm keeping a low profile. Calder should've left by now. I hope Bren hasn't messed up.'

'What car?'

'A car I found.'

'Stolen?'

'Borrowed.'

'Oh, Narce.'

'It's for a good cause.'

Macy rubbed her forehead. She wasn't just fighting her own people for Jelvias to have equality. She was fighting against Jelvias, too. They didn't seem to understand law and order, which didn't help. But Jelvias, for all their faults, deserved the government's backing. They'd fight for that support for an eternity, though.

It was something that had always made Macy sad when she watched old newsreels of Jelvias protesting against segregation and demanding equal rights back in the 1980s.

'Do you really think Calder will lead you to Aldarn? Won't he know you're following?' she asked.

'He doesn't suspect, so it should be easy. I've a good feeling about tonight. I think it'll all be resolved. What are you up to?' he asked.

'I shall watch the Fenovo interview. I'm also going to research the WUMs more,' she said. They chatted some more, but then Narcifer had a text from Bren telling him that she and Calder were on the move.

Macy felt like she had her work mojo back, and for the first time since Greg pushed her from the car, she felt she was returning to normal. Then, she noticed a bright blue envelope marked *Private and Confidential* that she'd dumped on the table with the rest of the mail. Curious, she opened the envelope:

Dear Miss Shaw,

My name is Phil Oswald, and I founded WUM. Unfortunately, its growth has made it a platform for the uninformed, and this is a warning not to accept any meeting with

anyone without consulting Oliver Kennedy or myself to verify the name.

However, the best course of action would be for us to meet. I promise it will be an informal chat. I've included my personal phone number. If you don't want to meet me, maybe we could FaceTime or something?

Call me on 02399 598314.

Best wishes,

Phil.

So, the leader of WUM contacted her.

The letter was obviously rushed as the handwriting was messy. Macy turned the blue stationery paper over in her hands and raised it to her nose. It brought a wave of memories. She sniffed again. Sunflowers by Elizabeth Arden. It had been her mum's favourite perfume, popular ten or twenty years ago.

Bringing it down, she traced the curls of Phil's hanging letters with her finger. Phil Oswald was a woman. Macy refolded the letter, placed it back in its envelope, and put it on the shelf above the fireplace. She sat an ornament on top to keep it secure. She didn't want the letter to get lost among the others.

She would call Phil Oswald at the number she'd provided, but first, Macy wanted to research her. And, hopefully, she would find something on James, too. She wanted to know where he fitted into all this.

As she thought about James, she suddenly realised she had never given his number to Courtney. Mumbling an expletive, she rubbed her forehead. Then she grabbed her phone again and put in the number James had provided her. But, just as she thought, it was deactivated. James had said his number would only be active for a short while. She shrugged. She owed James nothing.

She settled in front of her computer. Then, opening YouTube, she searched for a WUM podcast and found one called **Jelvias are**

Aliens. Sniggering, Macy listened as several people talked about ten alien spaceships coming to Earth on March 9th, six years ago. And, apparently, nine of the 'spaceships' landed in the Arctic and Atlantic Oceans. The tenth was shot down over London. It all seemed ridiculous to Macy, but she listened as a middle-aged guy spoke animatedly about those nine spaceships which became the Jelvian islands.

The WUM organisation might have started small, but its growth was fast. In fact, it had trebled in just the last month. Soon the numbers would be big enough for the government to take them seriously—if not already. After all, they already had a TV station interested in them.

The video ended, and another started. Macy was about to click off when an image of James Sullivan caught her eye. It showed James walking away from the camera as reporters chased him up the street. She heard one say, 'Can you confirm that you're involved with the new WUM movement?' James ignored them and climbed into a car. He drove away, looking straight ahead.

Macy looked at the date: July of last year. She thought back to July. It had been during the Jon Johnsen madness when Aldarn had held her hostage inside the bistro. She watched another clip of James Sullivan. Again, a reporter asked him if he was involved with WUM, but this time James replied, 'No. But they have my support.'

Macy scratched her head. There was something fishy about James Sullivan. She clicked on another link and read that Leigh Sullivan, James' wife, had been a professor involved in the laboratory scandal that destroyed a Jelvian helicopter and kidnapped two of its occupants. It was all instigated by William Springfield, aka Jon Johnsen, who also used Macy to seek out his nemesis, Aldarn.

Leigh Sullivan had died when Jelvias stored the lab, freeing Aldarn, which made Macy think James was after some kind of revenge. Something stirred in Macy's memory.

Tapping her fingers, she tried to tease it out. She returned to the notes she had uploaded to her computer, located the date she'd first met Narcifer, and began to read. Finally, she found the name she was looking for: Tsung Zmin.

Tsung Zmin was another scientist killed due to his involvement in the incident. He died last year. Narcifer had killed him. Macy recalled Narcifer admitting to killing him, saying, 'Aldarn wants revenge for everyone involved that night.'

And it was all tallying up. Everyone involved had become a target, and that's why Macy had never met James. He was in hiding! She rubbed her hands together as the revelation made sense. She'd only ever spoken to James on the phone. The last time she'd spoken to him was when he asked for Courtney's number, and he said his phone number would only be active for a short time—now she knew why!

But James had found out about Aldarn's brain damage and was going after him in some counterattack revenge.

'But why is Narcifer looking for Aldarn?' she muttered. Her mobile rang, and she reached for it absently.

'Hey,' said a woman's voice. 'Is it safe to come in? Narcifer home?'

It took Macy a moment to recognise it.

'Ah, Angela. Hi. Er... no, he's out—'

'Great. I'm outside your house with a bottle of strawberry gin. I know I'm early, but I thought we could have a few nibbles and drinks before going out.'

'Go out?'

'I knocked, but there was no answer. I'm outside in my car. You do still want to go out tonight, don't you?' Angela added in a small voice.

Macy glanced at the time. It was almost eight in the evening. She closed all the computer apps she'd had open, left the back room and walked around to her bedroom. She could see Angela in her BMW, her mobile clamped to her ear from the window. Macy groaned. Angela was a nice enough woman, but she was a little clingy and over-awed by Macy's involvement with Jelvias.

Finger-combing her hair, Macy went downstairs and opened the door for Angela. Angela's look of relief made Macy feel a little mean. Angela pushed out of her car like an eager puppy, grabbed a bag, and trotted over.

'Hi,' Macy said when she got closer. 'Come on in. I can never resist the mention of strawberry gin.'

'Thanks. I brought ginger ale to go with it—I know how much you hate tonic. I don't like it much either. Oh, and I brought the nibbles.'

Macy smiled, wondering when she had mentioned that she hated tonic water—and when she had agreed to go out, for that matter.

'Better and better,' she said as Angela stepped through the door.

Angela eyed her critically. 'Oh, my God, you've been crying. I hope Jack was kind when he fired you?'

The meeting with Jack seemed an age ago.

'I wasn't fired!' Macy peered into the mirror to check her eyes. They were a bit red, but she didn't think she looked that bad. She licked a finger to get rid of a smear of mascara. 'Jack offered me a considerable amount of money to resign. I haven't decided yet if I will accept or not.' She turned from the mirror and realised she was talking to an empty room. She hurried to the kitchen, where Angela was making herself at home.

'I've brought nachos, cheese, and salsa,' Angela said as she emptied the crisps and the shredded cheese into a bowl. 'Stick the oven on,' she commanded as she spooned salsa over the top of the cheese and crisps. 'This will go perfect with gin. Have you got any gin glasses? It doesn't matter; those will do.' She pointed to wine glasses visible through the glass door of the cupboard. 'There,' she said, smiling at her creation of cheesy nachos and salsa. She picked up the bowl and bent to slide it into the oven. 'These will be ready in ten minutes or so. We can have a proper catch-up, and then you can get ready. Tonight is going to be so much fun.'

Macy turned with the wine glasses clutched in her hands. 'Get ready?'

Angela took the glasses from her and set them on the kitchen counter. She looked back at Macy. 'Yes, duh! For our night out... ah. You've forgotten,' she added, her face dropping.

'I'm *so* sorry, Angela,' Macy said, genuinely feeling sorry. 'I can't remember saying we were going out. I've so much on my mind it's unreal. Anyway, I thought you wanted to watch the Fenovo interview?'

'I saw that yesterday. Rubbish, if you ask me. He wasn't given free rein to speak his mind.'

'Wait—you saw it *yesterday*?'

'Yeah, I was in the studio audience when they recorded it.' Humming, Angela turned towards the lounge.

After a shocked moment, Macy followed her. She watched as Angela grabbed the TV remote control and scrolled through the channels until she found MTV. Macy took the remote from her and turned the volume down.

'What do you mean? It's not airing live?'

Angela's hand flew to her mouth as she realised her lapse. 'I'm so sorry, Macy—didn't you know?'

Macy stared at her, disbelieving her insensitivity. 'Of course, I didn't know. I would have gone!'

'Not all of us went, just a select few.'

'And I bet it was Jack's idea that I wasn't one of those "select few"!' Scowling, Macy plonked herself down on the settee.

Angela sat next to her. 'Me and my big mouth. I wish I hadn't said anything.'

Macy sighed. None of this was Angela's fault. 'It doesn't matter. I would have known if I'd had my head in the game. What was Graham Barringham like?'

'He was meant to be a Jelvia expert, but as it turned out, he was just a mediator between Fenovo and WUM. Every question he asked had been carefully scripted—you'll see for yourself when you watch it. And we don't have to go out tonight if you'd rather not. I forget you're not long out of the hospital.'

'Thanks for being understanding. I'm really not in the mood for partying.'

But Macy's breath of relief was short-lived because Angela continued, 'We can stay in and get hammered instead.' Then, looking pleased with herself, she stood up and went into the kitchen. She returned shortly with the two glasses and the gin. The bottle of ginger ale was tucked under her arm. She grinned at Macy as she set them down on the coffee table, grabbed the TV remote and turned the volume up again. She poured their drinks, thrust a glass into Macy's hands, then stood up and, on a cry of, 'Come on! Dance!' she twirled around the room.

Angela's chattiness and buoyancy irritated Macy, but she could vaguely remember being just like Angela once.

It was probably only last year, yet it seemed a million years ago.

TWENTY-THREE

'*Controlling Jelvias makes us superior, and therein lies the problem,*' Fenovo said.

'I'm all nacho-ed out!' Angela said, popping the last one into her mouth.

Macy didn't look round. Instead, she sat glued to the Fenovo interview, but Angela was right—his questions were scripted.

'*They need to comply with our ethics or stay on their islands. It's that simple.*' Graham Barringham bent and picked something up. '*Before Johnsen was murdered, he discovered that once a Jelvia's throat was constricted, it couldn't spit venom. This is an anti-spit collar.*' He held the item up to the camera, and Macy leaned forwards to get a better look.

'It's like a gimp collar,' Macy said.

Angela laughed as if she'd heard the best joke. She was still sniggering into her gin long after the joke stopped being funny.

Macy turned the volume up on the TV. Barrington was still holding up the collar. '*This metallic brace locks around the neck to restrict the throat from expanding. Oliver Kennedy, the developer, is a member of the WUM organisation.*'

'*Who isn't popular at the moment,*' quipped Fenovo.

A ripple of laughter ran around the audience. But Macy sat up straight at the mention of Oliver Kennedy. She felt it had to be the same Oliver who'd spoken to her on the telephone.

Angela downed her gin and reached for the bottle. Macy put her hand over the top of her glass before Angela could top her up.

'*Why are we afraid of the Jelvias?*' Fenovo asked. '*We never had this worry ten years ago, and they haven't changed since then.*'

'*They weren't here ten years ago!*' a heckler shouted from the audience.

'And that's as exciting as it gets,' said Angela. 'That heckler was a WUM member; he was marched out of the studio.' She stood up and disappeared into the kitchen.

'*This fear of Jelvias has released intense stress hormones in our bodies,*' Barringham said, '*and because it happened to all of us, we saw it as normal. Have you heard of mass psychogenic illness? Also called mass hysteria?*'

'*Ah, yes. When Princess Diana died, there was an unprecedented outpouring of public grief,*' Fenovo said. '*I remember experts describing it as a communal spirit or mass hysteria.*'

'What a lot of pretentious crap,' Macy said and lowered the volume as Barrington began discussing the physiological distress the majority of the population had felt at the death of Princess Diana. She heard Angela clattering about in the kitchen and followed the sound. In the kitchen, she found Angela pulling a bottle of Malibu from the pantry.

'I'm bored with gin,' she said on seeing Macy. Her voice was slurred. 'And where's your music? Let's play some tunes!'

Macy grabbed the bottle of Malibu before Angela dropped it. 'I'm going to make you a coffee, Angela. Crikey, girl, you've only had three gins.'

'I drank as much as you.'

Macy eyed her critically, took her arm, and led her back into the lounge. Once Angela was seated, Macy cleared up their glasses.

'Stay there. I'll get you a coffee,' Macy said.

'Stick a brandy in it,' Angela said, giving a little hiccup.

Macy took their empty glasses and the nacho dish out into the kitchen and put them in the dishwasher. She flicked the coffee machine on and took a mug from the cupboard. She needed Angela to sober up before leaving, but she wouldn't be able to drive. She would have to get a taxi.

'Three gins. Three! The girl has no staying power,' she muttered as she made the coffee.

Macy took the mug out to Angela but stopped short when she entered the lounge. Angela was sitting in a slump, fast asleep.

Great.

Macy put the coffee on the table and went upstairs to pull Courtney's old duvet off her bed. Back downstairs, Macy manoeuvred Angela so she was lying down and looking more comfortable and then draped the duvet over her. She watched her a bit, then for good measure—and to protect her carpet—she went to get a basin and put it close to Angela in case she was sick.

Macy turned the volume back up on the TV and rewound the documentary, then watched the rest of it on her own as Angela snored gently on the sofa.

TWENTY-FOUR

Cool hands slipped around her, pulling her close, and a hard thigh pushed between hers, parting her legs. Half asleep, Macy felt hands tug at her pyjama bottoms. Narcifer made love to her while she drifted on the edge of consciousness. It was slow, gentle, and a delicious way to wake up in the morning.

She turned over. Narcifer was propped up on his elbow, smiling down at her.

'Hey,' he said.

She smiled back at him. 'Morning. How did your trip go?'

'Not entirely to plan,' he said, losing his smile. He rolled to lie flat on his back and stared at the ceiling. 'Sorry about yesterday,' he added. 'I wanted to chase off the helicopter. I forgot humans like to make a drama out of everything.'

Macy remembered the aircraft spinning before it plummeted. 'I think they were right to make a drama out of it,' she said, frowning. 'But I don't want to talk about that. What happened last night? Did you find Aldarn okay?' she asked, then heard the toilet flush in the downstairs bathroom.

Macy had alerted Narcifer to their guest before she'd gone to bed last night. Sitting up, she pushed back the duvet but stopped to look back at Narcifer. His hair was dishevelled, and he looked weary, but besides that, he was her Narcifer. Her lover and her best friend.

Macy studied him. He looked tired. 'I take it Calder caught you?' she asked.

'He not only caught me following but will have moved Al again by now, so the headway I've made is gone.'

Macy climbed out of bed and grabbed her robe. Tying it around her waist, she said, 'I think it's time you told me why finding Aldarn is so important to you.'

Narcifer's all-black Jelvian eyes looked dry. There was no sparkle.

'Get rid of your friend,' he said.

Macy nodded.

Angela was seated at the dining room table when Macy came into the room. She was applying lipstick with the help of her compact mirror, but she turned, looking apprehensive, as Macy approached. On seeing who it was, relief flooded her face. Putting her lipstick down, she stood up.

'Hi,' she said. 'I didn't know whether to just leave or not. Would that be rude? I'd like to meet Narcifer, but then again, maybe not. Is he home? There's a black SUV in your driveway, so I'm presuming he came home while I was on your sofa. Sorry about that... oh, my God, did he see me crashed out?'

Macy held up a hand. 'Whoa! Morning,' she finally said. 'How are you feeling? Headache?'

'No, I'm fine. I never get hangovers,' she said. She looked over Macy's shoulder, and her face lost colour. She backed up several paces.

Macy looked around at Narcifer. He stopped in the doorway and flashed Angela a bright smile. 'Hello,' he said, stepping closer and holding his hand out to Angela.

She took it, somehow cringing simultaneously, and they shook hands.

Letting her go, Narcifer headed into the kitchen. 'Anyone for coffee?' he said over his shoulder.

'Yes, please,' Macy said, and Angela squeaked a reply.

Angela cupped her mouth with both hands and looked at Macy. 'I met a Jelvia,' she said, lowering her hands. Her eyes were so round that Macy feared they might pop out of her head.

'Your first?'

Angela nodded. 'Oh, my God! I met a Jelvia.'

'Easy,' Macy said. She'd never met anyone who got this excited over Jelvias before. Everyone had been terrified at the thought.

'He's gorgeous,' Angela said.

'Yes, but don't tell him that, please.'

If it was possible, her eyes became rounder. 'Why? Would he get annoyed?'

Macy laughed. 'No, he already has a big head, that's all. Narcifer doesn't get annoyed. He's pretty chill.' Out of the corner of her eye, she could see him in the kitchen; he was clearly listening. He glanced over his shoulder at Macy as if sensing she was looking and grinned.

Angela plonked herself down on the chair she'd vacated. 'He's a giant.'

'Yeah, he's tall,' Macy agreed. She came over and sat opposite Angela. 'How come you're not afraid?'

'Not afraid? I'm shitting myself.'

Macy laughed. 'You seem excited to meet him rather than scared.'

'Maybe both, then.' Angela sat forwards and tried to look into the kitchen, but it wasn't possible from her angle. 'He's making coffee? Like a normal person?'

'He *is* a normal person, Angela. This is what I need to get out to the general population. Jelvias are normal people, just like us.'

Angela nodded like her head was on a spring, but she became fossilised as soon as Narcifer came in, carrying three cups.

Narcifer placed the cups on the table, pushing two across to Macy and Angela. Then he picked his up. 'I'll take mine upstairs,' he said. He nodded to Angela and said, 'Nice to meet you.' Before he turned away, he exchanged glances with Macy. Macy could see the worry etched on his beautiful face.

After he left them, Angela pulled the coffee cup towards her. She peered into it as if expecting to see something other than coffee. Macy smiled. Despite wanting Angela to leave, she felt an affinity with her. It was something she'd not felt with anyone for a long time.

After she'd drank the coffee, Macy gently steered the conversation to Angela leaving, and thankfully, she took the hint. She left, running to her car with her jacket pulled over her head as rain pelted the ground.

She waved a farewell from inside her BMW, and Macy closed the door gratefully as the car sped away. Then, turning from the door, Macy ran up the stairs to their bedroom. The door was ajar, and Narcifer was lying on their bed, facing the TV, but she could tell he wasn't really watching it. Instead, his eyes were staring off into the corner of the room, and he looked deep in thought.

'She's gone,' she said, stepping inside.

He sat up and turned the TV off. Then, swinging his feet off the bed, he came towards her. Taking her hands, he led her to the bed and pushed her to sit on the edge. 'I will ask you a question, and I want you to give me an honest reply.'

Macy nodded.

Narcifer squeezed her hand. 'Did James visit you in the hospital?'

'Oh,' she said. Whatever question she might have been expecting, it wasn't that one. 'No. All our conversations were over the phone or FaceTime.'

'Could he have visited you without you knowing?'

'Yes, that's possible, I suppose,' she said, frowning at him. 'I was in and out of consciousness for the first few weeks, and then again when I contracted septicaemia. But he would have said, I'm sure. So, what is this about, Narcifer?'

He let her hands go and stood up.

'I can't see the problem in him visiting me,' she said, watching him pace the room.

He stopped pacing and looked as if he was about to tell her something but then seemed to change his mind. Finally, he said, 'I know you and James are friends, and I have to confess something that you're not going to like.'

Macy braced herself as Narcifer took her hand again and sat on the edge of her bed.

'Before you came out of the hospital, I was sent to kill him.'

She waited for his words to sink in. She shouldn't have been surprised, after all; this is what she found out yesterday by adding all the pieces together. James Sullivan was wanted by Jelvias for his involvement in Jon Johnsen's experiments on Aldarn and for the death of Scasone. It was a personal vendetta that the Jelvias needed vindicating.

'When was this?' she asked.

'It wasn't long after you had that second illness.'

He was talking about when she had septicaemia. 'This is because James was involved in Jon Johnsen's experiments?'

'Yes,' Narcifer said, confirming her theory. 'But I *didn't* kill him. He's your friend. I couldn't do it.'

She frowned, sensing he was exploiting her connection with James somehow. 'He isn't a friend. How can he be a friend when I've never met him? But that's not to say I want him *dead*.' She pulled from his hands and stood up. She turned to face him. 'Why do I feel you're skirting around the truth?'

'I never *want* to keep anything from you, but sometimes I can't tell you the complete truth.'

'Who sent you to kill him?' Macy asked. She knew it wasn't the committee. Narcifer told her they never gave names; they just gave commands to kill. It was down to the Jelvia who they chose. That's why Jelvias chose criminals over ordinary people. It relieved them of the committee's relentless assault inside their heads and, at the same time, protected normal humans.

'Cal,' said Narcifer. 'Calder wants James dead because he was involved with the Jon Johnsen project, and killing James would have brought me relief from the committee's orders. I haven't been controlling the committee very well since your injuries.'

She remembered the argument she'd walked in on between Narcifer and Calder.

'*You're going rogue,*' Calder had said to Narcifer.

It had been easy to ignore Narcifer's killing side, focusing instead on the injustices Jelvias suffered under the hands of humans. Then when she did think about it, she consoled herself that Narcifer was killing evil people such as murderers and rapists.

'Babe, come and sit here,' Narcifer said, patting the space next to him. Macy walked over and sat down. Narcifer took her hands between his. 'Since meeting you, the committee's commands are weaker. I don't know how or why, but your presence helps control them. Then you nearly died, and the committee became stronger and stronger.' His thumb rubbed the top of her hand. 'I wasn't in any place to regulate the noise. I just killed when it got too much. Calder tried to help, giving me names of criminals, including James Sullivan, but what he gave me wasn't enough.'

'But this isn't just about you going rogue, is it?' she asked, using Calder's words.

'No,' Narcifer admitted. Letting her go, he brushed a hand over his face. When he brought it down, she saw real anguish on his face. 'We've barely been together a year, yet you mean so much to me,' he said.

'Seven months,' she said. 'And you mean a lot to me, too.'

'James can't die,' he said through a clenched jaw. 'Calder wants him dead, but he can't die.'

'Right,' said Macy. She felt utterly baffled.

Narcifer took her hands in his again, squeezing them. 'James has asked me to find Aldarn, and I need your help,' he said earnestly. His eyes searched her face. 'I think Courtney knows where he is, but she won't tell me.'

Macy stared back. All she could see was the worry etched over his face, and she reacted by pulling her hand from his to cup one side of his face. 'Sweetheart, I don't understand. You're searching for Aldarn because of *James?*'

'I know how this must sound,' he said. 'I can see your confusion.' He pulled away, and her hands flopped back in her lap. He stood up and went to stare out of the bedroom window. Macy watched his back. It was taut with strain. 'I need Aldarn to assure Calder that James had nothing to do with the laboratory incident. Then the order on James' life will be lifted. But I can't find Aldarn.'

Macy narrowed her eyes at his back. 'Okay, you don't want James to die, but why would you *help* him? It makes no sense.'

Narcifer shoved his hands in his pockets and turned around. He wasn't going to answer her.

'Let's get this straight,' Macy said, trying to understand. 'You go to kill James, can't do it, and he suddenly *asks* you to find Aldarn, which you go to extreme lengths to do?'

Narcifer's black stare lowered. Then, taking a deep breath, he looked back up. 'I'm protecting James. That's where I go most days.'

'You're—*protecting* James? From Calder?' Macy burst out.

'Yes.'

'But why?'

'And there's the question I can't answer,' he said.

'Can't or won't?'

He looked at her, his face firm. 'Won't,' he said.

Macy raised her hands in a gesture of surrender and let them flop back into her lap. 'Okay, I'll see if I can wheedle Aldarn's location out of Courtney. I can't promise anything, though. Any mention of Aldarn and she goes on the immediate defensive.' At her words, Narcifer seemed to relax. His big shoulder lost a bit of tension, but Macy couldn't take the annoyance out of her voice. 'But since you won't tell me what's going on, I'll continue researching the WUMs. I've found out that Phil Oswald is a woman. She sent me a letter smelling like an old lady's handbag and gave me her personal number.

I'm going to arrange a meeting with her,' she said, expecting him to disagree and prepared for an argument. Still angry with his reluctance to share his problem, she almost *wanted* a fight.

'The WUMs *are* just nobodies.'

'Maybe, but they are irritating nobodies. Locked up in a pub with two of them yesterday proved that.'

'You're annoyed with me,' he said. 'I'll show you our interrogation room, and if you want to use it, I'll bring you the WUM leader,' he said as if that made everything okay again. 'Calder's away tomorrow, so I'll take you then.'

'Sneaking behind his back again?'

'I've lost Cal's trust and possibly the trust of everyone at Keats. Babe, how about you? Have I lost your trust, too?'

He looked so dejected and utterly despondent that Macy went over and put her arms around him. She pulled his face down to look at her. 'No, you haven't lost my trust. Despite how little you share with me, we're in this together.'

He lowered his head until they were forehead to forehead. Somehow, he seemed more vulnerable than she'd ever thought possible. 'Remember when I said I'll always be your hero?' he asked.

'I remember.'

'I think I failed.'

TWENTY-FIVE

Narcifer went to take a shower after that strange statement—and, for the first time, he locked himself in. There was something more than ensuring James stayed alive.

Perturbed, Macy went downstairs and made another coffee and took her drink and stood at the window. The rain pelted against the pane, and the shrubbery and trees outside bent to its fury. She watched the skies while thinking about her personal storm with Narcifer.

After their few days at the Rose, where he'd promised they'd spend more time together, Macy had looked forwards to cooking him a roast dinner and cosying up on the settee in the afternoon watching old movies. But, instead, Narcifer wanted her to coax Aldarn's whereabouts out of Courtney, so he could plead James' case, and in turn, Aldarn would tell Calder to back off and leave James alone.

It was utterly bizarre and a little depressing. All Macy wanted was a little normality and to do what ordinary couples do.

He's not human, she told herself. *Yesterday proved that, and isn't this what you want? Excitement?*

Knowing she'd not change things for the world, she put her coffee cup down and turned away from the window. Then, sitting down, she grabbed her phone. Macy hadn't spoken to Courtney since she had been distant on the phone a few days ago. Macy had texted her last night, but texting one another was the level of their conversations lately.

'Hi Mace,' Courtney said.

'Yo!' Macy said lightheartedly. 'Haven't heard from you in ages, so I thought I'd call. How're things?'

'We texted during the Fenovo interview last night,' Courtney reminded her. 'You told me your friend was passed out on the settee.'

'Ha, yeah. Couldn't handle her drink. Not hardcore drinkers like us.' Macy laughed, trying to cajole Courtney into a bit of banter. 'So, how are you?'

'Fine. Work's crazy busy.'

'I forgot to tell you, but a few days ago, James Sullivan called me, asking for your number. Did he get in touch with you?'

'Did you give him my number?' Her tone was suddenly arctic.

'No, of course not.'

'I hope not, Macy,' Courtney said.

'I said I didn't!' Macy said, stung. 'Are we okay?' she added. 'I know things have been fraught lately, and you're missing Aldarn, but—'

'Look, crap's going on at the moment. Let's just say, I don't trust many people at the moment.'

'And that includes me?' Macy felt as if she'd slapped her.

'I don't know, Mace. I really don't know.' Courtney sounded tearful. 'You're living with Narcifer. Is he listening on the other end of the line?'

Macy was silent. She didn't know how to answer Courtney. Instead, she said, 'I'm sorry you feel like that. Narcifer's in the shower—'

Her fake laughter took Macy by surprise. 'Of course, he is. Look, tell him I don't know where Aldarn is.'

'Christ, what *is* it with you?' Macy snapped.

'It's not me. It's your boyfriend,' she said and hung up.

Frowning, Macy put her phone away. Then, hearing movement from upstairs, she went into the kitchen to make a coffee for Narcifer, trying not to feel upset at the phone call. But a door crashing open from upstairs rocked the house, and she jumped, spilling coffee beans. Thunderous footsteps followed, hurtling down the stairs, and then Narcifer burst into the kitchen as she turned.

'What the—' She was lifted off her feet in a bone-crushing hug.

He buried his head between her neck and shoulder, and Macy could feel his lips pressed against her skin. He was shaking. She couldn't hold him as she would have liked to—her arms were pinned.

'Hey, what's happened?' she said.

Slowly, she was lowered, and Narcifer stared at her, then dragged a hand over his face. His expression was one of pure pain.

'Narcifer,' she said again, 'what's happened?'

He drew a ragged breath, and a shudder rippled through him so violently that Macy felt it vibrate through her core. Her strong Jelvian man was overtaken by some inner emotion, and she felt powerless to help him.

'Yash phoned and told me that Calder killed James,' he said.

'And that has you in this state? *Did* Calder kill James?'

'No,' he said. His voice was shaky.

'Even so, why...' she broke off, noting the pallor of his face. 'Come on, let's sit down.' Macy ushered him into the front room, trying to keep the confusion off her face. They sat together on the settee, and she took his hand. 'Look, whether James' life hangs in the balance or not, maybe this is something you will have to let go of. If he was involved with Jon Johnsen's crazy plan, he's probably not someone worth saving.'

Narcifer didn't reply but stared at their entwined fingers.

'Even if I understand you want to help James,' Macy continued, 'I can't figure out why you're acting as if he's your best friend. You don't know him. *I* don't even know him, not really.' When he didn't reply, Macy nudged him. 'Narcifer?'

'It's not his death I'm worried about,' Narcifer said cryptically.

'Then what—'

'I need to call James to make sure he's okay,' he said, standing abruptly and leaving her staring at him in shock. She watched him head upstairs, feeling helpless. She waited, worrying and listening to the silence of the house until the sound of Narcifer's footsteps brought her out of her thoughts. His tread was lighter as he moved downstairs. Macy sat forwards on the settee and tried to keep her face neutral.

'He's okay,' Narcifer said brightly as if Macy should be happy with the news. And she was—she didn't *want* James to die—but this obsession was getting out of control. 'It must have been Yash's idea of a joke,' Narcifer added.

TWENTY-SIX

She woke up alone the following day. The imprint of Narcifer next to her was cold.

He'd either gone to protect James—and what *that* meant, she didn't know—or he was tearing the world apart to find Aldarn. After telling him about Courtney's obscure phone call, he was back to fretting over the whereabouts of Aldarn. She reached for her phone on the bedside table. She had three texts from Narcifer.

His inability to read and spell had made texting complicated until Macy showed him how to use voice-to-text on his phone. But he sometimes spoke too fast or was frustrated if technology didn't work immediately.

babe I can show you the interview room at kids later xxx
The second:
Keets not kids.
Macy smiled and opened the third.
Good luck at the office. xxxxxxxxxxxxxx
She'd already told him about her appointment with Jack Gonzalez over the roast dinner she did eventually cook yesterday. And despite Narcifer's distraction, they spoke about her decision to agree to the payoff and hand in her notice.

Macy flipped back the duvet and headed into the shower. She had a light breakfast and then dressed in a pale blue two-piece trouser suit. She stuffed Jack's documents in her handbag. She'd written **I love Narcifer** all over them. It gave her some satisfaction, even though she knew it was childish.

Then she went to retrieve Phil Oswald's letter, wanting to add it to her handbag. She intended to call Phil and arrange a meeting. But the letter wasn't where she thought she'd left it. She hunted for it briefly but decided it was making her late for Jack's appointment, so she left it.

Knowing she looked good, she drove to *London Echo*. She deliberately parked her Mini in the executive parking around the back of the building, then marched towards Jack Gonzalez's office. She didn't let the receptionist hold her up this time.

She was on time for her appointment, and Jack didn't keep her waiting. Macy realised he was just as keen to get all this done and dusted as she was.

'Good morning, Macy,' Jack said. He waved a hand towards a chair, but Macy had already seated herself. She didn't want to waste any more time either.

'So, I've discussed the situation with Narcifer,' she began before he'd even settled in his chair, 'and we want a hundred thousand. Jon Johnsen's newspaper was fictitious, but it's given me the idea to start one myself, and that's my price.' The previously agreed-upon £20,000 had been on her lips; asking for another £80,000 was purely an impulsive decision. It even took *her* by surprise.

Jack stared at her for a moment. 'That's a ridiculous payout,' he said, finally.

'Is it? Look at it from my point of view. I was an ordinary in-house reporter until the late editor-in-chief, Jon Johnsen, hired me to interview Jelvias. It's down to *him* that I met Narcifer. It's down to *him* that I was kidnapped by Aldarn and held in Johnsen's own bistro, and it was down to *him* I was recovering from it all by staying in Cornwall. Therefore, it's down to *him* that I was left with life-changing injuries.

'There isn't a place on my body where I haven't a scar.' She lifted her heavy fringe to show her droopy eye and the scar on her eyebrow. She stood up and took off her jacket, hanging it carefully over the back of her chair. Watching him, she rolled up the sleeve of her blouse and offered him her arm, turning it to show its numerous scars. Pulling the sleeve down, she rolled the other up.

'There's no need,' Jack said.

'There's every need,' she said. She thrust out her other arm to show Jack the scars, then parted her blouse to show him her collarbone. 'Want to see my legs?'

'Macy—'

'I'll never be able to lie on a beach and sunbathe without people pointing and wondering about my scars,' she interrupted him and bent to roll up a trouser leg. 'I'll never walk without a limp. And doctors have warned me that I may develop arthritis in my right leg.'

She rolled that trouser leg down before rolling the other one up.

'Macy!' he said, clearly vexed.

She enjoyed herself much more than when in Jack's office last time. She hadn't expected to get the vast payout, but Jack agreed to it almost before she'd finished straightening her clothing. He was probably worried she was going to strip naked.

A hundred thousand pounds in her bank, and it had taken less time than she'd thought.

Result.

Feeling buoyed by her successful negotiations, Macy headed to her old office to collect a few personal things. She texted Narcifer her good news as the lift took her down and slipped her phone back into her handbag with a happy sigh.

Apart from Narcifer's mysterious problem, life was looking up. Macy stepped out of the lift and headed into her old office. It was lunchtime, and it was mostly empty. She glanced around for Angela, hoping to tell her the news, but she wasn't at her desk.

Paul saw Macy, waved at her, and then came out of his office to greet her.

'You're looking great, Macy,' he said.

'I feel great. But this is goodbye. Jack has accepted my resignation, and I accepted a hundred thousand in return.'

Paul's mouth fell open. 'A hundred thousand pounds. Bloody hell, that's fantastic, Macy. You're well worth that. Oh, come here,' he said and gave her a hug. 'Don't be a stranger. Keep in touch.'

'I will,' she promised, pulling out of his arms and stepping back, preparing to leave. 'Where is Angela? I'd like to tell her the news, too.'

'Ah, Angela,' he said. He scratched the back of his neck.

'Something wrong?' she asked hesitantly.

'She isn't the friend you think she is, Mace. Watch out for her.'

'What do you mean?'

'She's a sly one. She's the one who tipped Jack off to your welcome-back party.'

Macy stared at him in disbelief. 'Are you sure?' she said at last.

He nodded. 'I'm afraid so. She'd sell her gran to the devil for an exclusive.'

The phone in his office rang, and he turned towards it. He raised a hand to Macy, saying, 'Good luck!'

She waved back and walked out of her office for the final time. She held her emotions in check until she stepped onto the pavement outside of *London Echo*, and then a wave of grief crept up on her. *London Echo* held fond memories—it had given her the biggest break in her journalism career. She was going to miss it.

She straightened her posture and secured the strap of her handbag over her shoulder. This was a new chapter in her life. She was now a freelance journalist—a professional, self-employed reporter with a spare hundred thousand pounds in the bank.

Sqeeeeek.

Leaving her car, Macy hailed a cab to Knightsbridge. She instructed the driver to take her to Harvey Nick's, where she bought several new suits—and a saucy lingerie set. Then, back out on the high street, her purchases swinging from one arm, she stopped outside a bakery and eyed the delicious-looking cakes on display in the window.

Narcifer was acting as if he had the world's worries on his shoulders, and Macy thought a special treat might cheer him up and help celebrate her payoff at the same time. The bakery looked busy with local workers buying their lunchtime goodies. Someone familiar caught Macy's eye across the road, and she looked to see Angela on the other side of the street. She appeared to be waiting for someone. Remembering what Paul had said about her, Macy hesitated to call out, but then Angela was joined by a broad-shouldered man and a woman. They shook hands, and then all three disappeared down a busy side street lined with coffee shops, cafés, and pubs.

Curious, Macy crossed the road. She followed them until they disappeared inside a café. Macy drew closer. People were sitting at several little tables outside, even though it was February and freezing.

A customer came out, and the smell of food trickled out. Pulling up the hood on her coat, Macy edged closer still and tried to spot Angela and her friends through the window. She kept her head bowed to avoid detection and pretended she was waiting for someone. Then Macy saw Angela and her friends waiting to be seated. Macy watched in astonishment as Angela took off her woolly hat to reveal red and curly hair.

Macy touched her own red curly hair behind her hood, feeling shocked. *She wouldn't! Would she?*

Paul had said she was sly, but this was underhanded.

Macy almost forgot she was trying to remain incognito in her disbelief, and the man Angela was with looked up and caught her looking. Macy turned away from the window, grabbed a menu off an empty table, and pretended to read. The heavily-built guy was Caucasian, and the woman was a petite Chinese lady. Then, out of the corner of her eye, Macy watched as a harried-looking waitress seated the three and gave them menus.

A group of people entered the café, and dropping the menu, Macy hurried to keep behind them as she followed them inside. The warm air hit her immediately, sliding over her and making her hot. But keeping her hood up, she pretended to look for someone while keeping Angela in sight. The three were looking at the menu. The Chinese lady said something, and they all laughed.

Macy excused herself to squeeze past the group she'd followed in and faked interest in the cakes on the counter closest to Angela and her friends. It risked being spotted, but she wanted to listen to their conversation.

'Well, it's good to meet up with you, Macy,' the man said. Macy had expected to hear her name, but the muscles in her body still clenched at the confirmation that Angela was pretending to be her. She clutched the countertop to stop herself from spinning around and challenging Angela.

'I'm very pleased to meet you both,' said Angela.

'What made you finally decide to meet us?' he asked. Macy recognised his dictation-paced voice: It was Oliver, the man she had spoken with on the telephone. His soft voice didn't match his huge frame. Without looking too closely, Macy noticed he wore a sharp suit, making him look smarter than Manbun, who she'd been locked up with on Saturday. The Chinese lady was more casual in jeans and a blouse, which Macy could see now as she took off her coat and hung it on the back of her chair.

'Matt Fenovo's interview,' Angela said. 'He raised a lot of questions. I thought your group came over very well.'

Macy controlled a cynical laugh. When Macy watched Fenovo's programme, she'd felt the WUM had come across as unresponsive and unable to speak up for their cause—apart from the heckler.

'There are still many questions we want answers to,' Oliver said. 'But, as I explained in our phone call, we can only ask those questions when the entire human population has woken up.'

'What do you mean by "woken up"?' Angela asked. Macy itched to turn around. She guessed Angela was sitting forwards, maybe recording the interview on her phone. 'Your slogan is "Wake Up". In fact, everything about you is telling the rest of the population to wake up. Wake up to what?'

'To the fact that aliens arrived on Earth six years ago. You, and most of the world, think the Jelvias have been here forever. They haven't. They came here six years ago, in ten spaceships.'

Angela gave a spontaneous laugh, which stopped when she realised Oliver was serious. Macy smirked. She'd never be that unprofessional! '*Ten* spaceships?' Angela said. 'So where are they? You can't exactly hide a spaceship, can you?'

'You can't hide them, but you can disguise them,' the woman said, who Macy suspected to be Phil. She spoke with an upper-class English accent.

Macy put her handbag down on an empty table and pretended to rifle through it to get a better look. Phil wasn't as old as Macy thought. Probably the same age as her. She was stunning but dressed in a way that told Macy she underestimated her looks. Beneath the table, one of her legs was jiggling as if nervous, but her elfin face appeared passive.

'Disguise ten spaceships? How?' Angela's tone clearly wasn't having it.

'First, their ten spaceships imitated meteorites,' Oliver said, 'then after landing, nine masquerade as islands in the Atlantic and the Arctic Ocean around Iceland, Norway and the UK. The tenth was—'

'Disguised as a tree?' Angela said and laughed.

If you want to steal my identity, at least be good at it! Macy swung around, unable to keep quiet any longer. They still hadn't noticed her, so lowering her hood, she walked up to the table and plonked herself down next to Angela.

TWENTY-SEVEN

'Hello, *Macy*. Are you going to tell me what's going on?' she asked.

Angela went the same colour as her badly dyed hair. Oliver and the woman Macy believed to be Phil looked on blankly before realisation dawned on their faces.

'You're not Macy?' Phil asked Angela. She looked annoyed. In fact, she looked ready to push her chair back and storm out, but Oliver placed a placating hand on her arm.

'No, she isn't,' said Macy. 'She is—*was*—a friend. You should probably check your back for knives before you leave.'

'How did she get my personal number?' Phil asked.

'She's also a thief,' Macy said, 'who steals people's mail. You wrote me a letter. I take it you're Phil Oswald?'

'I'm so sorry, Macy,' Angela wailed. 'But you have everything! You have the contacts, people wanting to talk to you—you even have the Jelvian boyfriend. I just wanted some of it, that's all.'

'What are you, three years old?'

'I'm sorry.' Angela stood up and pushed past Macy, almost knocking her from her seat in her hurry.

Phil's hands were clasped over her mouth theatrically. Macy thought she was hiding a laugh, but she looked furious when she brought her hands down. Then Oliver snickered.

'Sorry,' he said, sobering up quickly when he realised he was the only one amused, 'but you have to admit, that was some icebreaker.'

Phil turned her angry look on him, and Macy was sure she kicked him beneath the table. Then, finally, Phil turned to Macy. 'I'm sorry,' she said. 'We probably should have checked her credentials. Can I see yours?'

'No,' said Macy and folded her arms.

'That proves she is who she says she is,' Oliver said. He still looked amused.

The flustered-looking waitress interrupted them just then, and they each ordered a coffee.

'Let's make this quick,' Macy said once the waitress had gone away. 'I don't want to interview you, but I *need* to interview you. But not here. Somewhere more private,' she said, thinking of Narcifer's interrogation room at Keats Avenue. 'I need to find out what you have against Jelvias.'

'I can answer that simply,' Phil said. 'They don't belong here, and they are destroying us.'

'If I said that about your nationality, you would call me racist,' Macy said, thinking she'd won the first round.

'I'm as British as you are, and Jelvias aren't a nationality,' Phil said, making Macy think she'd offended her. But her beautiful elfin face and dark eyes didn't hold any offence. She answered matter-of-factly.

Macy pulled her gaze away from Phil as Oliver said, 'The Jelvias aren't a race. Or not a *human* race. They're aliens. I called you a couple of weeks ago, and we had this very discussion,' he said. He smiled as if the memory amused him and added, 'You hung up on me.'

'What did you expect?' Macy said. She didn't know anything about these people other than their names, but she knew they were clearly insane. She felt grateful she hadn't agreed to meet them alone. Oliver was hench. Not bigger than any Jelvias she'd met, but bigger than any normal human man. 'You're trying to tell me that the Jelvian boyfriend I'm living with is a space alien? Can't you see how ridiculous that sounds?'

'Yes, I know how it sounds—but it's true. All we want is for you to listen to us, maybe come to one of our meetings,' Oliver said. The slow pace of his speech annoyed Macy.

The waitress returned with their coffees, almost spilling them in her hurry to rush off to the next table. The hubbub of the café was quite loud.

'I've read your letters and texts,' Macy said. 'I've read your website, listened to your voicemail, listened to your podcasts, and you say the same things over and over. And no matter how often you repeat yourself, I still think you're talking bullshit. So why would I want to come to one of your meetings to hear it again?'

'I really wish it was all bullshit. But the truth is, we're running out of time. We're alarmed because our world is being taken over, and nobody does anything about it. Six years ago, Jelvias did not exist on Earth.'

Macy sighed long and hard. She picked up her coffee cup and took a sip. Then, looking at Oliver over the rim of her cup, she said in a tired voice, 'Jon Johnsen and his sorry team tried to destroy a group of Jelvias six years ago. It was documented in the newspaper I used to work for.'

'No. That's when Jelvias *arrived*. They arrived in small space pods. The ship you're talking about is the tenth spaceship and would've landed in the English Channel, but Johnsen intervened and shot them down. Nobody will ever know if Johnsen was awake, but we suspect he was.'

Shaking her head, Macy lowered her coffee cup back into its saucer. 'Can you hear yourself?' She glanced at Phil, wondering why she wasn't saying anything. She sat low in her chair, looking like a sulky teenager. 'You're the founder of WUM?' Macy asked her.

Phil straightened her posture. 'Oliver and I are cofounders. We were the only people at the time who could remember life before Jelvias.'

'Every day, we wonder if a Jelvia will take us out because of what we're doing, but every day they don't,' said Oliver. 'Have you wondered why that is?'

'Not worth the effort?' Macy asked with a shrug.

Oliver smiled, and Macy's palm itched. She wanted to slap that smile.

'No. Jelvias think we're mad, just like *you* think we're mad. But, you see, Jelvias are asleep, too. Macy, six years ago, the *entire* population worldwide fell asleep. That's the only way I can explain it. Our minds become fogged, and we remember only what *they* allow us to remember. We've been given false memories, Macy.'

Macy snorted. 'Are you telling me that Jelvias are so technologically developed that they have come up with—with what, a hallucinogenic drug or something? To warp the minds of every person on the planet?' She laughed, shaking her head. 'You're even crazier than I thought you were.'

'Not the Jelvias. The committee,' Phil said.

Macy's head spun towards her. Hearing 'the committee' from someone outside of Jelvian society startled her.

'We don't know who, or what, "the committee" is. They could be a hierarchy of Jelvias or another life form entirely. They might not even be organic. But whatever they are, they control Jelvias,' Phil said. Her voice carried more authority than Oliver's, and she clearly wasn't the petulant teenager she seemed to be. Neither was she nervous. Macy suspected her leg jiggling was just part of her nature. Phil's dark gaze stared into Macy's eyes. It was almost as if Phil could see into her thoughts. She was intelligent, very intelligent, which made Macy wonder how she became sucked into believing Jelvias were from another planet.

Macy was the first to look away.

'Let's start again,' Oliver said. 'Emotions tend to get the better of us lately. Phil and I began this movement two years ago, and it was slow to get off the ground. But even now it's up and running, it still feels like we aren't being taken seriously.'

Well, duh! Macy wanted to say but held back.

'I'm Oliver Kennedy,' he said.

Macy sipped her coffee, then reluctantly put it down to grip Oliver's hand when he reached across the table for a handshake. She looked at Phil, expecting a formal introduction from her as well. Instead, Phil kept her hands clasped on the table, so Macy picked up her coffee again.

'I call myself Philippa Oswald,' she said. 'I was born British, but as you've already pointed out, my origins are Chinese. My father was Tsung Zmin.'

Macy's eyes grew round as she took in the information. Finally, her coffee cup clattered back into the saucer.

'I see you've heard of him,' Phil stated without emotion.

'I know he was involved with what Jon Johnsen started,' Macy said.

'Yes, and I'm sure you have both versions: Narcifer's and the well-known versions. But you don't have the *correct* version,' Phil said.

'And I suppose you'll tell me your version?' said Macy.

'No, that would be pointless right now. The Jelvias memories are also implanted. Our aim is to wake the human population before the Jelvias awake. Has Narcifer done anything that has made you question his authenticity?'

Macy remembered the cat food, then recalled other small things Narcifer had done or said that she had thought odd, like the Christmas and birthdays he didn't celebrate or even understand.

'No,' she said.

'People are waking up, and while the committee is still unaware, we can formulate a plan of action,' Oliver said. 'We've realised Jelvias take no notice of us, and we're taking advantage of that by trying to wake up more and more people. Although, last Friday, we had a scare. I'm sure you heard about the Jelvia attacking the helicopter over Notting Hill?'

'You know that I have. I'm sure Mr Manbun and Dulcie contacted you as soon as they realised we were locked together in the pub,' Macy said tartly.

Oliver smiled. 'And they got close enough for you to hear Dulcie's name, obviously,' he said.

'Ferdy,' Phil said.

Macy looked at her blankly.

'Mr Manbun, as you called him, is called Ferdy.' It was down to Oliver to elaborate. 'And yes, they couldn't believe their luck when they noticed you. We advised them not to approach you. They can be a little, er, enthusiastic, and we didn't want to scare you off completely.'

'Narcifer attacked the helicopter because it was following us,' Macy said. 'Nobody got hurt.'

'Luckily,' Oliver said. He pursed his lips. 'You know, some people wake suddenly from the brain fog with all their old memories intact. Some remember gradually, recalling little bits, while others become confused, maybe making notes or telling themselves it's just a Jelvian quirk.'

Macy felt a jolt. His last had described her. She made notes all the time about things that didn't make sense. She remembered the strange déjà vu moment she'd had after the helicopter fiasco. In her mind's eye, she could still see the pulsing UFOs streaking across the sky as, one by one, they stopped as if to observe the land below before continuing. The unidentified fear she'd felt wasn't there, and again, she brushed off the moment as nonsense.

Oliver was still talking, 'Unfortunately, most humans live in oblivion, thinking the Jelvias have been around forever. You, Macy, are unique. You are living with a Jelvian man, happily and willingly. If you wake up, it would not necessarily mean the end of your relationship with Narcifer—you would just know what he is.'

'An alien?' she scoffed.

'Yes.'

Macy half laughed, and stood up. 'I've heard enough.'

Phil stood up with her. She reached out with both hands, and Macy thought she might restrain her for a moment. Then Phil's arms fell to her sides. This was the first time Macy saw emotion, other than sulkiness, on her face.

'He's an alien who is desperate for an ordinary life. An alien who doesn't *want* to live the life the committee wants him to. We think that's why your relationship is working. You make Narcifer believe he is normal,' Phil said.

'Bullshit,' Macy said. She turned to go.

'Wait, you said you wanted to interview us somewhere more private. Name the place, date and time, and we'll be there,' Phil said.

Macy looked over her shoulder at her. 'This afternoon, 4 p.m. at Keats Avenue.'

'That's where Jelvias have taken up residence,' Phil said, and her sulky expression changed. She suddenly looked interested. Her eyes glowed with excitement. 'Is that where you mean?'

'No,' Oliver said, standing. His bulk seemed to fill the café. He put a meaty hand on Phil's arm. 'That'll be too dangerous.'

Phil didn't even look at him. 'It'll just be me then,' she said. '*I'll* be there.'

Macy left them arguing and strode out of the shop. She didn't get far when she heard a familiar voice.

'Macy!'

Macy closed her eyes in annoyance and kept walking.

'Macy!' Angela said again, falling into step next to her. 'I'm really sorry. I don't know what came over me. It—it was an impulsive thing. I didn't think.'

Macy eyed Angela's hair. 'Woke up and clicked your fingers to turn that mop red, did you?'

Angela coloured up again. 'Not my hair. I meant meeting the WUMs was impulsive.'

Macy stopped walking and turned on her. 'Pretend you're me again, and I will have a lawsuit on you so fast the word "impulsive" will seem inhibited.'

Then she turned and walked away.

Angela didn't bother to follow.

TWENTY-EIGHT

The morning hadn't gone exactly as Macy had envisioned.

She'd had a hundred grand deposited into her bank account, seen Angela in her true light, met and secured an interview with the Wake Up Movement, and discovered Phil's true identity. That was significant. It made Macy wonder if WUM was a crusade of one woman's fight to avenge her father's death.

And she only speculated that because she felt James Sullivan was somehow part of it, but he couldn't be part of it for that reason. She didn't know how he fitted into the Wake Up Movement. But she aimed to find out, and she was going to find out this afternoon at Keats while interviewing Phil. She felt she would have her questions answered in one sitting. Phil's father, Tsung Zmin, had joined with Jon Johnsen to destroy the Jelvias. And Narcifer had been the Jelvia to kill him. That was enough for Macy to realise this was why she'd been targeted by WUM. They were using her to get revenge.

There were still so many uncertainties, but Macy finally felt she was on the right path to destroy WUM and all it stood for.

The morning and early afternoon had empowered Macy.

Back home, she dumped her packages on the settee before returning to the car for the cake she eventually bought for Narcifer. She put it on the kitchen counter and flicked on the coffee machine.

Narcifer wasn't home, but she'd called and warned him about Phil's identity. He didn't seem shocked, but he promised Macy he'd get a recorded confession out of Phil so Macy could share it over social media and get WUM shut down for good. Macy didn't tell Narcifer about the payoff from *London Echo*. He didn't understand money and the complex issues it carried or solved.

Narcifer came home an hour later with a bouquet of flowers in his arms, which he presented to her proudly.

'I've seen men give women flowers on TV,' he said as she buried her face in the delicious scent of the blooms.

'Usually, it's because they've done something wrong,' she teased. Then, standing on tiptoe, she kissed his chin. 'Thank you. You've never bought me flowers before.'

'After what I revealed yesterday, I felt you earned them,' he said. 'And I know you hate my Jelvian privilege, so I paid for them, I promise.'

Macy looked up from the flowers. 'You told me nothing yesterday, and you know it.' She turned to put the flowers on the counter and unwrapped them from their packaging. Then, spotting a card attached to the flowers, she pulled it off to read: **HAPPY BIRTHDAY, NANCY.** 'No Jelvia privilege, eh? Narce, these flowers aren't mine,' she said, turning.

'Of course, they are, babe. It's not my fault the women ran out of the shop squealing. I left money on the counter,' he added. He cupped her face with his hands and then kissed her nose.

Macy was torn between amusement and frustration. 'I don't hate your Jelvian privilege,' she murmured as his lips dropped to hers.

'What time have you arranged with WUM?' he asked softly.

'We've time,' she said and hungrily pawed at the zipper of his jeans. The flowers were forgotten.

Narcifer's throaty laugh followed, but they didn't make the bedroom. They had sex in the kitchen, up against the sink.

TWENTY-NINE

As they drove along Keats Avenue, Macy's heart got heavier and heavier on seeing the number of police vans lining the street.

'They followed you home anyway?' she asked.

'No, they've been here several days. They're just monitoring our movements,' Narcifer said.

'Monitoring?' They passed the police vans, and Macy spotted the camera on each vehicle. 'What for?'

'Just to show us they have the authority, I guess.' He glanced at her. 'Are you okay?'

She let out a breath. 'I am now I know they're empty vehicles. Is that why you overreacted to the helicopter?' she teased.

He gave her a side-glance. 'Overreacted?'

'Just a little.'

His lips quirked.

'Those cameras might have a zoom lens straight into your house,' she said as they passed the last van. 'Maybe not,' she added as the road led them to the black gates that secured the property. They opened as they drew near, and Macy craned her neck to see the house. But it sat over a crest of a hill, and she couldn't see from here. But then, neither would the police cameras. Narcifer was right; their presence was just a show of power.

She relaxed.

Macy was excited as they made their way up the long, winding drive towards Keats House. They rounded a corner, and Macy spotted something she'd only seen on TV.

'A helicopter pad! You have your own helicopter?' she asked, but her eyes widened further as the big house came into view. 'Oh, bloody wow. Narce! It's a frigging *palace.*'

Gravel crunched beneath the tyres as the road changed to a stone driveway. Macy had unclipped her seatbelt before Narcifer had even parked.

'Easy,' he said, putting a hand on her arm.

She turned to grin at him. 'Don't worry. I'm so over falling out of cars.'

'Don't even joke about it.' He opened his door and came round to help her out, but Macy was out of the car before he'd circled it.

She pushed her arm through his, and they walked up a paved path towards the massive front door. Narcifer pushed open the door and then stood back to let her enter. Macy walked into a marble-floored foyer with panelled walls and a high ceiling. Her heels clicked on the tiles. There were doorways to the sides, a wide staircase in the centre, and two archways leading to other rooms beyond the stairs.

'Impressive!' she said. She eyed the framed photos on the walls. There were family portraits dotted around—all showing the same human family. She remembered the house belonged to a viscount, an earl, or something. 'Are they the original family?'

'No idea. The pictures were there when we came. Come on.' Narcifer took her hand and led her across the marble floor towards one of the doors. Their footsteps echoed around the room, and then Narcifer opened the door to a spacious area with shelves of books lining the walls. Various high-backed chairs were placed around an unlit fireplace.

'Library,' Narcifer said. He left her peering into the room and strode off to another door. He opened it. 'A lounge area.'

Macy scurried over to have a look. This time, it was another large room with settees and two-seated sofas overlooking a wide window. The view was an unspoilt scene of the lawn. Macy noticed a picture on the wall over an unlit open fireplace. It was the same family—a man, a woman, and three children—but this was a painting, not a photo like what she'd seen in the foyer. Like the library, this room also looked unused. It was as though the family had just picked up and left.

She wanted to probe more, but Narcifer had walked across the hall to another room. Macy followed. Narcifer opened the door to a blazing fire in a living room. This room was occupied. A muted TV was on, and a Jelvian man lounged on the deep red settee. He looked over as they entered.

Macy recognised him straight away—Yash. His spider tattoo was all too visible. Seeing him brought back a wave of memories—mostly of her being tricked into being taken hostage. She hadn't seen Yash since, though she had made her peace with Aldarn—until he'd attempted to kill her!

Yash leaned back, relaxed, but his gaze was stern on Macy. 'Why'd you bring a human here?' he asked Narcifer.

'Macy is my girlfriend, unlike the victims you take to your room,' he said, putting an arm around her.

Yash snorted and closed his eyes, dismissing them.

'Victims like Bethany Roberts?' Macy asked, suddenly thinking of the scruffy woman who'd visited her in the hospital. She had a problem with Yash, though Macy couldn't remember the details.

Yash's eyes snapped open, and Narcifer howled with laughter.

'Oh, Mace, don't mention that name around Yash. She broke his heart—ran off with another man,' Narcifer said between bursts of laughter.

Yash stood up, his face a high red colour. Macy couldn't work out if it was anger or embarrassment. 'No, sweet cheeks,' he said, glaring at her, '*you're* the victim. You just don't know it yet.' He shifted his gaze to Narcifer, whose mirth rapidly died. 'If you love her like you say, you'll let her go.' Then he turned and strode towards a door at the far side of the room.

'What was that about?' she asked when Yash was gone.

Narcifer shrugged his broad shoulders. 'Nothing. You touched a nerve, that's all.'

Macy plonked herself down on the settee where Yash had been sitting. She rubbed her leg—she had been on it too much today, and it was hurting. 'Yash fell in love with Beth?' she asked, looking up at Narcifer.

'He never admitted it, but I've never seen him that protective of anyone. He had her boyfriend tagged and watched to ensure he was treating her properly.'

'I can't imagine what poor Beth went through dealing with him. And that awful tattoo on his face!'

'It covers his scars after he was injured in the helicopter crash.'

'I never knew he was involved! I thought it was just Aldarn and Scasone?' Macy asked, rubbing her legs.

'Scasone was Yash's brother. Yash almost didn't join our group. He just wanted to obey the committee and kill every human they asked him to. He only joined us when Cal and Aldarn said we'd go after all those involved in the helicopter crash.' He held out his hand. 'Come on, I'm supposed to show you the interrogation room before the WUM turns up.'

Macy took his hand and allowed him to pull her from the settee. Narcifer led the way out of the room and across the marble hallway. Around the back of the large staircase was a lift. He pressed a button.

'Bloody hell, a lift in your house. Do you have a butler, too?'

'A what?'

'Never mind.'

The lift doors slid open, and his hand urged her gently inside. The lift was as luxurious as the rest of the house. It took them down, and the luxury gave way to cement and brickwork. Lighting flicked on automatically as they stepped out of the lift and into the basement.

After the warmth of the house upstairs, it felt chilly down here. It wasn't like an ordinary basement—it wasn't dark or anything—and it looked clean. Narcifer led her up a corridor filled with various bits of covered furniture, which had been pushed up against the walls.

Finally, he stopped at a large sliding door. 'This is the interrogation room,' Narcifer said and slid the door open to reveal a room full of polythene-covered furniture, wooden boxes, and other containers.

The entire basement, including the interrogation room, was a storage area.

Macy stepped into the room and looked around, imagining it empty of all the stored furniture. But, even with the boxes and furniture, the room had an uncomfortable air of menace.

'Once we seal the room, it becomes soundproof.' He nodded to her. 'Go on, look around.'

'Impressive,' she said, turning to look at the door. She was glad he'd left it open.

Narcifer pointed to a mirror that ran the width of one wall. 'That's a two-way mirror. We can see in, but the prisoner can't see out.'

'I don't want to *scare* Phil,' she said, turning to Narcifer, leaning against the doorjamb, watching her. 'I just want to speak to her on my terms and get her to reveal the real reasons for persecuting you on camera. This room is more of a... a prison. I was expecting an office or something. So, what do you use this room for? Just storage?'

'Mainly, yes. The previous owners left much of their stuff, and we've moved some of it down here. Come on, I'll show you the control room,' he said. He turned towards the corridor, and Macy followed him. The passage housed more furniture, including several pieces covered with sheets.

The next room was the control room, and like when they stepped out of the lift, the light flicked on automatically. It was brighter than the corridor. Stored furniture had made it to the control room, too. Stacked boxes, various chairs, and even a bed were stockpiled.

Narcifer told Macy to sit at the controls and pointed to various buttons. 'You press this to talk, that one to mute. Volume. Lighting. This makes a high-pitched noise right into the interrogation room.'

Macy pressed it, but she couldn't hear anything. She turned it off. 'What does that one do?'

'Controls the temperature, I think. I'll go into the room; see if you can speak to me from there,' Narcifer said, leaving her sitting at the controls.

A moment later, Macy saw Narcifer enter the interrogation room. He waved, and she could see him talking. It took Macy a moment to realise she had to press a button to hear him. When she did, his voice was pitched straight into the room as if he was sitting next to her.

'...Once I get you upstairs, I'm going to undress you slowly. Spank you and then kiss every spare inch of you before making love to you hard.'

She laughed, then pressed the button so she could speak. 'How hard?' She took her finger off the switch so Narcifer could answer.

'Oh, *very* hard. So hard you'll squeal.'

He winked at her and then left the room. When he returned to the control room, she jumped off the chair. 'My turn!'

Narcifer's face dropped. 'But—sex?'

'Later,' she said as she passed him, laughing at his crestfallen face. She liked this Narcifer, this playful, boyish Narcifer. It was such a contrast to yesterday.

Macy made her way to the interrogation room and slid the door semi-closed after her. She wanted to get a feel of the room with the door closed without locking herself in. She faced the two-way mirror and viewed her reflection.

'Can you hear me?' she asked.

'I can hear you,' Narcifer said—or at least she hoped it was Narcifer. His voice was slow and robotic.

'You sound... strange.'

'That's because you've left me hanging.'

She smiled. It was definitely Narcifer behind the mirror.

'Can you change the way your voice sounds?' she asked.

'Is that better?' he asked in his normal speaking voice. 'Or how about this?' he said. His voice was now high-pitched.

Despite Narcifer making her chuckle, she could see how this room could intimidate someone. Especially with the door almost closed. She wasn't sure if it was suitable, but maybe she could make it look more office-like and share the space with Phil while conducting the interview. She pulled out her mobile and checked the time. She only had an hour before she met Phil outside the gates.

Putting her phone away, she looked at the mirror. All she could see was her own reflection. 'Would anyone mind if I rearranged some of the furniture here?'

Narcifer didn't answer her, and she suspected he was playing with the controls on the other side. Taking a last look around, she headed out to the corridor. She closed the door, and it glided effortlessly with a slight click sound to show it was locked. She caught a panel with a qwerty keyboard to the right of the door and saw it had a red light. Macy opened the door again, and the light changed to green.

The surrounding silence suddenly struck her. The corridor, however bright, was eery. She hadn't noticed it before, but there was no sound down here. Not even a hum from the lights. Macy cocked an ear and held her breath. Nothing.

Then she realised Narcifer hadn't spoken for a while.

Her instinct was to call out for him, but an inner sense stopped her. A sixth sense.

Bending, she removed her shoes, ditching one carefully on the floor. Then, holding the other with the heel pointing forwards like a weapon, she crept along. She kept close to the wall and listened hard, but all was quiet.

She stopped before she got to the open door of the control room. The brighter light spilt out into the corridor, but two shadows suddenly interrupted the light flow, making Macy jump. She pressed a fist against her mouth to stop herself from making any noise. Narcifer would've spoken if the people in the control room were harmless. She thought she heard hushed voices and held her breath to listen. But she didn't hear anything.

Macy inched forwards.

The grip of the shoe in her hand felt waxy. Then, with her heart thumping and adrenaline putting every sense on high alert, she flattened herself against the wall and peeked around the door. Oblivious to Macy, two Jelvias stood over Narcifer as he slumped over the control desk.

Narcifer faced Macy, and his eyes, open and dancing with sparks, widened when he saw her. Macy stared into his eyes, her own filling with tears as one of the men withdrew an inch-long syringe from Narcifer's neck.

They'd immobilised him, but his eyes said, *Run!*

THIRTY

Macy turned quickly—too quickly.

She knocked into a sheet-covered table, and the legs grated across the concrete floor. For an instant, Macy froze, but then, hearing movement, she turned and threw her shoe down the corridor opposite her. She slipped to the floor almost instantaneously and hid beneath the sheeted table just as one of the Jelvias came running.

Macy heard his pounding feet as he ran towards the noise of her tossed shoe. She didn't dare look to spy on him; instead, she lay still with her eyes tightly closed. His pounding feet came back, and he ran past her hiding place, making the sheet swish in his wake.

Macy watched beneath the gap of the sheet before it fell back into place. If he saw her, he'd kill her. There was no doubt about that. Macy squeezed her eyes closed again, feeling sick, worried about Narcifer, and scared for herself.

The Jelvias footsteps halted, and Macy's eyes pinged open.

He'd spotted her first shoe by the interrogation room. He bent to pick it up, and she glimpsed his face and long black hair. At first, she thought it was Yash, but his face was clear of tattoos.

He tossed the shoe away with a clatter, making Macy start. She pressed her face to the ground to muffle her breathing.

He knows I'm hiding.

She opened her eyes and saw his feet directly in front of her. She pressed her face back to the ground, and put her hands over her head in a futile effort to make herself invisible. Her heart was hammering so loudly that she was sure he would hear it. She squeezed her eyes closed and hoped her death would be painless.

The sheet rustled, and Macy opened her eyes cautiously. The Jelvia was walking back towards the interrogation room. He stopped outside the room, and then Macy saw a green light reflected on the opposite wall as he opened the door. Then his feet disappeared inside.

Not thinking, not even breathing, Macy bolted from her hiding place and slid the door closed on the shocked Jelvia. The door panel lit red, and Macy sagged against the door.

Footsteps told her the second Jelvia was coming, and she pushed from the door and ran for the lift. Inside, she jabbed the button as the pounding footsteps got closer. But the doors closed. Relief made her legs boneless and she sank down the wall as the lift moved.

When the lift stopped and the doors opened, Macy found she couldn't stand. But afraid the doors would close and take her back down, she crawled out, her eyes searching the luxurious marble hallway for enemy Jelvias.

Empty.

Forcing her body upright, she staggered towards where she had seen Yash in the sitting room. The TV was still on, but the room was empty. She felt spent, but she forced her protesting legs to carry on.

'Yash!' she yelled, then cut herself off. She didn't want rival Jelvias to hear her shouting for help. So instead, she ran towards the door she'd seen Yash go through earlier. The door led to a short corridor that fed into a large kitchen. She entered the kitchen and glanced around. It looked empty. Macy rubbed her forehead where a headache raged.

'Yash!' she called again as loudly as she dared.

Then she spotted him. A walled courtyard was attached to the kitchen, and Yash stood outside insolently watching her progress. A dark-haired Jelvian woman was by his side, also watching Macy. They glanced at one another in joint derision.

Ignoring their contempt, knowing they'd help Narcifer, she ran towards them and almost collided with Yash as he came towards her. He watched impassively as she stumbled backwards, trying to avoid him, then grabbed the door to steady herself.

'What the fuck are you—' he began.

'Narcifer's been attacked!' She cut him off impatiently. 'They—'

Without waiting to hear more, Yash ran past her. Macy tried to follow but couldn't keep up as he ran from the room, one of his hands reaching for a mobile phone from his back pocket.

'I locked one in the interrogation room!' she yelled to the empty room.

She dragged her hand through her hair; her head felt sweaty. Her leg throbbed, and her heartbeat was erratic. She limped to the lounge but didn't sit down. Once she sat, she didn't think she'd get up again. Instead, she hovered by the door, looking anxiously out into the passageway.

'What's happened?'

Macy jumped and swivelled around. She'd forgotten about the Jelvian woman.

'Two Jelvias... in the basement.' Her lips felt wooden. 'They injected... something into Narcifer's neck.'

The Jelvian woman's face was hostile. She had a boyish figure and short, dark hair, but like all Jelvias, she was tall. She swept past Macy and headed up the wide staircase as if her friends were constantly attacked.

Macy felt sick, and her heart was out of control. It made her breathing erratic. She tried to calm herself down, but her body was highly alert. She listened for noises—voices, anything—but all was silent in the large house. Still, she waited. She didn't know how long she stood there, but then, with a start, she realised she was standing in almost darkness. Macy pulled her phone out of her pocket and checked the time. It was after four in the afternoon.

Hands shaking, she searched for Narcifer's number.

She wasn't expecting it to be answered and jumped when a male voice said, 'Who are you?'

'I—er—I'm looking for Narcifer,' she said.

'And you are?' he repeated.

'A friend,' she said and was about to hang up, but the other person hung up first. She was left staring at her phone. 'Shit,' she said, pocketing her phone. She stepped outside into the hallway.

Yash had been gone for ages. She moved towards the lift but then darted back to the kitchen, where she found a carving knife in one of the drawers. Grasping it in her hand, she returned to the large hallway. She glanced up the stairs, wishing she'd stopped the Jelvian woman from leaving—there was always safety in numbers—then she continued towards the lift. The door was still open. Taking a breath, she stepped inside.

Hesitating only a fraction of a second, she pressed the button for the basement, then chewed on a nail as the door slid closed. The knife in her other hand was poised for action as her body geared her for danger. She jumped a mile when the lift doors opened again, almost dropping the knife.

'Calm the fuck down,' she muttered to herself and stepped cautiously out of the lift. She stood in the corridor, listening for any sounds, then edged her way towards the control room, keeping close to the walls. She stopped and pressed an ear against the door of the interrogation room. It was silent inside, but the walls were soundproofed—or maybe the Jelvia's accomplice had freed him.

Macy carried on to the control room, flattening herself against the wall, then peering around. She must have made a noise because the two Jelvias inside swung towards her, making her jump.

'Jesus, Macy,' Calder said, and Yash turned back to what he was doing. He hadn't forgotten her—he'd just deemed her unimportant. Calder came over and took the knife from her. 'Coming to save our arses, eh?'

She looked up at him, her eyes filling with tears.

'Ah, honey, don't,' he said. He pulled Macy into the room and sat her down on a chair. 'Hey, you're bleeding.'

She looked down at her bare feet. One of her toes was bleeding, and she vaguely remembered stubbing it on the table before she hid under it. Her smart blue suit was crumpled, and the knees had dirt marks.

'What's going on? Where's Narcifer?' she asked.

Calder pulled up a chair and sat next to her. 'They've taken him,' he said. He pointed to the two-way mirror. 'We're questioning the Jelvia you locked in the interrogation room. That was quick thinking, Macy. Well done.'

'*Who's* taken him? And why?' she asked, throwing out her hands. 'They were Jelvias. Friends!'

'Being Jelvias doesn't make them friends,' Calder said.

'But... but why have they kidnapped him? For what reason?' She felt jittery, and her palms were slick with sweat. She wiped them on her jacket.

'We don't know. It could be a case of mistaken identity. The attacker may have thought Narcifer was me,' Calder said.

'You look alike,' Macy said, trying to think practically. Her chattering teeth failed to make her sound practical, though. 'But why would they want you?'

'Because I started this group. Or maybe they came to look for Al but got frustrated and took the first man they saw, which happened to be Narcifer.' He sighed. 'Aldarn is wanted by the committee, and they've sent their troops to collect him.'

Macy gave an involuntary shudder. She buried her head in her hands with a gulp of emotion. A big hand rested on her back.

'We need to keep you safe until we know what's going on,' Calder said.

'No.' She looked up. 'No, I'm fine,' she said more firmly. She rubbed her eyes, feeling the wetness. She hadn't realised she was crying. She looked towards the two-way mirror to see the Jelvian man prowling the room, kicking the stored furniture and thumping the walls. 'What's he saying?' she asked as he stopped to face the mirror; she saw his lips move.

'Crap. He's saying fucking crap,' Yash answered. He moved a dial, and the Jelvia sank to his knees, clutching his ears.

Macy saw blood oozing between the Jelvia's fingers and, with a jolt, realised much of it wasn't fresh. Yash pushed the dial further up, and the Jelvia in the interrogation room collapsed. He spun around on the floor, using his legs like a propeller as if the motion gave relief.

'What are you doing to cause that?' she asked. The dial read 155 dB.

'Noise. A convenient method of, er, getting your interviewee to talk,' Calder said.

Yash moved the dial further up. The limit was 300 dB, and the Jelvian man spun faster.

'Stop!' she cried, unable to turn her eyes away from the spinning Jelvia. His mouth was open in a silent scream. Whether they had taken Narcifer or not, this was barbaric.

But Yash turned the dial further. Macy jumped up and attempted to move the dial back down to zero without thinking. Yash slapped her hand away, making her gasp in pain, and pushed the dial round to the maximum limit.

The man stopped spinning. He lay on his back, panting heavily, and blood dripped from his ears to pool on the floor.

Rubbing the back of her hand, she sat back down. 'He's no use dead,' she said, but her voice was small, and it wobbled. She sniffed, trying to get a hold of her emotions. She focused on her bare feet. They looked cold. A warm hand touched her shoulder, and she looked up.

'Let us deal with this,' Calder said. He smiled at her. 'It's okay, Macy. We'll get Narcifer back.'

Macy watched the Jelvia in the interrogation room. He rolled over to lie face down with his hands pressed against his ears—the only indication that he was in discomfort. Macy tore her eyes away and looked up at Calder.

'Why are some Jelvias enemies?'

Calder glanced at Yash, then back at Macy. 'We disobeyed the committee,' he said. 'Aldarn was told to return to his island. But they'd exterminate him if he went, so we hid him.'

'*We?* Don't include Narcifer in that. He's been trying to find Aldarn.'

Calder's smile was affected. 'And do you know *why* he's trying to find Aldarn?'

Macy didn't like the way Calder had turned the question on her. But she knew why Narcifer was looking for Aldarn: It was because James had asked him to. Her eyes widened as it all came together in her head.

James hadn't *asked* Narcifer to find Aldarn; he'd *blackmailed* him just like he'd forced Narcifer into protecting him. Only she couldn't fathom *how* Narcifer was blackmailed. So what hold did James have over Narcifer?

But keeping her face neutral, she looked at Calder and said, 'I wish I did.'

'We're all on the same team,' he said. Macy searched his face for hypocrisy, but she didn't find any—but then, he looked so like Narcifer it could be making her biased. Finally, he smiled as if understanding her thoughts. 'Recently, Narcifer has been acting oddly, making us believe he's working against us to find Aldarn for the committee.'

'*What?*'

'Ever since your accident, Narcifer has been trying to find Aldarn. He even went after Harry.'

'Harry?'

'Beth's boyfriend.'

'Beth? Ah, Beth, the scruffy woman who...' She glanced at the back of Yash's head. 'What's Beth's boyfriend got to do with all of this?' she asked instead, but Yash swung around on the chair, causing her to flinch.

'She doesn't know anything, Cal. Let's keep it that way,' he said, talking about her as if she wasn't in the room.

'She might shed some light on why Narcifer's been acting the way he is.'

'Narce is working for the committee,' Yash said. He waved a dismissive hand and turned back to the two-way mirror. 'Our alliance is with Aldarn,' he added. 'Your head will be fucked up if you continue to play happy families.'

'I'm not giving up on Narcifer!' Calder snapped.

Yash made a sound of disapproval but didn't turn around. Instead, he played with the dials, making the man in the interrogation room spin again.

'Narcifer hates the committee,' she implored Calder, and he turned back to her. 'He was gutted that he had to go against you and look out for James. But he's doing that for me because I don't want him to die. James has become a friend over this last year.'

'So you *do* know something?'

'I...' Macy floundered and looked helplessly up at Calder. 'I only know that James is my friend, and Narcifer couldn't bring himself to kill him,' she finally said.

'"Couldn't kill him" and "protecting him" are two different things,' said Calder, 'and Narcifer *is* protecting James. Do you know why?'

She shook her head but felt heat steal over her face.

'I think you know.'

She shook her head again. 'I don't, honestly. Narcifer admitted he was protecting James, but he never told me why. Lately, he's seemed so confused and distressed. I've been worried about him.'

Calder searched her face, making her feel like he was trying to get into her thoughts. Finally, he smiled.

'I believe you,' he said. 'And Narcifer would want to protect you by keeping you in the dark.'

'I've begged him to tell me what's going on, but he always just says it's Jelvian business.'

'Unfortunately, it's more likely that Narcifer is working for the committee and killing people when they instruct. That isn't his fault,' he added. 'The committee can be vicious if they are refused. The longer we distance ourselves from them, the weaker their influence becomes, but Narce returned sometime last year. He'd struggled to manage them until he met you. Somehow your presence helped him, but then—'

'Then I ended up in the hospital, and he reverted,' Macy finished for him.

Calder nodded.

'Earlier you mentioned Beth's boyfriend. What did you mean?' Macy had barely thought about the straggly-haired woman who had come to her hospital bedside months ago. Now she was suddenly important.

'Her boyfriend, Harry, is related to James. Through Harry, we discovered James' whereabouts, except that we sent the wrong man to kill James.'

'You sent Narcifer,' she said pointlessly.

Calder nodded. 'We wanted him to do it because he struggled with the committee. We thought killing someone on our own personal list would give him relief. Since then, Narcifer's tried to find Aldarn, and we all know James is looking for Aldarn. So the question becomes—Is Narcifer working for the committee, or is he working for James?'

Macy felt her bottom lip tremble. She bit down on it and gathered her emotions together. Her heart was still hammering, and she felt sick with unspent energy.

'No,' she said. 'The question is, who's taken Narcifer?'

THIRTY-ONE

Yash escorted Macy to Narcifer's room. She tried not to notice that he locked the door behind him when he left. She hadn't wanted to be here and had protested that she could get a taxi home, but Calder and Yash wanted her to stay. She wasn't sure of Yash's intentions, but Calder insisted it was for her safety, and she had no option but to believe him.

Macy stepped inside, and her cold feet sank into a luxurious cream carpet. The room was wide and spacious, and two steps ran its length, dividing it into two levels. On the higher level were a large four-poster bed, a dresser, and a spacious wardrobe with Narcifer's clothes neatly folded or hung up on hangers. They were all freshly washed, and no matter how hard she pressed her face into the clothing, she couldn't smell him. She moved around the bedroom, looking for things that might make her feel close to Narcifer.

She turned to the lower level, which held a circular table, two chairs, a poorly stocked fridge, and a coffee dispenser. She flicked it morosely with a finger, watched a light come on, then sighed and looked around the room again. Her gaze fell on the large bay window dressed with cream curtains tied back with pale green ties. It had a pastel green window seat beneath it. There were two smaller windows on either side, their green curtains tied back with cream ties. Everything in the room was perfectly matched.

It was a minimalist room decorated in cream and pale green; nothing about it reminded her of Narcifer. There was no *mess*—nothing that told her the room was lived in. It was all very sterile. Beautiful but sterile.

Macy leaned over the window seat and looked out. She had a clear view of the helipad from here. It was lit up and cast an eerie orange light over the ground. She was about to turn away when she heard the *chugger-chugger* sound of a helicopter. Pressing her forehead against the windowpane, she searched the starry sky.

Suddenly, something black broke her view, and she jumped back. With her heart thumping, she moved to turn the light off, then crept back to the window and peered out again, in time to see the helicopter land smoothly on the helipad. The *chugger-chugger* sound vibrated through her bones as the blades rotated in a blur. She blinked, almost missing the figures jumping from the helicopter and running towards the house.

She pressed her face against the window and made a tunnel with her hands, trying to see if one of the men was Narcifer. But the figures quickly moved out of the orange light and were impossible to see. She couldn't even make out whether they were human or Jelvian.

She sat back on the window seat and nibbled on a nail. She hoped they were friendly, whoever they were. She was in a precarious position and had no way to protect herself.

The helicopter's blades were still whirring, and the sound had got into her head. It felt like her brain was pounding. Then, the noise suddenly changed, growing louder before the volume dropped.

Macy scrambled to her knees, looking out just as the helicopter disappeared overhead. She looked at the starry sky long after the helicopter's noise had faded. Then, finally, the orange light of the helipad faded into the dark, leaving Macy staring at her reflection in the window.

She sat with a thump on the window seat. She felt useless—useless and hopeless. She didn't even know if Calder or Yash were helping him. Neither Jelvia seemed to be on Narcifer's side. They thought he was working against them to hand Aldarn over to the committee.

Suddenly, Macy was crying. Not bothering to control herself, she drew her knees into her chest and sobbed. There was no one to hear her, and she felt as if she'd been opened and had her heart wrenched out.

At last, her sobs became shudders rippling through her body. She sat up and dragged her hand over her face. She didn't feel any better. She reached over and flicked on the light. The glare stung her eyes, and she winced. She thought she heard a knock, but her head was still filled with the *chugger-chugger* of the helicopter, and she couldn't be sure.

The knock came again.

'Just a minute,' she said, uncurling her legs and groaning at the stiffness. She wiped her face with the back of her hand. Her eyes felt heavy. Her injured leg was uncooperative, and she hobbled to the door. 'Okay, you can come in.'

She expected to see Calder or Yash, but the Jelvian woman she'd seen earlier unlocked the door and pushed it open. Macy's shoes were dangling from one hand, and in the other, she held a pizza box; a bottle of cola was tucked beneath her arm. She must have heard Macy crying, but there was no empathy on her face.

She came in, dropped the shoes on the carpet, and set the pizza and cola roughly on the table.

'I'm Macy. You must be Bren?' Macy said, attempting friendliness. She held out a hand.

The Jelvian woman strode back towards the door without glancing Macy's way. Macy thought she would leave without saying anything, but then the woman stopped and turned to run a brief glance over Macy.

'Why has he brought you *here?*' Bren asked, ignoring Macy's hand. She looked so hostile and unfriendly that Macy shivered under her cold Jelvian glare. 'It's usually the blue room he brings his bitches back to.'

'Excuse me?' Macy said.

Bren turned and slammed out of the room, and Macy heard her locking the door a moment later. Macy stared at it, reeling at the woman's belligerence. She drew a ragged breath. She wasn't going to overthink it. She had more important things on her mind, like trusting Calder and Yash to help Narcifer.

Macy looked at the table where Bren—or whoever she was—had tossed the pizza box. The cola was fizzing, and Macy wouldn't have put it past the woman to have shaken the bottle so it would explode when she opened it. Above the fridge was an alcove with glasses, and Macy limped over and took one down. She opened the cola carefully, and although it fizzed and spat with each twist of the lid, finally, she was able to fill her glass.

Macy was thirsty but didn't think she could eat anything. She opened the pizza box just to look, and the aroma told her differently. She tore off a piece and ate it standing. Macy had missed lunch, and breakfast had been a long time ago.

Stuffing another slice in her mouth, she pulled out her mobile phone to check the time—almost eight in the evening. Her thumb hovered over the keypad. She was tempted to call Narcifer again, but the strange voice from earlier had scared her.

Macy dropped her phone on the table beside the pizza box. She closed the lid; its aroma was suddenly nauseating. Her leg was still throbbing, but it was nothing compared to the pain in her heart. Suddenly, her stomach lurched. Holding her hand over her mouth, she ran for the bathroom, where she purged her pizza into the toilet bowl.

She hung over the bowl, feeling drained. Finally, she stood up and washed her face in the sink. It was a beautiful bathroom, but Macy was too overwrought to appreciate it. She dried her face and went back into the bedroom. The lingering smell of the pizza threatened more nausea, so she held her breath while she moved the box to the bathroom, firmly closing the door on it.

She needed to sleep.

The sooner she slept, the sooner tomorrow would come, and Calder and Yash would have found Narcifer. And everything would be all right again. She took off her jacket and hung it in the wardrobe next to Narcifer's clothes, feeling some sort of comfort that their clothes were together. Her hands moved to her trousers, but she glanced at the window. Nobody could see in, but Macy was prudish about her body.

Only Narcifer was allowed to see it.

She moved to the bay window to draw the heavy, lined curtains. She found the pull cord and swished them into action when a pair of reflective eyes on the other side of the window sent her reeling backwards with a shriek.

She scuttled around the table and ducked down. When she raised her head to look again, the window was dark and blank. She briefly wondered if she had imagined it—but no, there had definitely been somebody out there looking in at her.

'Fuck,' she said. Her heart was thumping again. With all the stimulation it was getting, she felt lucky she hadn't had a heart attack. She shot out from behind the table and ran to the door. She banged on it.

'Help! Yash! Calder! *Help!*'

She stopped shouting and pressed an ear against the door. She couldn't hear anything. She banged her fists against the door again and screamed at the top of her voice until she heard voices on the other side. She stepped back as the key turned in the door.

It opened, and Yash stood on the other side. He looked like she'd woken him. His long hair was dishevelled, and he was naked from the waist up and barefoot.

Macy pointed to her window. 'Someone was out there!'

Yash passed her and headed towards the window. He looked out. 'What did you see?' he snapped, still peering out the window.

'Not out on the grounds,' she said. 'I saw a face looking in at me. Jelvian—reflective—eyes looking in. And earlier, there was a helicopter, and some men ran out of it. I thought they might have been your friends, but now they're at the window looking for a way in. They're outside, Yash. We're surrounded!'

'What's going on?'

Macy swivelled around to see two more Jelvias at her bedroom door. She hadn't met them before.

'Is Narcifer's girl okay?' asked one.

'She's fine,' Yash answered. He looked back at Macy. 'Look, we swept the grounds. Each and every room has been swept as well. The guy who took Narcifer escaped in a chopper; we know that because some of us saw them leave. The chopper was masquerading as ours, which had gone unnoticed until then. Our dogs are patrolling the grounds—*we* are patrolling the grounds. The helicopter *you* saw was ours. You're safe.'

Macy pointed to the window. 'But I saw reflective eyes!'

'Maybe you had a bad dream?' one Jelvia asked.

'I wasn't asleep,' she said.

He shrugged at her. 'Then I don't know. But I do know I'm missing out on my beauty sleep. I'm going back to bed.' He tossed over his shoulder as he left. 'Hey, Talin, maybe it's time you told Yash what you saw last week.'

Yash and Macy turned to the one he'd called Talin, who looked from Macy and back to Yash again.

'Tell me what?' asked Yash.

Talin pulled a face. 'You want to hear it? Okay, I caught Bren climbing the walls to watch you when you bring your women home.'

'Bren? The Jelvian woman?' asked Macy.

Talin nodded, looking amused. 'I think it was probably her paying you a visit. She's harmless.'

Yash spun away towards the window. Kneeling on the bay window seat, he opened the window and stuck his head out.

His roar, when it came, caused Macy to scuttle backwards.

'Bren, when I catch you, your arse will be a shade of red never seen in a fucking rainbow!'

THIRTY-TWO

Macy clicked her seatbelt into place. Yash's face was dark with suppressed anger as he joined her in the car—or maybe he had vented his anger last night on poor Bren.

The sullen Jelvian woman was apparently in love with Yash. She followed his sexual exploits more intently than he'd realised, leading to her peering in through the window at Macy. Bren must have thought Yash was in the room with her, which would explain why she'd been weird with her. But Macy barely cared. She looked straight ahead as Yash turned the ignition on, not wishing to talk to him.

He drove in silence, which suited her. She disliked him immensely, but her mind was everywhere anyway, and she wouldn't have been capable of a conversation. She was still shaken from yesterday's events; her head pounded, and her stomach churned. So, instead, Macy focused on an idea growing in her mind. When Narcifer returned, she would sell her house, and they'd go somewhere far away, where the committee and Calder wouldn't ever find them. A remote part of Australia, or maybe Tasmania—somewhere nobody would bother them.

Her head was woolly and her eyes were puffy from crying much of the night. Her mind was trapped in reruns of the things that had happened yesterday. She blamed herself for not acting sooner. Instead of hiding under the table, she should have run for the lift and found help straight away.

Trying to regroup her thoughts, she pulled out her phone to check her messages. There were many from Angela, all apologetic and begging for forgiveness. Macy deleted them. She wasn't upset with Angela. She just didn't care.

She opened a text message from Mumma Lisa, checking in on her. There were a few other messages from her old colleagues at

London Echo. They had obviously heard the news that she had resigned and wished her well. She texted them back, thanking them and telling them she hoped they would all keep in touch. Then there was nothing more to occupy her mind. She tucked her mobile back into her handbag and looked out the window.

Yash slowed for traffic lights. Traffic was busy on the road. People were milling around on the pavements, either window-shopping or going about their business. They had no idea of the turmoil inside her head. Such was the chaos of her life that she expected the world around her to be different.

As the lights changed and the car moved off, Macy glanced at Yash, asking, 'Where did you say Calder went?' Before leaving the house, she'd asked where Calder was, but Yash had just shrugged at her.

'I don't know,' he said this time.

She stared at him. He didn't look at her. Instead, his eyes focused on the road as they moved out of traffic and onto a dual carriageway. He either didn't care how she felt or hadn't noticed. She wished she'd been left under the care of one of the other Jelvias she'd seen last night. Nobody could be more unfriendly than Yash.

She had to ask. 'So, Calder's looking for Narcifer?'

'We are not looking for Narcifer anymore,' Yash said.

Macy's eyes filled with tears, and she did her best to keep them at bay. She closed them, determined not to give Yash the satisfaction of crying in front of him.

'Why? *Why* aren't you looking for him?' she asked. She couldn't let it go—she'd *never* let it go.

He didn't answer her at first. Instead, he manoeuvred the car to overtake a slower vehicle, pressing Macy back deep into her seat. Then he indicated to come off at the next junction but changed lanes erratically. Macy checked again to make sure her seatbelt was on.

'We know where Narcifer is. He's been taken back to his island,' he said, finally.

'And nobody thought to *tell* me?'

'You?' The look he gave her suggested that the thought would never have occurred to him.

'Yes, *me!*' she snapped. She rubbed her temples as a flare of pain caught her unawares. He shrugged again. He wasn't going to answer. She fell silent and felt angry and upset.

Soon they were in Richmond, where Macy lived. Yash turned onto Macy's road and parked outside her house. She hadn't expected him to turn the engine off and was surprised when he did. Then, unclipping his seatbelt, he said, 'I'll come in and make sure your house is secure.'

'You don't need to,' she said. She didn't want Yash poking around her and Narcifer's house. She took off her seatbelt and pushed open the door as Yash circled the car to help her.

'How are your injuries?' he asked.

'Fine,' she snapped again. She didn't like Yash, and he didn't like her—he probably didn't like anyone—and the sooner she saw the back of him, the better. 'I told you I don't need any help.' She pulled her house keys from her handbag, but Yash grabbed them from her and unlocked the door. He went in first and moved around the lower floor as Macy glared at his back.

She looked down. There was a lot of mail on the carpet. She bent to scoop it up from the floor while Yash ran up the stairs, two at a time.

Among the mail, Macy saw another handwritten letter from WUM. Listening to Yash move up into her loft, she ripped it open.

Macy,

Phil and I waited outside the gates for two hours. I'm sorry you decided you'd rather not interview us. Please change your

mind. **I know this is hard, but it's imperative that you hear us out. Please stay in contact.**

Oliver.

Shit! She'd forgotten all about the meeting with Phil yesterday. Yash dropped back down from her loft space in the attic, and she folded the letter up, returned it to its envelope, and put it in her pocket.

'All secure,' Yash said, coming down the stairs.

Tossing the letters onto the coffee table, she sat on the settee and massaged her bad leg. It ached after all the activity last night. She hadn't slept either and felt jetlagged and disorientated.

'You said your leg was fine,' he said.

She looked up. 'You didn't really want to know how it was?' she said sarcastically.

Yash cocked his head at her. 'I don't ask unnecessary questions.'

'Neither do I. And when *I* ask a question, I like it to be answered, not ignored.'

'When did you ask me a question that I ignored?'

'This morning, when I asked where Calder was, you just shrugged at me.'

He shrugged again, saying, 'Doesn't that mean "I don't know"?'

'I... Yes, it does,' she said with a sigh.

'I *don't* know where Calder is at this precise time. All I know is that he arranged to meet another group of Jelvias last night. But he never got there.'

Macy raked her hair. 'I don't believe this! He went on a jolly while Narcifer was missing? And why didn't anyone tell me where Narcifer was taken until now?'

'You've only just asked me, and I answered you.'

She stared at him, trying to decide if he was mocking her. His face was as surly as usual. 'I can't work you out,' she said at last.

'Narcifer will be okay. They've taken him back to his island, probably to question him over Aldarn's whereabouts. He'll be questioned, and he'll be released if his answers are satisfactory.'

'So, I... what now? Do I just wait for Narcifer to come home?'

'That's exactly what you do.' He dug into his back pocket and brought out a small box. He handed it to her. 'Before Calder left, he asked me to give you this,' he said.

She opened it to reveal a dark blue bracelet. She looked up at him. 'What's this?'

'Security,' he said. 'Wear it all the time. When you press the button, someone from Keats will call you. We'll come to you if we don't get an answer.'

'A tracker?' she asked, turning it over in her hands. It looked like a fitness tracker. The screen showed the time with several small buttons around the side.

'For your safety, any button will link back to Keats. Don't hesitate to use it. Are there any questions?'

She dropped the bracelet back into its box and shook her head at him.

'Put it on,' he said.

Wordlessly, she took it back out of the box and fixed it around her wrist.

'Don't take it off. It's waterproof.' Abruptly, Yash turned to the door. As he stepped into the hallway, Macy suddenly had a million questions.

'Yash, wait,' she said and scrambled from her sitting position, wincing as her leg protested at the sudden movement. Then, worried he wouldn't stop, she grabbed the back of his T-shirt as he opened the front door.

'I do not like clingy females,' Yash said, jerking his body away from her as if she repulsed him.

Her hand dropped away. 'I'm not clingy! Christ, my boyfriend's been kidnapped. Don't you understand how I'm feeling right now?'

Yash had offered only a flimsy reason why Narcifer had been kidnapped by his people—at least, it seemed flimsy to her.

'No, I don't know how you're feeling,' Yash said. 'Feelings and emotions are bred out of us.'

'Narcifer's weren't!'

'Narcifer has always wanted to be human. You may see a change in him once he's back.'

They stared at one another.

'Anything else?' he asked.

She shook her head and watched him leave, pulling the front door closed after him. She locked it, then limped into the kitchen and pulled open the drawer that held the painkillers the hospital doctor had prescribed her. But she hesitated: the pain in her leg was bearable. Taking the pills would make her sleepy, and she couldn't afford to be tired. So she closed the drawer on them. She would have to put up with the pain. Her headache could be cured with a couple of aspirin.

She made herself a coffee, making it extra strong, feeling she needed to be alert. She glanced in the fridge, knowing she should eat something. She'd eaten next to nothing last night, but her stomach was clenching and unclenching in worry for Narcifer, and she didn't want to be sick again. Closing the fridge door, Macy moved into the dining room with her drink.

She sat with a sigh on the settee, setting her coffee on the low table. The mail she had tossed aside earlier reminded her of the WUM letter in her back pocket. She pulled it out and dropped it on the table with the rest, but the bracelet on her wrist caught her eye. It was pretty, not clunky, like most fitness trackers, but its prettiness didn't take away it was a tracking device.

She lowered her hand and fell back against the settee with a grunt. She couldn't sit here and wait like Yash instructed. She *had* to do something. But even as she thought about the events leading to Narcifer's kidnap, the logic wasn't there. Even if it made sense that James was blackmailing Narcifer, *how* was he achieving it so effectively? And did that have anything to do with his abduction?

And then there was Phil Zmin and Oliver, wanting to avenge Tsung Zmin's death and creating WUM to do it—and if that was true, where did James fit in with the group? Again, James seemed to crop up all the time.

So many questions. Not enough answers.

Macy picked up her coffee and took a sip.

Most of all, she wanted to know why and how James was blackmailing Narcifer. But then, a thought struck her, and she sat up, suddenly alert. Grabbing her phone, she searched for James Sullivan's nephew, Harry. He was easy to find. He and his father owned a pub chain called the Everson Pub Company.

Frustrated with her phone's small screen, Macy grabbed her coffee. She took it upstairs to her office to continue to cyberstalk James' nephew, Harry. She discovered that he and Beth lived in a pub called the Rabbit Warren in Bromley. It was listed as a 'premium pub, bar, and restaurant with a garden and courtyard centrally located in the heart of the picturesque town of Bromley'. Not wanting to waste time, Macy telephoned the Rabbit Warren. But she was disappointed and told Mr and Mrs Everson-Watts were on their honeymoon in Jamaica.

'And do you know where I can find James Sullivan?' she asked.

'I don't know anyone by that name,' the person on the line replied.

Macy was glad the shabbily dressed woman had sorted her life out, but Macy wouldn't learn anything from Beth or Harry anytime soon. Back on her computer, Macy found the Everson Pub

Company's details and took down the phone number for its head office, thinking she could speak to Mr Everson-Watts, Senior.

She clicked a link that brought up photos and bios of Mr Everson-Watts and his son. The son, Harry, was blond and looked very handsome, Macy thought. The father was grey-haired, posing next to a woman Macy presumed was his wife. The bio told how the family had been rocked by a tragic death, which moved Mr Everson-Watts, Senior to come out of retirement and begin the Everson Pub chain. Macy wondered if that tragic death had been Leigh, James' wife, the scientist who had worked undercover alongside James for Jon Johnsen.

Macy found an image of Leigh Sullivan, and her likeness to Harry's mum was remarkable. They were obviously sisters, which meant James' only connection to the family was marriage.

Macy yawned. She needed more coffee.

Grabbing her empty cup, she left her office and went back downstairs. Then, a freak gust of air, perhaps divine intervention—Macy couldn't think what caused it, but the WUM letter she had tossed to the table fluttered to the bottom of the stairs as she descended.

She stared at it. She had nothing to lose, and she wasn't going to get anywhere with Harry Everson-Watts.

She turned and ran back upstairs to grab her phone before she changed her mind.

THIRTY-THREE

Within minutes of calling Phil Zmin, Macy had arranged another meeting.

The woman was definitely peeved with her failing to show up yesterday, but Macy ignored her annoyance and refused to apologise or give any excuses.

Macy didn't want Phil to come to her home; neither did she want to be far away if Narcifer returned. She suggested they meet in a pub near her house, and Phil said she'd be there in two hours. Macy didn't know where she was coming from and didn't ask.

Upstairs, she changed out of the business suit she'd worn so proudly yesterday and pulled on a pair of jeans, a T-shirt, and a hoodie. She didn't think she was mentally strong enough to meet Phil, but it was too late to back out now.

The half-mile car journey to the pub felt like a marathon. She climbed into her car, her body feeling like an eighty year old's, and reversed off her driveway. She almost hit an old, black Volvo parked across the road. Her headache was still raging despite taking painkillers, and her leg ached, yet her body was awash with endorphins that made her jittery.

The Black Horse pub was a hotspot for the local youth, but it was usually quiet during the day. Macy thought she was the first to arrive, but as she headed to the bar to order a Coke, she saw a thick-set man approaching. She recognised him as Oliver.

'I'll get this,' he said with a smile.

Macy didn't argue. She followed him to the table where Phil Zmin was waiting. She stood up at Macy's approach and held out a hand. Macy didn't see any point in formalities, but she shook her hand anyway. She couldn't be bothered to annoy the woman.

'Thanks for coming at such short notice,' Macy said, sitting down and taking control of the situation. 'This interview is neither formal nor recorded, but before we start, I want to know what you *think* you know about Jelvias.'

Phil's dark eyes studied her as if wondering what she had failed to grasp during their last meeting. She was dressed more casually this time—they'd obviously left in a hurry, and Phil hadn't given much thought to her clothes. Her hair was pulled up in a quick ponytail held with a scrunchie, and there wasn't any makeup on her face.

'I know a lot about Jelvias,' Phil said, sounding arrogant. 'We know that SOHO, the Heliospheric Observatory, first brought to our attention six years ago that extraterrestrial objects were on a collision course with Earth. We know that NASA and HAARP worked together to study them. The world was on high alert, but as they got closer, it all changed. The world stopped caring. Even before the aliens landed, they were controlling us. We were all put under the same illusion you're under at this very moment. We were blinkered to the alien invasion, believing them to be meteorites—our air defence wasn't even activated. Then, on the ninth of March, almost six years ago, nine alien spaceships masquerading as meteorites landed in the Atlantic and Arctic Oceans around Iceland, Norway, and the UK. The tenth was shot down.'

While Phil spoke, the words rolling out of her mouth with enthusiasm, Macy glanced at Oliver. He nodded along, looking fiercely proud.

'Those nine spaceships are still there. You call them the Jelvian islands, but they're spaceships. Somehow, when *you* look at them through a telescope or fly over them, you see a blanket of fog around them, which you've labelled as a weather phenomenon. No human has claimed to have visited them—some even say they're an environmental haven for endangered animal species. But to those who have woken up, they are nine hideous charcoal-black spaceships.' Phil came to a halt and looked across at Macy smugly. 'Maybe you should have recorded me, after all.'

She had a lot of confidence—too much confidence. Macy studied her. No, it was more than that. Phil seemed to be one of those brainy, geeky types who looked down on ordinary people.

'You haven't said anything yet that I haven't already heard. It's all on your podcast,' Macy said, hoping to wipe the smugness off Phil's face.

'So, what do you want to know?'

'How come *you* know all this, yet intelligent people—no offence—are under the same so-called illusion that I am? Why doesn't anyone from NASA or anywhere else know about it?'

'My guess is that many people do know but believe themselves crazy,' Oliver interjected softly as Phil's face finally lost its arrogance. They were an odd couple but finely tuned. Macy wondered if they were an item.

'We used to be under the same illusion you're under now,' Phil said. 'I can't speak for Ollie, but I woke suddenly knowing that alien spaceships had landed in the sea. My memories were confused. I couldn't understand why I remembered televised reports of meteorites heading our way, yet I also remembered seeing them as spaceships.

'My dad thought I was having a breakdown and paid privately for me to see a psychiatrist. The psychiatrist believed I had a psychotic episode. He prescribed anti-psychotic drugs, which zombified me. Eventually, I was given electroconvulsive therapy, which wasn't the most pleasant experience, so I pretended I was cured. It was frustrating and scary to know that aliens had landed and were walking among us, killing us, yet everyone called them Jelvias, shrugged their shoulders, and allowed them to do whatever they wanted. I'd tried speaking out, but I was labelled "mad", so what else could I do? I shut up.'

Macy stared. While Phil spoke, her eyes were fixed on Macy as if she could read her thoughts.

'You didn't, though. Instead, you started the WUM group,' Macy said.

'Yes, eventually, Oliver and I started WUM. My dad was a cytologist. He was very clever, but the Jelvias fascinated him. And I think he felt partly responsible for my "illness" because he often brought his work home. I don't know how he got involved with Jon Johnsen, aka William Springfield, but he did, and you know the rest.'

'Yes. Johnsen tricked the Jelvias and killed many when he blew up their helicopter. Aldarn has never recovered, not properly,' Macy said.

'Except it wasn't a helicopter,' Oliver said.

'So you claim,' Macy said, 'but I beg to differ.'

'My dad made mistakes,' Phil said. 'His biggest one was getting involved with Johnsen. But once he *did* get involved, I think the stress woke him up. He remembered everything and was beside himself for not believing me. He remembered the facts as I remember them—not as a fantasy forced upon us by alien beings.'

Macy sat back in her seat, sighing at the word "alien". She picked up her drink and took a sip. Then she looked over the rim at Phil and asked, unable to control the sarcastic undertone, 'Where did these *aliens* come from?'

Phil shrugged. 'No one knows. All we know is that they've invaded Earth.'

I love you to the moon and back.

I love you to Itor and back.

Itor? Where's that?

It's a planet, isn't it?

Never heard of it.

The memory of her conversation with Narcifer hit her like a sledgehammer. She usually remembered all his quirks or wrote down all the amusing or silly things he said or did. This one she had forgotten until now. She remembered her sense of déjà vu after

Narcifer attacked the helicopter. Then she remembered her incorrect drawing of the Jelvian islands.

'There are only four Jelvian islands,' she said, thinking she had caught Phil out. 'Earlier, you said nine spaceships landed and masqueraded as islands.'

'Yeah. You'll probably *remember* that there are nine islands when the Jelvias want you to know there are nine,' Phil said casually. She picked up her drink and clinked the ice cubes around the glass, watching them bash together.

Macy stared at Phil as she continued to play with her drink. One moment she gave the impression she was younger, the next, she seemed older than her years. Then, finally, Macy swung her attention to Oliver, who had listened to their conversation but was not saying much.

'What's your story? Are you two an item?'

He smiled. 'No, we're not an item.'

Phil gave a hoot of laughter, and his smile waned. He looked hurt.

'My story is similar to Phil's, but I woke up a lot later than she did,' he said, recovering. 'It was probably about two years ago, and like Phil, I thought I was going mad. She saved my life. Without going into all the very personal details, I lost everything when I remembered. I ended up in the hospital. Phil was working there, and she took the time to listen to me—probably because my madness was her truth.'

Macy glanced down at his hands, cradling his glass of orange juice, and noticed the scars on his wrists. Then, as if he felt her stare, he dropped his hands into his lap, pulling his sleeves down over his wrists to hide them.

He had attempted to take his own life. Macy lifted her gaze and met his across the table. He was a giant of a man, but he was a gentle giant. Obviously unnerved by her stare, he tried to mask nonchalance by picking up his drink and taking a swig.

Macy looked over at Phil. 'Which hospital did you practise in?'

'Chigwell,' she said. 'I resigned not long after I met Oliver.'

How she switched from Oliver to Ollie made Macy wonder if Oliver was his preferred name outside their group and if "Ollie" was spoken by mistake. They probably had a vote and decided that "Ollie" was too unprofessional. Macy sipped her drink to hide her smile.

'Long story short,' said Oliver. 'As far as we were concerned, the world had gone mad. Aliens, calling themselves Jelvias, had arrived in ten small spaceships, killing us, and governments worldwide were allowing it.'

'Oh, come on!' Macy couldn't help herself.

'I don't expect you to believe us,' he said, 'not yet, anyway. But maybe we can change your mind?'

Macy rolled her eyes.

Smiling, Oliver reached underneath the table and picked up a backpack. He rested it on the table. 'We realised they'd corrupted not only our minds but the Internet, so to prove our cause, we use books and historical documents from the library. May I show you?'

Resigned, Macy nodded.

Still smiling, Oliver unzipped the backpack and took out a book, followed by another and then another. They all went on top of each other.

'Information online simply did not match physical books or documents. So we concluded that since the memories were so strong in people's heads, why would anyone check anything in a book? Books couldn't be changed without being destroyed, but the technology was distorted.' He nodded at the books. 'Please. Take a look.'

Pushing her Coke to one side, Macy reached for the top book. It was a small Ladybird book she recognised from her school days, titled *James I and the Gunpowder Plot*.

Feeling bemused, she paged through it. Then, frowning, she flicked back, then forwards again. Finally, she looked up at Oliver.

'There's no mention of Jelvias.' She closed the book and looked at the cover. The picture was of a human man, not a Jelvia. But her memory was clear from what she had read on the Internet: A group of Jelvian men had banded together to overthrow Parliament by using gunpowder to blow it up. Every year on 5th November, England commemorated its failure with a ritual of letting off fireworks and building bonfires with an effigy of the Jelvia called Guy Fawkes.

She picked up another book, which was also designed for children. There was no mention of Jelvias in it either.

'Of course, there isn't,' Phil said with a scoff. She pushed across a hardback book called *Faith and Treason: The Story of the Gunpowder Plot*. 'Try that one,' she said.

Macy opened it and scanned the pages. No Jelvias.

'And now this,' Phil said, pulling out an iPad. She jabbed at it and then pushed it towards Macy. 'I've just searched "gunpowder plot", and you can see the difference.'

The article was about a Jelvia named Robert Catesby, the brains behind the terror act in 1605. Guy Fawkes was a Jelvia who, along with others, attempted to blow up King James I and Parliament on 5th November 1605.

'All this proves is that you carefully picked books that deleted Jelvias from history. I've seen that sort of thing happen countless times.' Macy pushed the iPad back across the table. 'The Jelvias were rallying against the poor treatment against them.'

'No, you can pick up any book from a library, bookshop, anywhere, but they'd be no mention of Jelvias. It was obviously overlooked. Maybe they thought their memory-altering drug, or whatever they'd done to us, would make us not believe what was written in books? Well... it didn't make *us* not believe, just the majority of the human race.'

Macy scowled at her, but Phil looked back deadpan, and Macy couldn't tell whether she had been flippant with her. Phil typed something else into the iPad. She pushed it back towards Macy before delving into the backpack again and taking out another book. Looking excited, she handed it over. The title read *Suffragettes and the Fight for the Vote.*

Phil tapped the iPad. 'And here is the same book online.'

Macy looked at the iPad. It was an identical cover to the book in front of her, but the title read *Jelvias and the Fight to Live.*

'The proof is all around you,' Phil said, tapping the book's cover. 'You just need to see it.'

Macy rubbed the back of her neck. These people couldn't help her. They were out-of-control bigots. Macy pushed her chair back to give herself a little space. They both must have thought she intended to leave because Oliver put his hand on Phil's as if to stop her from obstructing Macy's exit.

'We can't make her remember, Phil. Her memories, like our memories, are authentic to her.' He looked at Macy. 'I know it's a lot to take in, especially when you believe your memories are real.'

Phil's bottom lip protruded in a pout as Oliver gathered up the books, tucked them away in the backpack, and then put it back on the floor by his feet.

'Sorry,' he said, noticing Macy eyeing Phil's petulant expression with distaste. 'Phil can be very passionate about this, but we both feel we don't have much time. It's taken too long for us to realise we aren't crazy, too long to gather together the few people who have the same memories as us.'

Macy raised her eyebrows. 'When I was caught up in one of your protests the other day, all the roads were blocked, and it sounded like the whole of London was protesting. You have more than a *few* people.'

'It looks like it, doesn't it? But the reality is that many just want Jelvias controlled, locked away, or blown up,' he said with a regretful smile. 'The majority still believe Jelvias have been here forever, just like you. James Sullivan is the most prominent person we know who has woken up, but he doesn't want to be involved with our group.'

'He's woken up?' Macy frowned. 'Has he told you this?'

'Yes. He woke up at a similar time when my dad woke up. I think it was the stress of working for Johnsen.' Phil took up the conversation. 'He told us after Johnsen's death. He was scared. He knew he was next on the list to be exterminated and wanted us to know he was awake before he died.'

'James *rescued* the Jelvias! He let the other Jelvias in to release them,' Macy said. This was something that had always puzzled her. Calder was baying for James' blood, but James wasn't responsible for them being in Johnsen's hands.

'So James says,' Phil said.

'You don't believe him?'

'Whether I believe him or not doesn't matter. It's whether the Jelvias believe him that counts.'

'James wasn't directly involved with the laboratory experiments, but his wife was. And she subsequently died for it,' said Oliver. Macy's face swung towards him. 'There is so much misinformation out there. It really is hard to sieve the truth from lies. You can go mad trying.'

'Want to know the name of a *Jelvia* who has woken up?' Phil said casually. The triumph on her face was unmistakable. 'Aldarn.'

THIRTY-FOUR

Macy made a great show of picking up her Coke and taking a few sips. She hoped her face didn't betray the agitation roaring through her body and that Phil couldn't hear the racket of her thumping heart. She tried to calm herself but could see the liquid tremble in the glass from the force of her pounding pulse.

'I'll get us another round of drinks,' Oliver said, breaking into her thoughts. 'Is anyone hungry? I noticed they do bar food here. I can order a few bowls of chips for us to pick at.'

Macy barely glanced at him. Her phone pinged an alert on the table next to her. Macy grabbed it, but it was just Angela realising she'd been blocked and using another method to leave a message. Macy put the phone back down, feeling emotionally whipped.

'Problem?' Phil said.

Macy glanced up. It was just the two of them. Oliver had gone to the bar.

Desperate for a distraction, Macy blurted the first thing that came to her mind, 'Why do you call yourself Oswald and not Zmin?'

'It's my mum's name. It connects me to her. Her name was Philippa Oswald. I'm Li Jing.'

'She died?'

'Yeah. Cancer, when I was twelve.'

'My mum died when I was the same age,' Macy said, wondering if she'd judged Phil too harshly. At such a young age, the death of a parent could affect a child immensely. 'I'm sorry to hear about your mum's passing.'

'Thanks. Sorry about your loss, too.'

Macy forced a smile. She hadn't missed the change in Phil's demeanour. She'd gone from tense to soft moments after mentioning her mum. So while Phil's guard was lowered, Macy tried to get more details from her. 'So, what makes you think Aldarn has woken up?' she asked nonchalantly.

'I don't think it. I *know* it,' Phil said.

And that quickly, the hardness was back. The quiet insistence in Phil's voice rubbed Macy the wrong way.

'He's recovering from the experiments Jon Johnsen and *your father* did on him,' she said. 'They opened up his head to study his brain. They broke and re-broke his legs to see how quickly the Jelvian body could repair itself. They tried to remove his venom sac. They almost killed him. Aldarn hasn't "woken up"; he's brain-damaged,' Macy said, but Phil slowly shook her head.

'So why me?' Macy asked when it was clear Phil wasn't going to say anything. 'Why do you want *me*, in particular, to wake up? If I were you, I'd be hounding my local MP.'

'Believe me, we have. It was either you or Courtney.'

Macy baulked at this, but Phil didn't seem to notice. Rubbing her eyes, Macy wondered how much more she could take. She hadn't got much sleep and was tired and probably still in shock from yesterday evening.

'What made you agree to see us now?' Phil asked suddenly.

'I'm going to debunk you,' Macy said and felt genuine pleasure at the irritation on Phil's face.

But Phil recovered quickly. 'I also know that Narcifer, the Jelvia you live with, is the person who killed my father.' Macy's smile dropped from her face, but Phil continued talking as if she hadn't dropped that bomb. 'Narcifer isn't to blame. He does what the committee tells him to. But, like all Jelvias, he's a puppet of the committee.'

'Narcifer and the rest of the team only kill criminals. Criminals like your father.' Macy couldn't help but throw a bigger bomb back.

'We're not here to change your mind about Jelvias. We're here just to give you our side of the story.'

'Then I'll give you mine,' Macy said, leaning forwards. 'My life with Narcifer was a constant struggle from the get-go. We fell in love—it was so instant it felt clichéd, but that's how it was. Narcifer and I *clicked*. It was as if he knew what I was thinking and vice versa. And so far, we've had every possible hurdle thrown our way. But you know what? We're still together, and we're still in love.'

'And those hurdles will keep coming because you and Narcifer can't be. You just can't be.'

Macy stared at her. She was unaware that her eyes had filled with tears until she caught Phil looking at her in astonishment. Then her hand snaked across the table and clutched Macy's.

'I'm sorry. I can see I've touched a nerve,' she said.

Macy pulled her hand away and wiped her eyes. 'You haven't. I'm still feeling the effects of the car crash.'

Oliver came back with three drinks clasped in his hands, but Macy stood up, pushing her chair back and almost knocking into him in her hurry. He looked at her in alarm.

'I've heard enough,' Macy said, grabbing her phone. 'I'm going.'

'Hey, what?' Oliver said. 'I've ordered three bowls of chips!'

But Macy was already walking out of the pub. She didn't care what they thought of her. She didn't care about the dynasty of the Jelvias, the committee, or anyone.

All she cared about was Narcifer and finding him.

THIRTY-FIVE

It was getting dark as she drove out of the car park. Her hands were jittery on the wheel, and her entire body felt heavy. She drove home on autopilot and pulled into her driveway, feeling numb. The black Volvo still sat across the road. She didn't recognise the car, nor was there any reason for it to be parked where it was. The windows were blacked out, and Macy was almost sure it was a police surveillance car, but she barely cared.

She pushed open the car door and caught sight of the bracelet on her wrist. It reminded her of Yash. She wished she had taken his phone number to check if Narcifer had called anyone at Keats. Still sitting in her car, she chewed on her lip and stared at the bracelet. She could always press the button, making Yash call *her*. Heart hammering, she pushed it before she could change her mind.

It was only seconds before her mobile phone rang with an unknown number.

Macy answered her phone with a hesitant, 'Hello?'

'Answer "yes" if you need assistance or "no" if you don't,' an unknown voice said. It wasn't Yash's surly voice. Neither was it Calder's more dulcet tone.

'I...' Macy floundered. 'No, I'm fine. I just want to know if you've heard anything from Narcifer.'

There was no answer.

'Hello?' They'd hung up on her. The climb out of her car was like the last ten-metre climb up a mountain. She heaved herself out, almost too tired to put one foot in front of the other.

Her house was in darkness, and it was quiet—horribly quiet. Without turning on any lights, Macy threw her handbag onto the settee and limped upstairs. She changed into her pyjamas and wrapped her dressing gown around her body. It was barely evening, but Macy suddenly felt utterly deflated with overwhelming fatigue.

Her head was pounding, and her leg was still aching. It was probably psychological, but it was as if someone had pressed an off switch on her body, and it was shutting down. She sat on the edge of her bed. It looked so inviting right now. She lay down, telling herself she'd close her eyes for a minute.

Macy opened her eyes, wondering what had woken her. She felt cold, and remembering how she fell asleep, she sat up to drag the duvet over her. Her eyes caught the time on the digital clock on the TV. It was two in the morning. She groaned and pulled the quilt around her head.

Then she heard it. The rattle of the back door. And she knew it wasn't the cold that had woken her.

She pulled the duvet down and lay listening. The rattling stopped, and then there was no more noise until a loud smash made her sit up in alarm.

Flipping back the duvet, she swung her legs out of bed. She moved to her bedroom door and pulled it open. All was dark out on the landing. She closed the door and thought about pushing something against it to hold it closed while she called the police, but remembered her handbag, with her phone, was downstairs.

Another smash made Macy jump.

She opened the door a crack, knowing she had to leave. Her bedroom had no lock. Whoever had got into the house could easily get into her bedroom. She needed to move somewhere safer. Macy tiptoed out onto the landing as she heard someone coming in through the back door downstairs. She heard the cracking of glass under the intruder's feet.

She scuttled towards her office. That room had a lock. She crossed the part of the landing where it met with the stairs and came face-to-face with the intruder climbing up.

Remembering the bracelet, she geared to press it but locked eyes with the intruder instead.

She gasped.

THIRTY-SIX

'Narcifer.'

Her voice was a squeak. She fell back against the wall, her legs suddenly boneless. Her hands flew to her mouth as he climbed the last step and filled the landing with his bulk.

Narcifer looked dishevelled. He was wearing the same clothes, but they were tattered and wet. His black eyes danced with electricity as he met her gaze across the small space. He looked ill.

Macy's hands fell away from her face. She took a step towards him.

'Are you okay?' she asked. She wanted to run into his arms but sensed something different about him. He looked more than ill—no, he looked worn down. Like he'd been to the other side of hell and wasn't fully back yet. She held out her hand towards him. 'Narcifer?'

He stepped towards her; his tread was hesitant. His eyes never wavered from hers. It was as if he didn't want to lose sight of her. Macy held his gaze, her hand still reaching out for him. He didn't look at her hand. He probably didn't even see it.

Macy grabbed his arm as he got closer and ushered him into the bedroom. She sat him on the wing chair beneath the window. He was compliant, his gaze never moving from her face.

'Hey, let's get you dry, eh? You're frozen.'

Narcifer didn't reply, and Macy turned, intending to get a towel from the en-suite bathroom, but Narcifer grabbed her hand and pulled her back. His all-black eyes searched hers. They looked so confused.

'It's okay,' she said, forcing a smile. But inside, she was a turmoil of emotion.

'Macy?' he asked as if he couldn't believe it was her.

'Yes, it's me.' Her eyes filled with tears. 'What have they done to you?' she asked, almost to herself. She sank to her knees and looked up at him. 'It's okay. You're home now. Narcifer? What happened?'

He gave an involuntary shudder as he stared into her shimmering eyes.

'I... not sure,' he said.

He looked and felt cold. Then, pulling from his grip, Macy stood up. She wiped her eyes with her fingers and rolled up the sleeves of her dressing gown.

'Let's get you under a hot shower,' she said. 'Come on, up you get.' Then, speaking to him like a child, she ushered him into the bathroom. 'Can you manage by yourself?' she asked.

Narcifer didn't show her he could, so Macy peeled off his wet clothes and coerced him into the shower. As the water poured over him, he turned to face her through the glass cubicle.

Macy's throat was a solid lump, and her eyes filled again as she watched him looking back at her, so confused. He didn't attempt to wash but stood there gazing at her. He looked so lost. She bent to grab his wet clothes from the floor to disguise her tears.

'I'll just put these in the washing machine,' she said, her voice croaky. She gathered them up in her arms and left him in the shower.

Downstairs, in the kitchen, she shoved the clothes into the washing machine, put them on a quick cycle, and then flipped the kettle on to make Narcifer some hot, sweet tea. While she was waiting for it, she grabbed her mobile phone. The Jelvia who called her after she pressed the bracelet didn't leave a number she could call. She'd have to use the bracelet if she wanted them to know that Narcifer was home.

Back upstairs, she could hear the shower still running. She placed her phone and Narcifer's tea on the dressing table, then poked her head around the bathroom door. Narcifer stood with his hands on the wall. He bowed his head under the shower. The water was pounding down on his naked back.

Almost unconsciously, Macy took off her dressing gown. Narcifer still hadn't noticed her. She pulled off her pyjama top and tossed it to the floor, followed by the bottoms. She stepped into the shower behind Narcifer and slipped her arms around his waist. She pressed her lips against his back and then turned her head to rest her cheek against his flesh. He said a few words in a language she didn't recognise.

She gave him a little squeeze. 'Honey, I don't understand.'

His pause was lengthy. Then he said, 'I don't know if this is real.'

'It's real.' She wanted to question him about the strange language he'd spoken but felt the timing wasn't right. She could feel his body shaking as if he were cold, yet the hot water poured over them, fogging the shower cubicle with steam.

Narcifer turned around, forcing her to let him go. He took hold of her face with gentle hands and tipped her head back. His eyes searched hers.

'Macy, it really *is* you,' he said. Then, cutting off any answer she might have given, he lowered his head and lightly brushed his lips against hers. 'I wasn't sure... but I had to check...' he muttered between kisses.

'Sweetheart, what do you mean?' she said—or tried to. Narcifer took possession of her mouth, pushing his tongue deep inside her. Macy slid her hands up his chest to rest on his shoulders as he continued to kiss her. His hands left her face to run down her back until they rested on her hips, pulling her closer. Then he lifted her, and as her legs locked around his waist, he pushed inside her with a grunt.

They made love as the water cascaded over their heads. Normally, making love was an intense and romantic experience; this time, Macy felt it was a need in him—as if he was seeking shelter in her body.

When he came inside her, she remained locked to him; he continued to hold her, his face buried against her shoulder. She held his head against her, feeling him soften inside her.

'Hey, hun,' she said when she felt he might keep them locked in their embrace, inside the shower cubicle, forever. 'Shall we get dry now?'

As if reluctant, he let her slide to the floor. Macy turned off the shower, grabbed a towel, and wrapped it around Narcifer. She picked up her dressing gown from the floor and slipped it on as she urged Narcifer to follow her into the bedroom.

He sat on the edge of the bed while Macy got another towel and wrapped that around his upper body. Despite the hot shower, he was still shivering. She towel-dried her hair quickly while watching him. Then she sat next to him. She nudged him with her shoulder.

'Hey,' she said and smiled when he looked at her, 'it's okay. You're home now.'

He gave her a feeble smile in return. 'I feel so confused. Confused and weak.'

'Can you tell me what happened?' she asked. She reached for the tea she'd made, but it was cold. So she left it on the side.

'I... I'm not sure.'

'I've been so worried,' she said and almost started crying. 'Calder said you were taken back to your island.'

'Yes, I was.' He looked surprised for a moment, and then his face darkened. 'I had to face the committee for the crime of being a runaway. I knew what it meant at the time, but now... I don't understand anything.'

'Shh, hun, it's okay. They let you go,' Macy soothed.

'No, they didn't. I got out the same way I escaped the first time. They hadn't found our escape route...' His voice trailed away into nothing, and he sat there looking bewildered. Suddenly, he turned to her, his black eyes anguished. His body gave another involuntary shudder. 'They injected me with something, but I could hear and see everything. I knew you would come back to the control room, and there was nothing I could do to stop you or stop them from hurting you.' She realised he was talking about when he'd been kidnapped in the basement of Keats House. 'I saw you peer around the door. I saw the look on your face when you saw them. Then you ran away, and one of them came after you. I heard him kill you. I heard you scream... He *killed* you, and I couldn't move—'

'Shh—hey, it's okay. He didn't kill me. I got away.' She stood up and pulled back the duvet on the bed, uncaring that their bodies were still damp—she just wanted his shivers to stop. 'Come on, let's get in.'

He nodded and did as asked. She climbed in next to him, and he wrapped his arms around her and held her tight as if he didn't want to let her go. She rested her head against his chest. His heart rate was still erratic, and she didn't think it was because of their lovemaking.

'But it didn't matter that you'd died because you're not real. You're a dream. And this is...' He flung out a hand. '...a dream. A simulation.' His hand fell to the bed, and Macy caught his big wrist, bringing it under the duvet.

'I'm not a dream or a simulation. Your life here isn't a dream.'

He spoke in the weird language again, and this time Macy tried to hold on to the words.

Pounit un.

Whatever the words meant, they sounded urgent.

'Narcifer, they injected you with something. It will probably take a few days to wear off,' she said.

Acting agitated, he sat upright as if to climb out of bed, but Macy grabbed his shoulders and pulled him back. Narcifer turned and cupped her face with his big hands. He stared into her eyes. The confusion in his expression made Macy's heart break. 'There's no way you could escape the Jelvias. This *has* to be a dream,' he said. 'You're a simulation of a life I wish to lead, only I don't usually remember my other life when I'm in... in...' He stopped, looking at her blankly. 'You're real?'

'I'm real,' she said. 'The drug must still be in your system, making everything dreamlike. They didn't catch me. I hid under the table in the corridor.' Something told Macy that she had to answer Narcifer carefully. 'I heard one of the Jelvias run past my hiding place, and when I peeked out, I saw him head into the interrogation room. I think he thought I was in there. So I snuck out and locked him in. As far as I know, he's still there. Then I ran to find Yash.'

He relaxed against the bed, and Macy tucked the duvet around his shoulders again before snuggling against him. She rested her head against his chest, closing her eyes and breathing in his scent.

'He and Calder searched the house and grounds, but you and the remaining Jelvia had vanished,' she continued, her eyes still closed. 'It came out later that they'd put you in a helicopter disguised as one of yours.'

'I remember the helicopter. Three Jelvias carried me inside. Three Wardens...' His voice trailed off.

She raised her head to look up at him. His eyes were closed, and just when she thought he'd fallen asleep, they opened. They had a light in them, a light she'd seen before—like a million diamonds.

'All I could... can... think about is the other Jelvia coming after you. I thought he'd killed you, but it was a dream... you were a dream... so it didn't matter because it was just a dream, and you didn't exist.' His voice faltered until it faded into nothing.

She peered at his face. He looked shattered. His eyes were closed again, but she could tell he wasn't asleep. She pressed her lips against his chest, and in between kisses, she said, 'This isn't a dream, Narce. And he didn't kill me. Stop torturing yourself.'

'The committee wanted to know where Aldarn is... It's all they kept on about. "Where's Aldarn?" "You must bring him to us." "You cannot disobey us." ...Christ, if I knew where he was, I'd hand him over in a heartbeat! James!' His eyes flashed open. 'I need to make sure he's okay. He can't die...'

'Honey, do you mean James Sullivan?'

Narcifer's frown had deepened. 'I don't know,' he said, staring up at the ceiling. Then, slowly, his eyes closed again. His head lolled to one side, and his breathing became regular. He was asleep.

Macy watched him for a while, not liking how his eyes rolled beneath his closed lids. Then, finally, she climbed out of bed carefully, not wanting to wake him. She took off her damp robe and pulled on her pyjamas. Her body was dry.

Narcifer groaned a long and anguished sound. He flung out a hand, his claws exposed. Macy jumped on the bed and pressed her lips against his forehead.

'Shh, it's okay. I'm here,' she said. His clawed hand was inches from her face, but she wasn't afraid. She knew he would never hurt her.

Narcifer became still again, and his claws retracted into his fingertips. Macy slowly moved off the bed when she thought he was asleep again. But it was as if he knew she was leaving him, and he immediately became agitated.

'I'm here,' she said quickly, lying back down. When Narcifer was still, she pressed the button on the blue bracelet. She needed to inform someone from Keats that Narcifer was home. Almost instantly, her mobile phone rang on the dressing table.

Narcifer sat upright, his eyes wide and his throat engorged. His mouth had gaped open as if he were readying himself to spit his venom. Macy sat up with him and put her arms around him.

'Narcifer, it's just my phone. It's okay. I'm here. You're safe now. We're both safe,' she said.

Her mobile continued to ring, and Macy looked at it, knowing if she didn't answer it, Yash or Calder would come over. And, somehow, she thought they'd make it worse—they'd take him away from her to Keats or something.

Narcifer said something in that same foreign language again.

'*Kraovo sa.*'

'What was that, baby?' she asked.

He looked at her blankly.

'What does *kraovo sa* mean?' she asked gently.

'It means...' He trailed off. 'I don't know what it means,' he added helplessly. 'That's your phone ringing. I remember. A phone. Not a dream.' He flopped back on the pillows, looking like a lost little boy. Macy's heart went out to him. She bent and kissed him on the temple and tucked the duvet around him.

'That's right. Just my phone. Why not sleep now?'

His all-black eyes stared at her as she fussed over him. There was no strange diamond-like light there now.

There was only panic.

THIRTY-SEVEN

It hadn't taken long for Narcifer to fall into a deep sleep, so Macy tiptoed out of the bedroom with her now-silent mobile phone. She opened the bedroom door and stepped out on the landing, closing the door behind her. Then, leaning back against the door, she took a huge breath.

Narcifer's strangeness worried her. He looked so confused and scared.

Slowly, Macy went downstairs and unlocked the front door for Yash's or Calder's arrival. She figured they'd already be on their way, and there'd be no point calling to stop them. She swept up the broken glass from the door in the kitchen and threw the shards in the bin. It was the second time Narcifer had broken the back door, but Macy couldn't raise a smile at the irony.

Outside in the back, she hunted through the recycling until she found a broken-down cardboard box to tape over the smashed glass in the door. She worked on autopilot, feeling the need to keep busy. She'd just put the last strip of tape on when she heard a car pull up outside. She rushed through the house towards the front. Outside, Yash and another Jelvia, one Macy vaguely recognised, climbed out from a Rolls-Royce.

Yash approached her. His face was animated as if he was looking for a brawl.

'If you've called us out just to ask where Narcifer is—' he began, and she felt certain he wouldn't hesitate to backhand her.

'No, I called to tell you that Narcifer is home and safe,' she said quickly, 'but when you rang my phone, he became agitated, and I couldn't answer it in time.'

Yash swept past her and into the house, leaving her staring up at the other Jelvia.

'How is he acting?' he asked.

It seemed like an odd question, but Macy was too unsettled by the two Jelvias to give it much thought. 'I... he's acting confused. And he spoke a foreign language.'

She glanced at the surveillance car as the second Jelvia followed Yash inside. The dark Volvo sat there, silent and watching. *Well, let it! Stupid police.* She closed the door on it and followed the Jelvia into the front room.

Yash joined them from the kitchen, demanding, 'Where is he?'

'He's upstairs asleep,' she said. 'Please don't wake him. I think he needs rest.'

Yash looked over her head and addressed the other Jelvia. 'We'll stay until he wakes up.'

Macy didn't want either Jelvia in her house. She didn't like Yash, and the other looked just as unfriendly. His eyes were deep set and looked like holes in his face, and his mouth was down-turned as if he hadn't laughed once in his entire life.

'You needn't stay. I can take care of Narcifer,' Macy said quickly.

'So why did you call us?' asked Yash.

'I thought you should know he was home.' Then, suddenly, there was an almighty crash from upstairs. 'Oh no,' Macy exclaimed and raced for the stairs. At the top, she became aware of someone close behind her, and before she reached her bedroom door, rough hands grabbed her around the waist and pulled her back.

It was Yash. Moving her aside, he pushed the door open. Looking around his bulk, Macy saw Narcifer standing in the middle of the room. It looked like he was trying to get dressed. His jeans were undone at the waist, but the free-standing full-length mirror was in millions of bits on the floor. Narcifer looked up as they entered.

'I saw a man,' he said.

'Hey, Narcifer, it's Yash. Remember me?' Yash said, approaching cautiously, his hands raised.

'I saw a Jelvian man,' Narcifer said.

'It was just a mirror,' Macy said, squeezing past Yash. 'Narcifer, you saw yourself.'

Narcifer glanced from her to Yash. Macy saw the realisation settle on his face. He sat heavily on the bed, stared at the broken mirror, and then looked at Macy. 'A mirror?'

'Just a mirror,' she affirmed, sitting beside him.

He dragged a hand through his hair. 'So is this reality now, or...?' He looked up at Yash. 'What has the committee done to me?'

'I don't know, buddy.' Yash sounded unbelievably kind. 'I haven't been back to the islands for years, but everyone who comes back—if they make it back—they're not the same. Aldarn—'

'I'm not Aldarn,' Narcifer almost growled.

'Aldarn's confusion was caused by a brain injury,' Macy said.

'And he went back to the islands repeatedly until Calder realized the trips made his condition worse. Narcifer, you've been living here longer than on the islands. This will wear off. You just need to sleep.'

'Every time I close my eyes, I'm back *there*. And James Sullivan? Is he safe? He must be safe.'

'Sullivan?' asked Yash. He looked surprised at the sudden change of topic. He sat in the wing chair Narcifer had occupied earlier. He leaned forwards and looked intently at Narcifer. 'Why must he be safe? What's all this about James Sullivan?'

Narcifer looked up blankly. 'I don't know.' He drew a hand across his eyes. 'Fuck, my head is scrambled.'

'Does Calder know Narcifer's back?' Macy asked, looking at Yash worriedly.

'He'll be notified.' He was back to being curt. Yash clearly despised her.

'What's going on, Yash?' she asked. 'Why was Narcifer taken like that? You know something. I know you do.' She heard a noise and looked around. The other Jelvia was leaning against the doorjamb. He had been listening to their entire conversation. She looked at him, hoping he was friendlier than Yash. 'I'm in this deep,' she said. 'Please treat me like one of your—like a female Jelvia and tell me what's going on.'

The Jelvia smiled, his face softening. His teeth were startlingly white. 'Female Jelvias, unfortunately, aren't like human women. They are bred only for birthing and nursing the young. So, maybe not quite like a female Jelvia, eh? I'm Axelor,' he introduced himself. He dropped his gaze to Yash. 'How much does she know?'

'She witnessed Narcifer's kidnap.'

'For God's sake,' Macy said, clenching her fists. She relaxed her hands as she noticed Axelor glance at her. But he looked amused. 'Just tell me what's going on,' she said instead.

'Calder's not returned any calls. So we think our group has been infiltrated,' Axelor said.

'You mean they have Calder, too?'

Narcifer looked up at her shocked cry and put an arm around her shoulders. 'It's okay, babe.' He transferred his gaze to Yash and Axelor. 'I need to get my head back in the game. Calder went to see Aldarn? Has Al been contacted?'

'Yes, Al knows what's going on. Calder didn't go to see Aldarn. Meeting up with him would get them both killed,' said Axelor. 'There's another group of Jelvias who've disbanded from the committee, like us. He went to meet one of their leaders to discuss a coalition. But he never got there. We found his burnt car, but no evidence of his body.'

Narcifer looked crushed. 'Body? You think they've killed him and taken his body?'

'Not this other group, no,' Axelor said. 'We're pretty sure about that. It's those who are working for the committee. Those who kidnapped you. They want Aldarn, for some reason. As I said, we searched the area and found Cal's car, but there was no sign of him. Sorry, bud.'

'When was this?' Narcifer asked.

'We found the car Tuesday morning,' Axelor said. He stood away from the door. 'I'll continue to search the house in case Narcifer was followed.'

Narcifer kissed the top of her head as Axelor left them. 'I'm sorry, babe. Coming home was supposed to be relaxing for you... er... you *have* been in the hospital, haven't you? Or was that a dream?'

'No, all that was true. Greg pushing me from the car, Aldarn having a breakdown and trying to kill me—all that was true, unfortunately.' She looked up at Narcifer's worried face. 'It's okay. I'm okay.'

'And what day is it now? How long have I been missing?' he asked.

'Two days and two nights. How did you escape?'

'I had help. Fortunately for me, many Jelvias wish to escape the islands. I caught illicit rides on various lorries and vans to get me home.'

'You must be hungry. Can I get you something to eat?'

'That'd be great,' Yash said.

Narcifer chuckled, and Macy answered with a smile.

So Macy found herself in the kitchen at almost four o'clock in the morning, cooking bacon and eggs for three ravenous Jelvias. She felt tired, yet her mind was buzzing with worry for Narcifer. All she could think about was how Narcifer's behaviour seemed similar to Aldarn's when he'd had his breakdown.

She dropped bread in the toaster and made coffee. Then she turned and jumped: Narcifer was leaning against the doorjamb, watching her. She had been so engrossed in cooking that she hadn't noticed.

She smiled at him, and he smiled back. 'You know what the two best things are in the world?' he asked.

'What?'

'Watching you and the smell of bacon.'

She went over and, on tiptoe, put her arms around his neck. Then, with his hands on her waist, he bent to receive her kiss. Pulling apart, he said, 'We'll get through this, won't we?'

'There isn't any doubt about that.'

With his forehead against hers, he said, 'It feels like you're a dream that's become real. And if you are a dream, I don't want to wake up.'

Normally, she'd have laughed at the cheesy cliché, but this time she knew Narcifer meant it in its true sense. The eggs cracked and spat in the pan, and Macy pulled free from Narcifer's arms. She flipped the eggs and turned the heat off as the toast popped and the kettle boiled.

She filled three plates with bacon and eggs. Axelor and Yash came to sit around the table as if she waited on them all the time. Then, acting as if it was all normal, Macy filled their plates, placed the food in front of them, and set a toast rack in the middle of the table. She followed it with coffee and a pitcher of iced juice.

She didn't eat; she just made herself a strong coffee.

It was going to be a long day.

THIRTY-EIGHT

In the early hours, Macy fell asleep in Narcifer's arms in their bed, with Axelor just across the landing in Courtney's old room and Yash downstairs on the settee. They'd flipped a coin, apparently, and Yash had lost.

She opened her eyes slowly. It was light. Immediately, she rolled over and felt for Narcifer. His side of the bed was empty. She sat up with a jerk, then jumped to see Narcifer sitting at the base of the bed. He turned towards her with glowing eyes.

'Kraovo sa,' he said, followed by a chunk of foreign words.

'Kraovo sa,' she repeated, stumbling over the strange pronunciation.

He stared at her, then stood up and stepped towards the wall. Macy watched him, concerned yet unwilling to call for help. She watched as Narcifer put his hands on the wall and lowered his head to hang morosely down between his arms. He was a picture of torment. Flipping back the duvet, Macy went to him. She slipped beneath his arms and lodged herself between him and the wall. She put her hands around his neck.

'It's okay. You're back with me now,' she said.

He took his hands off the wall and wrapped them around her.

'Come on, Narcifer,' she said, 'let's go back to bed.'

She led him to the bed like a child, but then he pulled off her clothes, kissing her exposed flesh as if in a frenzy. Macy didn't bother to slow him down. There was no tenderness, just a hardness that Macy somehow welcomed. He cried her name, and then, sated, he fell against her, his body finally relaxing, while Macy lay staring at the ceiling, stroking his damp hair.

~

She woke slowly, and at first, she wasn't sure where she was. She'd dreamt she was back in the hospital.

'Morning, sleepyhead,' Narcifer said.

She looked up. Narcifer was propped up on one elbow; he had watched her sleep. She smiled at him. 'How long have you been watching me?'

'All night,' he said and pressed a kiss against her forehead.

They both heard Axelor come out of his room and head down the stairs, followed by his and Yash's muffled voice as they moved around the kitchen.

Narcifer sat up and flipped back the duvet. 'You stay there. I'll bring you some coffee and try to get rid of Yash and Axelor. I can hear them downstairs. I bet they're eating all our food.' He stood up and pulled his jeans on. Then, fastening them up, he said, 'Hope they're not eating all the bacon.'

Macy sat up, bewildered by his nonchalant behaviour.

'How are you feeling?' she asked, watching him pull on a T-shirt.

He pulled it down over his head and then flattened his hair. 'Fine.'

Macy frowned. 'You had some violent dreams.'

'Really? Sorry about that. I hope I didn't scare you, babe.' Then he opened the door and disappeared through it, leaving Macy alone in the bed.

She stared at the door, feeling uneasy about Narcifer's calm behaviour. It was as if his kidnap and the subsequent strange dreams had never happened. She swung her legs out of bed and had a quick shower. As she dressed, she heard the front door open and close and rushed to the window in time to see Yash and Axelor get into their car.

She couldn't help but notice the black Volvo was still there. A creak of the stairs sent her to the top of the landing to look over the banister. Narcifer was coming up with a cup of watery-looking coffee.

'Have they gone?' she asked.

He looked up. 'Yes,' he said.

'You're okay now?' she asked, taking the coffee he offered. She went back into the bedroom with Narcifer following. She glanced at him over her shoulder when he didn't answer. She could see he was trying to word his answer carefully. When he caught her looking, he smiled.

'It was the drug they injected me with. It made me hallucinate.'

'And speak an unknown language?'

He shrugged. 'Maybe. The hallucinations might return when I'm asleep, but they should wear off over time.' He sounded like he was reciting something someone had told him.

She put the coffee on the dressing table. 'Right, we've no time to delay. We need to swing into action now. Can you get your passport?' She had kept her suitcase under her bed, and now she pulled it out as Narcifer watched. She dropped it on the bed and opened it.

'What are you doing?' he asked.

'Packing. I've another suitcase in the loft if we need it.' She threw in her clothes haphazardly. She wanted to be quick, which meant packing couldn't be tidy.

'Packing?'

'You don't have a lot of clothes, do you?' she asked, going into her wardrobe and pulling several dresses off their hangers. Next, she grabbed a couple of hoodies and jeans. All went into the suitcase. 'I had a peek in your wardrobe at Keats, and you only seemed to have the same clothes in various shades of black.'

'Macy—'

She barely looked at him as she carried on throwing in clothes. 'We've no time. I've a plan, Narce. I'm going to sell up, and we'll move somewhere where the committee, Calder, or anyone won't be able to find us.'

'Run away, you mean?'

'It isn't running away.' She looked at the clothes in the case, then turned to the dressing table and collected her makeup and toiletries. She dropped it all in her case. 'It's survival,' she said and looked at Narcifer with her hands on her hips. 'I have it all planned. I'll sell this house, plus with all the other money from the *Echo*, we can afford to go anywhere we like. I was thinking Australia?'

Narcifer sat in the wing chair opposite Macy. 'It doesn't matter where I go. The committee is in my head. I can't escape it.'

'But—'

'And how would we get to these other places? On one of those aeroplanes that fly in the sky?'

'Well, yes, of course, we would. Or are you telling me you're scared of flying?'

He laughed, and she glared at him. Then, sobering, he said, 'I wouldn't be *allowed* on a plane, Macy.'

She chewed on her bottom lip as she thought. 'The train then,' she said. 'We don't have to go to Australia. We could travel to Europe—Italy or Spain, maybe. Somewhere hot.'

'I'm not running away, Macy.'

'It isn't running away,' she said again, her voice tense.

'Sweetheart, sit down a minute. Draw a breath.'

Macy sat on the edge of the bed and gave him a mutinous look. 'Tell me why you want to stay here. Do you want to risk a kidnapping again? You want to risk being taken to one of the islands and never escaping?'

Narcifer stood up and sat on the bed next to her. He took her hand and lifted it to his lips, kissing the back. 'I appreciate what you are willing to do for me—leave your friends and family. But it's not possible for someone like me.'

'I don't understand why not. The committee is only part of the problem. Calder and the other Jelvias are a bigger problem at the moment. And Calder's gone missing now,' she said. 'Do you remember that?'

Narcifer frowned. 'No, I don't. When did he go missing?'

'Monday evening. Apparently, he went to meet with another group of Jelvias but never got there.'

'Yash never said a word.'

'He did; you just didn't take it in at the time.'

Awareness caught up with him, and his face darkened. 'I remember now.' He rubbed his face. 'Christ, how'd I forget that? My brain is fucked.' Then, pulling his hands down, he stood up. 'I need to call Yash.'

'No!' Macy stood up with him and grabbed his arm. 'Please, Narcifer! Calder didn't even care about your kidnap. He thinks you're on the committee's side and working *for* them to kill Aldarn.'

'He thinks *what?*'

'I'm sorry to tell you that, but it's true. Calder told me himself.'

'I need to go and speak to James,' Narcifer said.

'*Why?* What has James got to do with things? Why is he so important?' She ignored the taunting voice inside her head that said James was blackmailing Narcifer. According to Phil, if James and Aldarn had 'woken up', maybe this is why he wanted to find Aldarn. The reason James was blackmailing Narcifer was all clicking into place. The only thing that puzzled her was *how* he was blackmailing him.

'Narcifer?' she prompted when he didn't speak. 'Come on, tell me what's going on with James.' She felt she was right in her assumptions but wanted it confirmed.

'I'm not sure. My mind's blurry. I know I have to protect him,' Narcifer said.

She observed his face. 'Because the committee's told you to?'

Narcifer stood up and strode across the floor towards the door. 'No, the committee has nothing to do with James.'

'Hey, wait,' she said, standing. 'I'm coming with you.'

'You're not,' he said. 'You're staying right here.'

She grabbed a chunky blue jumper from the suitcase and pulled it over her head. Straightening the jumper over her body, she looked at Narcifer. 'I almost went to a dark place when you were kidnapped. It was that same dark place I went to when my mum was murdered—and I almost didn't come back then. If you keep insisting my world and yours are separate, I can't guarantee that the dark place won't find me again.'

'Mace—'

'In short, you can't lock me out anymore,' she interrupted, 'because I'm as much a part of this as you are.'

THIRTY-NINE

In the end, Narcifer didn't put up much of a fight to stop her from coming along. It was as if he was resigned to the fact that she needed to know what was happening.

To avoid the police following them, Macy organised a hired car. It had taken longer than expected, making Narcifer pace the living room. He was anxious to get to James. He couldn't tell her why. He didn't seem to know himself this time, and he hadn't been able to phone him because he couldn't remember the number.

Macy chose a hire car firm from outside her hometown of Richmond. She also turned her mobile phone off and left the bracelet Yash had given her on her bedside table. Narcifer's phone was long lost.

They set off separately. Macy drove her Mini around the corner from the black Volvo and waited for Narcifer to join her. The Volvo didn't follow, making her more certain it was just an empty car videoing the house. They drove to the car hire place with Narcifer squashed inside and exchanged the Mini for an SUV. He seemed okay now. There was no more confusion from him, no strange foreign language slipping into the conversation. He could drive, but Macy felt it would be better if she drove in case the police pulled them over again. Unable to give her an address, Narcifer told her to head south. All he could say was that it was by the ocean. Soon into the journey, Macy realised they were heading towards Southampton.

It was early afternoon, and they drove through the rain. It splattered against the window screen, and the washers were going full tilt. Traffic was slow.

'Maybe we could spend the rest of the day in a hotel?' Narcifer suggested, looking out the window at the hotel they were driving past. He seemed jovial now. The confusion from last night and this morning had gone.

Macy glanced at him. 'Maybe, after we've seen James.'

Narcifer scowled theatrically, and she smiled at him. 'Has your memory come back about why you're protecting him?'

'Unfortunately, yes.'

'So why are you protecting him?'

'I can't tell you that.'

She slowed at a traffic light. Then, pulling the handbrake on, she turned to Narcifer. 'I'm going to find out when I meet James.'

'Not necessarily,' he said.

She stared at him. 'Are you being deliberately annoying?'

'The light is green. You can go on green.'

Macy set off again. 'When you were kidnapped, Calder seemed to think they had mistaken you for him. What has the committee got against Calder?'

'Calder and Aldarn began our group, and Al's inaccessible, so they've come for Calder. We've been trying to escape the committee's rule for years, but nobody can escape them even though many of us have left the islands.'

'Why didn't you bring the rest of your family to England? Why leave them behind?'

He didn't reply, and Macy looked at him. His face was blank. 'They didn't want to come.' Then, as if to stop any further questions, Narcifer began playing with the dial on the radio. David Bowie started singing—ironically, 'Life on Mars'—and Narcifer's fingers tapped on his thigh.

Macy sighed. She wouldn't get answers from him, no matter how hard she tried. She could only hope James would fill in the blanks.

Macy pulled up to a petrol station to fuel the car an hour into the journey. They'd also left without any food provisions. Macy declined Narcifer's offer to go into the shop; she wanted to keep his identity hidden. Narcifer pulled out his wallet and tossed it towards her.

'No, it's okay. I have money,' she said.

'It'll go on my expenses. Just buy what you want.'

She grinned at him. 'It's a shame they don't sell diamonds!' She took the wallet and stepped out of the car. It was freezing outside, and the rain was almost horizontal, hitting her side-on as she fuelled the vehicle. The wind had picked up, too. Filling the car to its maximum, she went into the shop to pay and buy their provisions.

She bought two toasted bacon rolls for Narcifer, a plain chicken sandwich for herself, and two bottles of water. There was a small queue for the cashier, and while Macy stood in line, she opened Narcifer's wallet.

It was crammed with notes, but most of the money was foreign—or toy notes, like children's play money. There were also debit and credit cards, and Macy looked through them. None of them belonged to Narcifer. Frowning, Macy closed the wallet and put it in her back pocket.

Something was unfurling in her mind. Lost memories tried to resurface.

She remembered the spaceships she'd pictured in the empty sky after leaving the backstreet pub she was forced into after Narcifer's stunt with the helicopter. The spaceships hadn't been there at that moment in time—it was a *memory* of them. A memory she'd forgotten.

'*Some people wake suddenly from the brain fog with all their old memories intact. Some remember gradually, recalling little bits, while others become confused, maybe making notes or telling themselves it's just a Jelvian quirk.*'

They were Oliver's words. And Macy, at the time, believed he was describing her—trying to get her to admit that she was waking up to their ridiculous notion that Earth had been invaded by ten spaceships on 9th March, six years ago.

She turned her head to look out the window. Narcifer was sitting patiently in their hired car, staring straight ahead. Suddenly, he moved and looked right at her. In the dimness of the car, his eyes glinted.

Macy's eyes widened, and her breath caught in her throat as she realised that Narcifer's little 'quirks' weren't cute characteristics. They were Narcifer learning how to be a human... Learning how to live on an alien planet. Learning *not* to be an alien.

Macy remembered the excitement, the fear, the public protests, and governments around the world appealing for peace as the alien spaceships made straight for Earth. Then there had been the quiet. The sudden nothingness as calm spread over the people on Earth, who believed meteorites had fallen harmlessly into the Atlantic and Arctic Oceans.

But they hadn't been meteorites.

They'd been spaceships—nine of them. The tenth had been shot down over the English Channel. The occupants—what was left—were taken into laboratories owned by Professor Jon Johnsen.

Memories...

Memories unfurling.

Unfurling and developing.

Macy remembered.

FORTY

'Hey, love, are you in the queue?'

Macy looked up at the man and then at the counter. She expected to see a line of people waiting to be served, but there was just one woman ahead and a wide gap between her and Macy. 'Oh, yes, sorry,' she mumbled and moved to stand behind the woman.

The man fell in line behind her.

Macy glanced out of the window again. Narcifer was looking straight ahead. She loved him—or was it just her perception of him? What if the human form wasn't his true identity? What if Narcifer was something else entirely? What if—

'No fuel, miss?'

Macy came back to the present. 'Yes, pump number four. And these,' she said, putting her purchases on the counter.

She paid using her own money. Then, moving away from the counter, Macy took her time walking towards the exit. She was thinking hard, but her thoughts were a mad ramble.

Everything Phil and Oliver had said was correct. Earth had been invaded six years ago by alien spaceships masquerading as meteorites. Nine had landed in the oceans near Ireland, Great Britain, Scotland, Norway and Iceland, and one between Greenland and Canada.

A higher technology had distorted people's memories, making everyone believe the Jelvias had always been there—making the spaceships appear as islands.

The automatic doors slid open as she approached, but she hesitated on the threshold. In the car, Narcifer watched a woman trying to get a screaming toddler back into the child's safety seat. Macy scrutinised him as he watched the activity.

'Excuse me, love.' The man who had been behind her in the queue was trying to get around her. She moved to the side. He threw her a look of annoyance, but Macy barely cared.

Her legs were stiff and heavy as she walked back to the car—back to Narcifer, her lover and best friend, who wasn't who he said he was. He didn't know. He thought he had been here forever. He even thought he had a family on one of the islands—an island that was a spaceship.

A shudder rippled through Macy, and her steps faltered. Her thoughts were conflicted. She didn't want to get into the car with an alien being—someone or *something* she hadn't even known for a year.

But it was *him*.

Narcifer.

And the few months they'd known one another, they'd laughed, talked, played, made love, argued, and cried together. She had subconsciously realised that he was different from other men but put that down to him being a Jelvia, not an alien.

'Macy?'

She looked up. Narcifer had pushed open the car door and was standing, looking at her over the top of the car's roof.

'What are you doing standing there? You're getting soaked,' he said.

Macy hadn't noticed the rain until it dripped off her hood and ran over her face. She stared at Narcifer. She still couldn't move. Her feet felt glued to the ground.

James has woken up.

The sudden thought gave her some reassurance. She trusted James—which was why she found it so hard to believe that he was on Jon Johnsen's side.

Oh, my God. It's true! Johnsen had been awake all this time!

'Macy!'

Taking a deep breath, she moved forwards and climbed into the car, handing the bag with her purchases over to him. She felt him watching her as she closed the door. She sat with her hands on the wheel, staring straight ahead. His hand on her shoulder made her jump.

'Hey,' he said. 'Why so tense? Did somebody say something to you in the petrol station?'

She forced herself to relax and shook her head. She pushed her hood back.

'Here, let me help you get this wet coat off.'

She said nothing but allowed him to help her with her coat. He dropped the coat behind them on the back seat, then grabbed a napkin from the bagged food and handed it to her. Macy dried her face and did her best to dry the parts of her hair that had become wet.

'Everything okay?' he asked.

'I... yes,' she said. What would happen if she told him she had woken up? Would he suddenly wake up too? What would that do to him? And what would he do to *her*? She loved him, but she was frightened, too. She also needed answers, and she had never been one to shy away from getting those.

Narcifer peered into the bag and pulled out one of the bacon rolls. He held it out to her.

'It's all yours,' she said. The thought of food made her stomach clench.

'Macy...' he began. He looked concerned. 'What's wrong?'

She reached round to her back pocket and pulled out his wallet. She handed it to him. 'There is no legal tender in there, and the credit and debit cards aren't in your name.'

Narcifer took the wallet and shoved it into his pocket. Then, he unwrapped his food. 'Is that all that's worrying you?'

'Do you know what legal tender is?' she asked. She remembered she'd used one of his illegal credit cards before. But back then, she'd not questioned it. She just assumed it belonged to another Jelvia.

'I never could understand your money system, but humans don't complain when I hand over a card.' He began to eat, his cheeks bulging as he made light work of the food.

'They don't complain because they're scared of you,' she said.

'Maybe,' he said in between mouthfuls.

And they're scared of you because their subconscious knows Jelvias are aliens.

Macy picked up the bottle of water and unscrewed the lid to take a sip. Then she put the bottle down and pulled on her seatbelt.

'We've still a way to go,' Narcifer said, finishing his food and unaware of the turmoil in Macy. 'We need to head east now. If you want me to take over the driving, I will.'

'No, it's okay. Don't you know the name of the town at all? I might be able to find a shortcut.'

She'd made up her mind. She would act like nothing had changed. She had another sip of water and started the car. She followed Narcifer's directions. He still couldn't direct her by place-names, relying instead on some inner spatial cognition, but according to the signposts, they seemed to be headed towards Bognor Regis.

Traffic was no less light towards the coast. They followed the coastline until they drove into East Wittering. The small town looked deserted as the rain hammered down. Narcifer directed her down a side road towards a car park, telling her they could only get to James on foot. She did as he asked, trying to keep a smile on her face and her voice light. She parked in the almost-empty carpark, facing the ocean. The English Channel was turbulent, dashing against the rocky beachside.

'James is here?' she asked, looking along the coastline. She had expected to see a house; instead, there was nothing but coastline, a closed fairground on the seafront, and the town behind them.

Narcifer pushed out of the car, a blast of cold air sweeping in to replace the warm. Macy grabbed her still-damp coat from the back seat and followed him outside. She shivered as she pulled it on, wishing she'd thought to bring gloves and a woolly hat. The hood on her coat blew off every time she pulled it up.

Narcifer took her hand, and she steeled herself to not pull away. They left the carpark, following a sign to the coastal path. A boat tethered to a pier crashed on the waves—even the jetty wasn't visible beneath the ocean's foam. An angry sea was always a beautiful sight to Macy, but it looked icy cold, and the chill that radiated from it pierced through her coat, making her shiver.

Narcifer pulled her towards the beach, and as they faced the Channel, he pointed to a lighthouse surrounded by rocks and foaming waves.

'That's where James is,' he said.

Macy stared at the lighthouse and then looked up at Narcifer. 'Is this a joke?' Her breath puffed around her face.

'Joke?' he asked.

She glanced up at Narcifer, and she could see that it wasn't a joke to him. He just hadn't considered the danger of getting to James.

'Do you normally swim to the lighthouse?' she asked.

'The ocean is usually calm. Sometimes it will be gone. I hoped it would be gone again, and we could've walked. It's muddy and wet, but I could've carried you.'

'The tide will be out, you mean?' She spotted a tidal board and walked over to it. Narcifer followed. 'The tide will start to recede at 19:01,' she read aloud. 'That's a couple of hours away.'

'Scared of getting your feet wet?' he teased. When she didn't laugh or punch his arm as she usually would have, Narcifer's brows drew together. 'Something *is* wrong, isn't it? What is it, Macy?'

She tried to formulate an answer, but there wasn't anything to describe what was happening inside her head. She had just woken up to a lie that she had been living for six years and needed time to process it. She opened her mouth to speak, only to close it again.

'All right. You can't answer, but that's okay,' he said. 'Stay there. I'll bring James to you.'

'It's too dangerous to swim,' she said, grabbing his arm.

He looked back at the sea, then pointed to the boat being tossed by the waves. 'I could use that.'

'Or we could wait until the tide goes out? Come on, I've spotted a café. I don't know about you, but I could do with a hot drink.' It was true: she'd seen a tiny café with an "Open" sign, nestled between a pub and a closed seaside shop. 'We need to discuss what we're going to say to James.'

'I don't need to discuss anything with him. I'm going to check if he's okay, take down his number, and then leave.'

But Macy was already striding across the soggy beach towards the café. Narcifer followed her, pulling out his sunglasses to disguise his eyes. It was a pointless exercise, but she didn't bother to tell him. People could always tell a Jelvia just by their bulk alone. Macy had thought she'd had envious looks when people saw her with Narcifer in Cornwall last year—but they hadn't been envious. Instead, they were anxious and fearful but, more than likely, pitying.

The door to the café gave off a little jingle as they entered. Narcifer sat by the window as Macy ordered their drinks at the counter—a hot chocolate for her and a coffee for Narcifer.

Taking the drinks back to their table, she sat down. They could see the lighthouse from here. The waves looked ferocious as they slapped against the rocks, some almost reaching the lighthouse's first window. Macy watched the waves splash up on the rocks. It was mesmerising. Narcifer must have felt the hypnotic pull because he was silent, too, and looking out of the window.

It was warm in the café, and Macy shrugged out of her coat, leaving it to fall back over the back of the chair. She curled her hands around the mug. She was cold, but it was more than being chilled. Something was unfolding, and had been since the Jelvias arrival. Even before Narcifer's kidnap, she'd subconsciously known that she'd only just touched the surface of what was behind Jelvias' existence.

Now she'd woken up, but the truth still eluded her.

If Phil was correct and James *had* woken up, then wanting to find Aldarn so he could speak to him made sense. She didn't know how James had blackmailed Narcifer into protecting him or finding Aldarn. It must be something big, and she couldn't imagine what. She looked across at Narcifer and considered asking him outright.

'While you were in the hospital, James did something to you,' he said without prompting. He wasn't looking at her, and she realised it hadn't been the mesmerising waves that had rendered him silent. Instead, he'd figured out a way to tell her the truth. 'He visited you while you were unconscious and alone and put something into your heart. A heart valve.' He looked at Macy. 'He has the same valve, and if his heart stops, so will yours. That's why he can't die.'

She stared at him as shock enveloped her. She opened her mouth, then closed it again.

Narcifer grabbed her hand that was lying limply on the table. He gave it a squeeze. 'That's why I have to do as he says. He doesn't care if he dies, but at the moment, he wants to avenge his wife's death, and I think he wants to do that by killing Aldarn. I can't see any other reason why James wants to meet him. I have no affinity with James. I hate the man, but I must keep him safe for your sake.'

'He's blackmailing you with *me*?' she burst out. 'All this time, you were worried that if Calder killed James, I'd die, too?'

'I'll sort this, I swear,' Narcifer said. 'We'll get the best doctors to take that valve out of your heart.'

Macy sat back in her chair, blowing out a breath. 'Inserting something like that is impossible, surely? I'm no medical expert, but... no, that's impossible,' she said. She unconsciously touched her chest, feeling for her beating heart.

'I'm not prepared to risk it.'

Macy stared at him. He was an alien, yet he'd risked the wrath of Calder and the committee to protect her. *He doesn't* know *he's an alien!* Her thoughts were in overdrive.

'One way to find out.' She pulled out her phone and then looked at it. 'Damn,' she said. 'If I use this, we'll be tracked here.'

'Too late. The girl behind the counter has called the police.'

Macy looked round. She could see the girl behind the window in the kitchen. She had a phone against her ear and was talking to someone while stealing glances at them.

'Shit. Shall we go?'

'No, you stay. It's cold outside, so you stay here.' He stood up. 'Who were you going to ring?'

'Courtney. She's a nurse, and she's also assisted in surgery. So she would know about that sort of thing. Wait, I'm coming with you. We'll sit in the car.'

She finished her drink and grabbed her coat, then exited the café. Narcifer followed. It felt even colder outside, and Macy pulled her coat on quickly. Narcifer put his arm around her and hugged her against his body, keeping her warm as they walked back towards the car.

Inside the hired car, Macy turned on the engine and put the heating on full. She looked at her phone. 'Dare I risk it?'

'It's not the police I'm worried about. It's Calder finding James.'

'Calder's missing, remember?'

Narcifer grunted. 'Phone her and ask,' he said.

Macy turned on her phone and waited for it to come to life. She had a text from Oliver—so much for his promise not to text or call her. She didn't bother to open it. Courtney was listed in 'favourites', and Macy pressed the screen to call her.

'Hi, Courtney,' Macy said when she answered. She didn't waste time on pleasantries, just got straight to her question. 'Please don't question me, but give me a straight answer if you can.'

'Oh, God. Look, I don't *know* where Aldarn is.'

'This has nothing to do with Aldarn. It's about a surgical procedure, and I need to know if it's possible or not.'

'Surgical procedure? What's happened? Are you okay?'

'I'm fine, never better. Listen, is it possible to have some sort of procedure where the hearts of two separate people are linked?'

'What on earth are you going on about? If you had two hearts, you would need double of everything—four lungs and double of all your blood vessels.'

Macy closed her eyes in frustration. It sounded so bizarre she didn't really know how to word it. She began again.

'Imagine this, and tell me if it's possible. A man is set to be killed by a hitman. To save himself, he surgically implants something—a valve, I don't know—into the heart of the hitman's daughter. If the man dies, then so will the daughter. This makes the hitman back off, and the man is safe.'

'Sounds like a shit sci-fi movie to me.'

'Not possible then?'

'Who is this man? Is he a cardiothoracic surgeon?'

Macy hesitated. 'Would he need to be?'

'It'd help! What is this, Macy? Even if this so-called man was a surgeon, it would be a massive job. He'd need an anaesthesiologist, possibly someone to operate the heart-lung bypass machine. Physician assistants. It isn't a job this *man* could do alone.'

'And the hitman's daughter would have a scar on her chest?'

'Of course. A big scar and lots of bruising. Mace, what's all this—'

'What about a nonsurgical procedure? Like being injected in?' Macy interrupted.

'A valve isn't something that could be injected. Anything large enough to work that way *and* stay in the heart, instead of circulating in the bloodstream, would kill the daughter stone fucking dead. What is this, Macy?'

'So this couldn't happen?'

'No, it bloody couldn't. Ridiculous question!'

'Thank you.'

'Are you all right?' Courtney asked in a softer tone.

'Can I ask you another question?' Macy asked instead.

'Do you want to know if teleporting is possible?'

Macy laughed. She *loved* Courtney. She was grumpy, bad-tempered, and bossy, but God, she missed her. 'I really miss you. Can I come up and see you soon?'

'Fuck's sake, of course, you can. Mace, are you okay?'

'I'm fine. There are a few things I need to tie up here first, and then I'll come.' She injected laughter into her voice, but Courtney didn't reciprocate.

'For the record, I've missed you too,' Courtney said. 'But will you be... No, it doesn't matter.'

'Will I be what?' Macy asked and heard Courtney sigh down the phone.

'I said it didn't matter,' Courtney said.

'It does to me, and I think I know what you wanted to say. You wanted to ask me to come alone,' she said before Courtney could add anything else. 'And I will be. I will be very much alone.'

FORTY-ONE

Narcifer slipped down in his seat just as Macy finished the telephone call and pulled his baseball cap low over his eyes. She glanced at him, then at the car that had just pulled into the car park, parking in a bay a few rows up from them. A police car. Macy sank lower in her seat and watched as two officers climbed out of the car and walked down the coastal path towards the café.

She looked at Narcifer.

'What do they want?' she asked. 'They never bothered us this much last year!' But deep down, she wondered if somebody high up—maybe a commissioner or something—had woken up to the truth of the Jelvias. It was highly possible.

'I don't understand it, either,' he said, watching the officers disappear around the corner. He sat up, and Macy wriggled upright in her seat. 'What did Courtney say?' He wouldn't look at her. Macy knew he had heard the entire conversation but wanted her to say it.

She dropped the phone into her handbag, feeling miserable but saying nothing.

'I understand,' Narcifer said. 'At least, I think I do. And it might be best if you go back to live with Mumma Lisa while I clear things up this end.'

Realising he had misunderstood, Macy breathed a sigh of relief.

'So, what did she say about the heart valve?' he asked.

'That it's an impossible procedure.'

'Is she sure?'

'I'd have a huge scar on my chest from where he would have had to cut me open. She said it was an impossible process, and if somehow it *had* been possible, James couldn't do it alone. He lied to you, Narcifer.'

Narcifer looked away, and it seemed like he was ready to kill someone.

'We need to give James a chance to explain,' she said.

'He used you as insurance to keep himself alive,' Narcifer said. He gave a choked laugh. 'And to think—the lengths I went to in order to keep him safe. I followed Calder practically everywhere and made enemies for life out of Courtney and Aldarn.'

'Courtney?'

'When you wanted to leave Cornwall and come home, I had to hide James again. After you were settled at home, I returned to Cornwall and demanded that Courtney video-call Aldarn in front of me. It didn't work. He took one look at me and hung up. I think he tipped Calder off I was looking for him. Courtney was never angry or annoyed with you. It was always because of me.'

Macy felt like a cornered animal. She had nowhere to go and no one to turn to. She closed her eyes, wishing she could hide. But, instead, a lump in her throat threatened to choke her.

A cloud suddenly burst, and rain hammered down. It pounded the car's roof, making talking hard. She was glad the noise of the rain caused them to be silent. It gave her time to think. She fixed her gaze on the deluge as it rebounded off the tarmac.

'I'm so sorry, Macy, but I only wanted to keep you safe,' Narcifer's voice suddenly boomed in the car above the noise of the rain. He clearly thought she was upset at his confession. But in truth, none of that was important anymore. 'She'll forgive you. It's me she hates. Macy?' he added, placing a hand on her knee. 'Please look at me.'

'I'm okay,' she said, glancing at him and offering a shaky smile.

'Your leg is twitching,' he said.

She looked down and saw her right leg jiggling up and down beneath the weight of his hand. She hadn't even noticed it. Her body was reacting to all the stress that she couldn't voice.

'Sweetheart,' he said, and leaned across to plant a kiss on the side of her face. But, without thinking, Macy jerked her head away violently. The back of her head banged against the window of the car.

Narcifer sat back in his seat, removing his hand and looking at her in shock. They stared at one another.

'I'm sorry,' she said, feeling miserable.

He gave her a sad smile. 'I'll give you some space,' he said suddenly and opened the car door, letting in a blast of cold air.

The door closed after him, and Macy watched him in the rearview mirror as he jogged across the car park towards the road. He approached a building and then scaled it, turning his body in ways impossible for an ordinary man. Then he was gone. Her eyes were unable to keep up with the speed he was moving.

She turned to the front to watch the raging sea. The image blurred as tears filled her eyes. She could sit here and watch the ocean in this state forever if things were different. It was nature at its best, but now all Macy could do was wonder if nature was under threat along with the entire human population.

She wiped her eyes and tried to think. When Narcifer had come back yesterday, he'd been unbelievably confused. It was as if he couldn't believe that she was real—he'd even admitted he thought she was a dream. What if they lived a parallel life on the spaceships, believing humans didn't exist or were just simulations? Narcifer had said the committee had criminalised him, labelling him a runaway. Could the label simply mean that he had joined with the others at Keats?

There was too much for her to think about. She leaned her head forwards and rested it against the steering wheel. She hoped James had some answers because she had no clue where to go from here.

But this was bigger than her and James. It was the *world's* problem, and she felt unbelievably alone.

She gave a strangled laugh and sat up. This was probably how Phil had felt when she first woke up. She suddenly had immense respect for the woman. And Aldarn... he, too, had woken up, but he could barely speak because of his brain injury. As Aldarn's scarred face swam in her memory, Macy had a moment of lucidity. She watched the ocean blindly as the awful awareness took shape in her head. Then she grabbed her phone and called Courtney again.

'Hey, Macy,' Courtney said on answering. 'I'm just leaving for work.'

'I have to tell you everything. And I have to tell you now.' Macy heard Courtney bleep open her car, and then the car door opened and closed as if she'd got into it. 'Do you have a pen?'

'What is this, Macy? I'm going to be late.'

'Do you have a pen?' Macy repeated.

'I'm just searching in my bag, right... I have a pen,' she said with a huff.

'Write down "Kraovo sa" and "pounit un". I don't have the correct spelling, but that's exactly how it sounded when Narcifer said them.'

'Gobbledygook,' Courtney said.

'I want you to repeat them to Aldarn, and I want you to tell me what he says. His reaction, everything.'

'Is this another ruse so your mad boyfriend can get to Aldarn?'

Macy didn't even prickle over the term "mad". 'Narcifer isn't here. He's—'

'Don't tell me. He's in the shower,' Courtney said sarcastically.

Macy turned on the speakerphone and placed her phone on the passenger seat. Her hands were suddenly slick with sweat. She cranked open the window a little bit. Drops of rain immediately blew inside the car, but she didn't care.

'Narcifer admitted to me today that he came to interrogate you. But I didn't know at the time. He's... he's acting strangely, and I thought he was seeing someone else. I was paranoid my scars had scared him off—'

'Oh, Macy,' Courtney said, but Macy ignored her.

'He was acting strangely because James Sullivan—remember him?—had blackmailed Narcifer into protecting him. Narcifer was sent to kill him, but James told him he'd inserted a valve or something into my heart while I was unconscious in the hospital. So if his heart stopped, mine would, too. Narcifer believed him, so instead of killing James, he's been protecting him from other Jelvias.'

'That explains your last call.'

'Yes, but there's a lot more going on, and I don't know where to start.' Macy took a breath. 'In short, James is forcing Narcifer to bring Aldarn to him, and now—because Narcifer is hunting for Aldarn—Calder thinks he's working for the committee, who wants Aldarn dead. And Narcifer thinks *James* wants to kill Aldarn, but I know he doesn't, and I know that because... because...'

'Because what?' Courtney asked, as if fed up with Macy's dithering. 'Maybe *James* is working for the committee.'

'That's not all of it, but no, James isn't working for the committee. It's because he's woken up. He and Aldarn both have, only Aldarn doesn't realise it yet. He thinks he has a brain injury.'

There was a long pause on Courtney's end.

'You sound like those delusional WUM protesters,' she said finally.

Macy pushed open the car door. She felt sick. Rain drenched one side of her body and the exposed parts of her seat.

'Are you still there?' Courtney asked.

Macy sat back in the car seat with the door open and the rain splattering one side of her. 'I'm here.'

'What you've just said is crazy, Macy. Utterly crazy.'

'I've woken up, too,' she said quickly. There was no other way of saying it. It had to be quick because it sounded so senseless. 'The WUMs have been telling the truth all this time.'

'Macy—'

'Narcifer was kidnapped Monday and taken back to the isl... er... spaceship to face the committee. He came back early hours Wednesday—last night—but he was very confused and thought I was a dream. I know it's hard to believe, but—'

'Hard to believe? Can you *hear* yourself?'

'The islands aren't islands. They're spaceships.' Macy pulled the car door closed. 'There's nine of them across the Atlantic and the Arctic Ocean. The tenth was shot down over the Channel by Jon Johnsen. He was probably awake too.'

'I don't know what you want me to say. Macy, this is ridiculous!'

Macy carried on talking. 'Narcifer seems okay now, but last night he was confused. He kept repeating the words "Kraovo sa" and "pounit un", which makes me think that once the committee's technology wears off, the Jelvias won't be able to communicate with us. Also, Aldarn became increasingly confused before Greg tried to kill me—what if that wasn't his brain injury? What if it was because he was waking up all along? And now he's fully awake, the committee's technology has worn off, and Aldarn can no longer communicate because he doesn't understand our language.'

'You're having a breakdown,' Courtney said.

'I wish it was that simple. Aldarn's confused because he's woken up, *not* because of an injury—that's why James wants to see him, because he's woken up, too, and he doesn't know what else to do. Now Calder's gone missing, probably taken to the committee just like Narcifer was, and he'll have some of his memory distorted. Have you written those words down?'

'What? Oh, yes. Yes, I have,' she said a little impatiently. 'But Macy, all of this is ridiculous. Have you overdosed on your painkillers? Are you hallucinating?'

Macy closed her eyes. 'When you next see Aldarn, ask him about his dreams.'

'I don't talk to him much,' Courtney said. Her voice was low and soft, and she sounded incredibly sad. 'His brain injury has left him almost completely unable to speak, and what he does say doesn't make much sense.' She sniffed, and Macy could tell she was on the verge of tears. 'But he knows who I am!' she added as if reassuring herself. 'He smiles when he sees me.'

'He *does* know who you are,' Macy confirmed. 'He's woken up, Courtney, and this is what I'm afraid of. He *can't* communicate. I think Jelvias have been speaking their own language all this time. Their technology has somehow converted their language straight to our minds so we can understand, and vice versa.'

'Where are you?' Courtney asked suddenly.

'Sussex, by the coast.'

'What the hell are you doing there?'

'I'm with Narcifer. He's gone somewhere because we...' She paused, closing her eyes. 'I'm having a bit of a crisis at the moment. Narcifer doesn't know I've woken up, but I'm struggling with finding out he's an alien. He knows something's wrong, but I can't tell him.' Macy gave a choked laugh. 'We've come to find James. I'm hoping he can give me some sort of reassurance. I just don't know what else to do, Courts. I'm scared. I'm really scared.'

'Sweetheart, I want you to hang up and call the police, and then I want you to ring me back.' Courtney spoke firmly and slowly, in the tone Macy imagined she used with her patients who were on the verge of ending it all.

'You don't believe me at all, do you?'

'I believe that *you* believe,' she said after a moment.

Macy laughed. 'I might not be speaking clearly—I'm certainly not *thinking* clearly—but all I can say is keep an open mind and listen to Aldarn. Write down what he says to you because it isn't nonsense. It's an alien language, and he's trying to communicate with you.'

'You're scaring me. Give me your exact location—'

'So you can call the police on my behalf? No, that's not going to happen.'

'Mace! Don't you hang up on me.'

'I wasn't going to.'

'Good. Because we're both in over our heads,' Courtney said. Her words made Macy realise that she knew something odd was happening and that realisation was a comfort.

'The entire human population is in trouble,' Macy said. 'I think some high-up people are awake because of the measures they've taken to block the media from broadcasting anything to do with Jelvias.'

'Mum spoke to Harry—you remember Beth? She came to visit you in the hospital, but we sent her away because you were too sick.'

'I remember. Well, not properly, but I remember you telling me about her. She's running a pub in Bromley with her boyfriend, Harry. Or husband, I should say—they're married now.'

'Yeah, well, Mum wanted to make sure that she was okay, but she got Harry on the phone. Mum explained to Harry what had happened, and he advised her to leave the UK and go and live in a warmer climate, taking us with her. He wouldn't tell her why and told her that living with Jelvias was a death sentence. He also told her to pay attention to the protesters,' Courtney said.

'The WUMs?' The world felt like it was closing in on her. She stared at the phone on the seat beside her, wishing Courtney was there instead of just her voice.

'I guess so. There aren't any other protesters wandering the country at the moment.'

'Do you think Harry's woken up?' Macy asked.

'Now you're asking me if I believe all this WUM business, and I don't,' Courtney said. 'I *can't* believe it; I remember growing up with the knowledge of Jelvias.'

'They're false memories. The knowledge is implanted.'

'I'll speak to Aldarn as soon as I can,' Courtney promised after a short pause.

'Thanks.' They spoke a bit more, and then Macy hung up. She closed her eyes and leaned her head back against the headrest. Macy was exhausted. She'd hardly had any sleep last night and practically none the night before. She turned to grab her coat from the back seat and then pushed open the car door. The rain had eased off, and Macy couldn't just sit in the car waiting for Narcifer to reappear.

She walked down to the beach and stood watching the sea. In another life, she'd have brought her camera equipment. The sea really did seem magical as it threw waves around the lighthouse. The tethered boat was still there, looking a little lost against the ferocious ocean. She wondered if it belonged to James. If so, then he wasn't in the lighthouse.

She walked back up to the car park. The police car had gone. She couldn't remember seeing it leave. There weren't many other vehicles parked, and she eyed them all suspiciously, thinking maybe one of them belonged to James. He would have to have a car, and where else would he park it?

As casually as she could, she walked to each car and peered in, looking for signs of the owners. But there was nothing. All the vehicles were empty and ordinary in their interiors. She wondered where Narcifer was and glanced at the buildings around the car park. Jelvias usually travelled from rooftop to rooftop, avoiding CCTV. She couldn't see any sign of him, but it was getting dark, and she couldn't see much anyway.

She checked her phone for the time and saw it was almost six in the evening. The heavy clouds hadn't helped in turning the day into evening. Macy felt peckish. She thought about returning to the little café again but didn't want to draw unnecessary attention to herself.

She left the car park and walked back into town to find a shop that sold takeout meals. She didn't want to eat in a café on her own. The smell of fish and chips invaded her nose, and her senses danced to attention. It was hard to miss that aroma, and her mouth watered. She found the fish and chips shop, quaintly called Codd's, and ordered two lots of fish and chips. She didn't know if Narcifer would be back to eat them before they got cold, but she bought them anyway.

The rain had picked up again, and Macy hurried back to the car. Inside, she shrugged off the coat and threw it on the back seat. She turned the ignition to warm up the car and demist the windows. Then she opened her food and ate with the supplied wooden fork.

She ate hungrily, occasionally drinking from the water bottle she'd bought earlier from the petrol station. Then, finishing her food, she scrunched up the rubbish and looked outside for a bin.

Something caught her eye in the rearview mirror, and she looked around over her shoulder. A car behind her beeped, its lights flashed, and a man pushing a supermarket trolley full of groceries came into the carpark. Macy watched him unload the trolley into the boot of the car. His light-coloured hair was flattened with rain against his head, but there was no mistaking him. He *was* James Sullivan. He returned the shopping trolley to its bay. But instead of returning to the car, he remotely locked it and turned around, heading back towards the town.

Macy scrambled out of her car as James disappeared around a corner. Grabbing her coat, she scrambled into it and ran after him. She called out, but he couldn't hear her through the heavy rain, so Macy ran faster. When she got close enough, she reached out to tap him on the shoulder, but he turned suddenly.

James locked his hand around her throat in one swift movement as he simultaneously pushed her into an alcove.

His other hand held a gun to her head.

FORTY-TWO

She didn't have time to make any noise. Neither did James before a dark-clad figure appeared between them and sent James skidding on his backside along the tarmac. He dropped the gun as he fell.

Narcifer picked up the gun while Macy stood there, mute and shocked. She didn't think her mind could take much more. Narcifer put the gun in the waistband of his jeans and looked at James, who was still sitting on the ground, holding his jaw. The three looked at one another as the rain continued to pour. Macy felt her teeth chattering.

'Did you have to wallop me so hard?' James finally asked, getting to his feet.

'After what you've done, you're lucky you're still alive,' Narcifer retorted.

A look of realisation crossed James' face. He glanced at Macy. 'Ah, you've told her? I suppose that's why you brought her here,' he said. He rubbed the back of his neck, then held a hand towards Narcifer as if expecting a handshake. 'Blackmailing you wasn't the best tactic for staying alive, but it was all I had. Can I apologise?'

Narcifer glowered at him.

James wiped his hand on his jeans and turned to offer it to Macy. 'Macy, good to see you looking so well.'

Manners forced Macy to step forwards and shake his hand.

'Sorry about the rough handling. Are you okay?' James asked.

Macy nodded. She gave a spontaneous shiver, and James looked around at Narcifer. 'Let's get out of this rain. I suppose you both deserve an explanation.'

Narcifer glanced at Macy, and she shrugged. Then they both followed James along the deserted streets until he stopped outside a small guesthouse. He pushed open the door and ushered them up the stairs and into room number twelve. No one was about. Inside, James offered them towels to dry themselves.

Macy took off her coat and held it awkwardly as rainwater dripped onto the carpet.

'Here,' said James, taking the coat from her. He grabbed a coat hanger from the wardrobe and disappeared into what Macy guessed was the bathroom. She picked up the towel James had given her and wrapped it around her shoulders. A chill ran down Macy's back, but she knew it wasn't entirely from the rain.

She met Narcifer's gaze as they heard James move around the bathroom, separated from them only by a thin wall. He had rented the cheapest bedsit, it seemed.

'Are you okay?' Narcifer asked.

'Yeah, you?'

James came back whistling a merry tune, leaving her question unanswered. Macy felt the phlegmatic air around James was superficial, but she preferred it to Phil's and Oliver's rushed panic.

'I've hung your coat up in the shower. It probably won't be dry by the time you want to leave, though,' James said,

'That's okay,' she said. 'I thought you were living in the lighthouse,' she added, trying to hang on to the normality of their conversation. She was scared of having her memories clarified.

'I do, normally,' James said. 'It depends on the weather. It's a little isolating when it's like this, so I tend to book in here for a night.' He looked at Narcifer. 'And I'm also a sitting duck. Can I make you a hot drink? A cup of tea, perhaps? Please, sit down.' He threw the duvet over the unmade bed and straightened the pillows as he spoke. 'I wasn't expecting visitors.'

Narcifer sat on a chair as if exhausted, his head hanging. Macy looked at him. He looked beaten. She sat cautiously on the edge of the bed, facing Narcifer. She wanted him to look up, to acknowledge her. But he didn't.

James filled the kettle with water from the bathroom. He came back shortly and placed it on its dock. He glanced at Macy.

'You look frozen,' he said.

'I'm fine.'

James said nothing but moved towards the built-in wardrobe, which he opened to take out a thick blanket. He placed it around Macy's shoulders.

'Better?' he asked.

She grabbed the edges of the blanket and smiled her thanks. James smiled back. 'Believe it or not, I *am* on your side,' he said.

'I don't know who or what to believe,' she said. She glanced at Narcifer, who looked back at her miserably. She felt awful and lowered her head.

If James noticed their exchange, he didn't say anything. Instead, he returned to the kettle as it boiled to make tea. He glanced over his shoulder at Macy. 'I'm sorry about the gun thing. I've been a bit spooked lately,' he said.

'What you told Narcifer was cruel,' Macy said.

'Cruel but necessary,' James said.

'It's not true, then?' Narcifer asked. Macy could see his hands on the arms of the chair. She watched his throat for any sign of him firing his venom. Seeing none, she looked back at James.

He poured the tea and brought two cups over to them. 'Of course not. It was a lie based purely on the friendship you and the others at Keats have. No one there would want Macy hurt because you would be devastated. It was pure luck that you were my executioner.'

'Why do they want to kill you?' Macy asked, knowing but wanting to hear it from him.

'Because of Johnsen.' James hadn't made himself any tea. He pulled out the small stool beneath the vanity unit to sit on. 'My wife and I were involved with the laboratory botch up.'

'But you were the whistleblower,' she said. Her memories still told her that James had known Aldarn years before, but she knew that couldn't be true.

'I was. I got to know Aldarn and Scasone while they were incarcerated. I liked them, and I liked to think they liked me. Security was tight, and I tried to rescue them many times. In the end, I enlisted my wife to help. She schmoozed Johnsen into giving her a job on the team, and together we managed to shut down all Johnsen's safety measures and then bring in other Jelvias to rescue them themselves.'

'That's *your* side of it,' Narcifer said. 'Scasone isn't here to corroborate your story, so you're turning to Al. He's ill, and what he says won't be worth anything. You're fucked, James.'

James dipped his head. 'I know. But finding Aldarn isn't all about saving *my* skin,' he said, looking up straight at Narcifer. 'It's saving everyone elses.'

Narcifer snorted. He obviously was still angry at James. Macy curled her hands around the mug of tea, appreciating the warmth from the cup to her hands. She still felt chilled despite the blanket around her shoulders.

'I'd appreciate it if you'd still help me find him,' James continued as if Narcifer had never made a noise.

'Why should I?' Narcifer asked.

'Because Aldarn has the answers,' Macy said. She felt Narcifer's questioning gaze on her and turned to look at him. 'Something's going on, and *he* knows what that "something" is. I think Calder also knows, and that's why he's protecting Aldarn.'

'Problem is,' said James, and Macy swung her head towards him. 'Aldarn has been labelled "mad". Who's going to believe a mad Jelvia? All we can do is hope that Aldarn can help.'

'What help do *you* want from Aldarn, James?' Macy asked softly.

James' cheerful smile waned. 'Just the truth, Macy. Just the truth of the Jelvias' existence.'

'Or is it because you and Aldarn have woken up?' Macy asked. She felt Narcifer's astonished gaze and glanced over at him. He looked so lost. He was hurting—still reeling from her rejection. She looked away, feeling utterly despicable.

'Have *you* woken up?' James asked, and she swung her face to his, feeling cornered. James must have read something in her expression because he added, 'Maybe better not to answer that. But, yes, I've woken up, and I believe Aldarn has, too. That's why I need to see him. But, unfortunately, it might already be too late. Courtney says he's lost the ability to speak coherently.'

'You *spoke* to Courtney?' Macy asked.

'Yes. After you and I last spoke, I tried her again and got through. But she wouldn't tell me where Aldarn is. She told me they video-call, but she wouldn't give me his number either.'

'She doesn't *know* where he is,' Narcifer said.

'You know that for certain?' James asked.

'It'd be too risky to tell her. I went to see her and forced her to call Al in front of me, but he hung up as soon as he saw me. He's been told I'm working for the committee who want him dead.' Narcifer put his tea down on the floor between his feet.

'Sorry. I guess that's partly my fault,' James said.

'Partly?'

James pulled a face. 'Okay, maybe wholly.'

'Things have developed since then. I was taken back to the islands, and now Calder's missing. We think he's been taken to the islands, too.'

'Shiiit,' James said with a long, drawn-out breath. 'When did he go missing?'

'Monday, apparently,' Narcifer said. 'Yash thinks our group has been infiltrated.'

'That's not good at all. You're leaderless.'

'Macy?' Narcifer asked, and she looked up in surprise to see both men looking at her. She had been listening intently to their exchange. But then she felt something warm spill on her leg and looked down. Her leg was jiggling again, and she'd spilt her tea.

'I'm fine,' she muttered, wiping at the spill with the sleeve of her sweatshirt.

James stood up. He reached the built-in wardrobe in two strides and took out a half-empty bottle of Bell's whisky. Then, twisting off the top, he poured a measure into her tea.

He held out the bottle to Narcifer.

'Alcohol?' Narcifer asked.

Narcifer picked up his tea at James' nod and held it out.

James smiled and poured a little into his cup. 'Jelvias need control to use their venom, right? So, in theory, this makes me instantly safer.'

Narcifer's mouth quirked into an answering smile. He took a sip and immediately pulled a face of disgust.

Macy giggled, and the sound was edged with hysteria.

FORTY-THREE

Macy's head was scrambled, and the whisky made her sleepy. She would have fallen off the edge of the bed had Narcifer not grabbed her arm when she fell asleep sitting up.

'I think we should continue this tomorrow,' James said as Macy blinked in disorientation at them. She looked at Narcifer in surprise, sitting beside her on the bed. He moved his hand from her arm straight away.

'Want me to see if they have any vacant rooms here?' James asked. His words washed over her, and sleepily, she heard Narcifer's deep tone as he replied an answer.

Macy forced herself to liven up. She yawned, dragging oxygen into her lungs, rubbed her face, and stood up. 'May I use your bathroom?'

'Of course,' James said and pointed needlessly towards the short corridor leading to the bathroom and the main exit. It was the only other room in the bedsit.

Macy nodded and stumbled towards the bathroom. Her leg was stiff and uncooperative. Inside the bathroom, she splashed cold water over her face to try and wake herself up. She grabbed a towel and stared at herself in the mirror. James' toiletries lay scattered on the shelf just below the mirror. He didn't have many: deodorant, a razor, toothbrush and paste, and a comb. She raised her eyes to her image in the mirror. She looked like shit.

Her coat was still damp, and she left it hanging from the shower rail around the bath.

She returned to the main room in time to catch the tail end of their conversation.

'It must be hard to go against Calder, but I appreciate your help finding Aldarn,' James said.

'I'm doing it for Macy now,' Narcifer said. He was back sitting in the chair, and he looked at her as she walked back into the room and followed her with his gaze until she returned to her seat on the bed. She felt they had a lot of talking to do, but had no idea where to begin.

'That's commendable,' James said. 'You must love her very much—maybe even as much as I loved Leigh.'

'Your wife?' Macy asked.

James smiled at her. 'Yes. She and I were both under the committee's influence and believed the Jelvias to be part of the human race. Neither of us knew of Johnsen's plan to shoot down the tenth spaceship and capture the occupants.'

'Spaceship,' Narcifer said with a snort. 'It was a helicopter!'

'When did you wake up, James?' she asked.

'Probably two or three years ago. It's hard to say because it was a gradual process, and like Aldarn, I thought I was going crazy.'

'It was sudden for me,' she said softly. Then, out of the corner of her eye, she saw the shock on Narcifer's face. She couldn't bring herself to look at him and kept hold of James' gaze. 'This afternoon, in fact,' she added.

'Fuck,' said James. 'Your head must be scrambled.'

'It is,' she said and glanced at Narcifer and then wished she hadn't. He looked so hurt.

'Whether we believe in this "waking up" thing or not, we must agree on one thing, and that's to help one another. If we don't, we'll *all* lose to the committee,' James said.

Macy pulled her gaze away from Narcifer to look at James through a blurry vision. She nodded.

'The WUMs are under the impression that if all Jelvias wake up, it'll be worse for humans,' James said, oblivious to the emotions at work in Macy's body. 'But I think it'll be the opposite. Narcifer, you know the committee and how they—or it—works. We need to defeat them together. We *have* to be on the same team.'

Macy rubbed her eyes. She looked at Narcifer. 'Narce?' she asked. The use of the nickname she held for him had its effect. He visibly softened.

'I said I'll help, and I will. But what good will it do to find Aldarn? It's not guaranteed he'll help or even have answers.'

'True. It's a shot in the dark,' James said. 'But we have no other ideas.'

'And Calder's the only one who knows where Aldarn is,' Narcifer added.

'So we find Calder first?' Macy asked, looking from one man to the other. She rested her eyes on James. 'Axelor said Calder went missing somewhere in Sussex. This is Sussex. Heard anything about burnt-out cars from two days ago?'

'If it's Jelvia related, it wouldn't have been broadcast, but you know who else lives in Sussex?' James asked.

'Who?' Narcifer and Macy both said together.

'Phil Zmin.'

FORTY-FOUR

It was late evening and dark outside. Macy was shattered and could scarcely put one leg in front of the other to walk the short distance to the car park. They had decided James would do some snooping on the burnt-out car, and they would regroup the following morning.

Narcifer grabbed her elbow and hurried her up the street towards their hired car. It was still raining, and the fish and chips she'd had at lunchtime lay heavy in her stomach. Reaching the car, he pushed her into the passenger seat.

The smell of the fish and chips she had bought for Narcifer hit her nasal passages hard, and she gagged. When Narcifer saw the colour of her face, he grabbed the offending bagged food and tossed it into a nearby bin.

He climbed into the driver's seat.

'You're not insured,' Macy said, but it was pointless. Jelvias had undoubtedly been driving uninsured the whole time they'd been here. Narcifer adjusted the seat and set the car in motion, swinging it around and moving out of the car park.

Macy nodded off again but jerked awake when the car's engine cut off. She looked up in surprise at her surroundings. They were in another car park and facing a very ambiguous-looking building. She spotted a sign reading 'Dale Hall and Annexe'. She sat up, yawning.

'Where are we?'

'At a hotel.' Without waiting for her to reply, he pushed open the car door, climbed out, came round to her side, and opened the door.

Without moving, she looked up at him. 'We're staying here?'

'James has already rung ahead and booked us in. There weren't any rooms at his place.'

'When did he do that?'

'You were in the bathroom. Are you coming?'

Narcifer got wet while he waited for her to climb out of the car. He took her arm and helped her upright. They didn't have much baggage—in the end, Macy had just dropped a few clothes into her gym bag. Narcifer had already taken that from the boot, and it was slung over his shoulder.

'I'm going to wait out here while you check us in,' he said, pushing open the door and ushering her inside out of the rain.

She was too tired to care whether anyone was bothered about him being a Jelvia, but she went inside to find reception. A round-faced woman handed over the room key and told her the restaurant and bar opening times. Macy nodded politely and then followed her directions towards the lift. Then, when the woman had gone, Macy doubled back to Narcifer and let him in.

Usually, sneaking Narcifer in would have them giggling like children, but they were very sombre as they rode the lift to their room. It wasn't like the Rose; it was just an ordinary room, but it had everything they would need.

Macy eyed the double bed. She wasn't sure if she could share it with Narcifer. She wasn't sure what she felt about him at all. Everything felt numb.

Narcifer pulled her coat off her shoulders and hung it up in the wardrobe. 'Why don't you have a bath or shower while I find us some food?'

Macy nodded. A bath sounded wonderful.

Narcifer picked up the key she had dropped on the desk by all the power points. This particular hotel was obviously frequented by businesspeople.

'Back soon,' he said, but Macy grabbed his hand as he was about to leave, suddenly anxious about being separated from him. She still loved him despite everything—despite the last six years being a lie. Narcifer looked at her, hope flaring in his black eyes.

Macy let him go without speaking. Her words had dried up, and he turned and left her alone in the room. Macy closed her eyes. She loved him. The committee hadn't induced or prevented her feelings for him. If they had, surely her feelings would have worn off the moment she woke up.

Still feeling confused, she ran a bath and was lying among the bubbles when she heard Narcifer returning. She didn't shout out to him as she usually would, and he didn't call out to her either. She sank down, wanting to stay there forever, but she knew she owed him a proper explanation. She pulled the plug and stood, reaching for a towel.

Macy came out of the bathroom wearing fresh clothes—her only fresh clothes. She'd towel-dried her hair, and it lay damp about her shoulders. Narcifer had put the TV on, and movie credits were rolling to the soundtrack of *The Greatest Showman*. Macy loved that movie.

Narcifer pointed to two pizza boxes. 'I even paid with real money,' he said, giving her a tentative smile.

She smiled back. 'Thanks,' she said. She felt shy like she didn't know him anymore.

'I'm not going to bite,' he said as she hovered outside the bathroom.

'No, no, of course not,' she said, pushing into action. 'Pizza smells so good. What sort did you get?'

'I just pointed to the menu,' he said as she opened one of the boxes. It was pepperoni. She sat on the bed, her back against the headboard with the pizza box on her lap, pulled a slice off, and tried to make appreciative noises as she bit into it. Narcifer sat eating the other pizza at the desk. Neither spoke as they ate.

Macy was surprised to find that she could eat most of the pizza. Finally, she closed the box, and predictably, Narcifer took it from her and ate her leftovers. She smiled.

'This is the end for us, isn't it?' Narcifer asked suddenly.

Macy's smile vanished. She began to answer him, but all that came from her mouth was a sob. She covered her face with her hands, and then Narcifer was beside her, putting his arms around her and gathering her close.

She sobbed against him, feeling utterly distraught and already grieving. She cried hard against him as he held her, occasionally stroking her hair. Macy couldn't contain herself. She felt wretched, but she knew she had to explain. She pulled away from him, sliding from his arms to go back into the bathroom, where she pulled off some toilet tissue and blew her nose.

Coming back out, she leaned against the wall and watched Narcifer. He was still sitting on the bed where she'd left him. He looked at her, his eyes dry and bottomless, seemingly without expression, but she knew his emotion was very much there. He was feeling as wretched as she was.

'We are both victims, you and I,' she said, watching as he moved from the bed to sit back at the desk. It was as if he knew she wouldn't sit on the bed while he was there. She felt cold suddenly. She sat back on the bed and tucked her feet beneath the duvet. 'While you were kidnapped, Calder told me he thought you were working with the committee to find Aldarn. And I must admit, it seemed strange how obsessed you had become with him. And then there was all this with James—which I understand now.' Macy finished on a bit of a shudder—the residue of her earlier sobbing.

'I did what I thought I had to do,' he said.

Macy nodded. 'I get it, and it's all straightforward, really. James and Aldarn have woken up, but Aldarn has been told he's mad, which he believes. James knows he's next on the list to die but feels he owes it to the world to reveal what he's found out. The WUMs are doing so badly at it.'

'The WUMs have got to you,' he said. It wasn't a question.

Macy shook her head. 'I realised it was all connected—the
WUMs, Aldarn, and James. And the more I researched WUMs, the
more it all tied together. I met Phil Zmin and Oliver, the group
leaders—'

'Hey, what? You *met* them? When?'

'Monday, I think. I don't know what day of the week it is.' She
rubbed her head. She lowered her hand and saw Narcifer's all-black
eyes flash, and a muscle in his jaw pulsated as his annoyance flared.
'I know you didn't want me to meet them without you, but you
weren't there. At the time, I felt they might have had something to
do with your kidnap, or at least could give me answers to why you
were kidnapped.'

'And now they've converted you to their way of thinking.'

'No! I didn't believe them at all. I thought Phil was a nasty,
manipulative woman taking advantage of Oliver, who clearly has or
had mental health issues.'

Narcifer rubbed his face. 'Oh, Macy,' he said. 'I can't lose you to
the WUMs. Anything else I can deal with.'

'Jelvias came to Earth on 9th March, six years ago,' she said, her
voice soft. 'Your technology clouded our brains, making us believe
that you were native to this planet. Your spaceships are dotted
around the Atlantic and Arctic Oceans. We don't know why you're
here. Probably to kill us and take over the planet. But some of you
have morals, so you've built groups, like the group Calder made, to
kill criminals instead.'

Narcifer sighed. He grabbed a glass from the shelf, which housed
the kettle and the complimentary sachets. Macy heard the cold tap
run when he disappeared into the bathroom. He came back, sipping
the water.

'You've joined a cult,' he said.

Macy shook her head. 'We have been made to believe that you
are the superior race and that our population is declining. We

believed the inevitable next stage was Jelvias taking over Earth's reign. Jelvias wanted a smooth transition. They didn't want to kill us all because we drive the world so well. You have a ready-made home with us working for you.'

'Babe,' he said, putting the glass down and coming to sit on the bed beside her. He took her hand. 'I was born on the island between Cornwall and Cork in Ireland to my mum and dad. I was the only child. My mum's sister fell pregnant with Calder, and you know the rest of that story. What you believe is not true. None of it.'

'Describe your parents,' she said.

Narcifer's face went blank.

'You can't because they don't exist. Memories have been implanted into your mind, just like they've been implanted in ours. There are so many things I catch you doing and saying that makes no sense. For instance, that money in your wallet is all fake money and stolen credit cards. You bought cat food, thinking it was food for human consumption. You hadn't heard of birthdays, didn't understand Christmas. And because of this *fake* terror humans have, you've never been challenged. That's the masterstroke,' she said with a humourless laugh. 'We're so terrified of you that you can practically do what you like.'

Narcifer pulled away from her and stood up. He went to stand at the window; the view was almost obscured by a leafless tree.

'I think some high-up people have woken up, and that's why the police are watching Keats. I think that's why the government have instructed the media not to print anything negative about Jelvias,' Macy said.

The TV was running the news. It showed protesters crowding the streets somewhere in the Midlands. The signs they carried said WAKE UP or JELVIAS ARE ALIENS. There was a lot of noise and jostling, and then some of the demonstrators threw rocks at parked cars and shop windows until it looked like a full-on riot.

She glanced at Narcifer. He'd turned and was watching the TV as well. He grabbed the remote and turned the volume down.

'They're getting desperate,' she said, watching him.

'I have no memories of being an alien,' he said.

'Where's Itor?'

He frowned at her. 'Itor?'

'Doesn't that mean anything to you?'

'Should it?'

'You mentioned it once.'

'Now you're analysing everything I say?'

Macy ignored his question. 'When you first came home after being kidnapped, you insisted that I—our life here—was a dream. You insisted I was a simulation. You were very confused.'

'I still am.'

'What does "Kraovo sa" mean?'

He shrugged.

'"Pounit un"?'

'Macy, stop. It's all rubbish!' he said, exasperated.

'You kept repeating those phrases when you came back.'

'I had violent dreams because of the drug they injected me with. I confused the dreams with real life.'

Macy shook her head. 'They aren't dreams, Narcifer. They're memories.'

FORTY-FIVE

Macy woke up slowly.

When they had gone to bed, they'd placed rolled-up towels down the centre of the bed. But now the towels had vanished, and Macy was on her side with her head on Narcifer's naked chest. Her leg was curled around one of his, and her arm was looped around his waist. Narcifer had an arm around her shoulders, holding her close. It was as if, in the night, they'd come together instinctively.

She moved carefully, untangling her body from his without waking him. It was still dark. She rolled over and glanced at the digital clock on the TV. It was the early hours of the morning. Macy groaned. Now she felt wide awake and couldn't sleep though she probably needed to.

'Kraovo sa,' Narcifer said.

Macy looked across at him, realising what had awoken her. He was dreaming again. She grabbed her phone and pressed the video button. It was dark, so she wouldn't get much visual, but she didn't want to disturb Narcifer by putting on any lights.

He rolled over, taking the duvet with him. Macy got out of bed. She was wearing her underwear and a T-shirt. She sat at the desk with her phone still rolling the video.

'Kraovo sa! Kraovo! Mu mizule! Mu!' He flipped onto his back. 'Kraovo Macy.'

Macy started at her name but continued to record him. His outline was only slightly visible.

'Kraovo, please kraovo. Wake up, for fuck's sake, pounit un! Kraovo us all.' His voice drifted, becoming quieter, and Macy thought his dream was over, but then he began shouting again. There was even more urgency in his voice.

'Pounit un! Wake up! Pounit un!' he shouted, leaving her with no doubt about what he meant. His subconscious was telling him to wake up.

Her teeth chattered with fear, and her hands shook as she held the phone, but she continued to film. Then Narcifer settled and became quiet, giving gentle little snores every now and then.

Macy turned off her phone and crawled back into bed. She stared at the ceiling, watching the little blinking light of the smoke detector. Finally, she closed her eyes but didn't think she'd fall asleep again.

Daylight was creeping in through the curtains when she opened her eyes. She looked across the bed for Narcifer, but his side was empty. Then she heard the shower from the bathroom. She sat up, flattening her hair, and swung her legs out of bed. Standing, she drew back the curtains and opened the window a little. It felt stuffy in the room. Through the leafless branches of the tree that obscured much of the view, Macy could see the rain had cleared. It looked brighter outside.

Moving towards the kettle to switch it on, she thought of Narcifer's strange dream last night. It had scared her. His subconscious was begging him to wake up.

She pulled out her phone as the kettle boiled and rewatched the video. There was nothing to see. If she looked hard enough she could make out the black-on-black image of Narcifer in bed, but it wasn't the visual that was important.

The kettle clicked off as Macy came to the end of the video. The footage still terrified her. Putting her phone down, she made two coffees and took hers back to bed. She put it on the side table and reached for her notebook from her gym bag. It was the same notebook where she'd written Jon Johnsen's phone number on the front all those months ago. It seemed years ago now. She pulled out a pen just as Narcifer came out of the bathroom with a towel wrapped around his waist. His body was spectacular; he would outshine any model gracing the cover of a magazine. Her body reacted to him, but it wasn't just physical. It was mental, too. She was drawn to *him*. Drawn to Narcifer, not a Jelvia. The committee hadn't grown those emotions. They'd come naturally.

'Hi,' she said and smiled at him.

His answering smile was hesitant, and she could hardly blame him for being cautious.

'I've made you a coffee,' she said, pointing to it with her pen. 'How'd you sleep? Any dreams?'

'Yeah, lots. I don't think I slept much, actually.'

'Describe them,' she said.

He picked up his coffee and sat on the edge of the bed. He nodded towards her pen, poised above the notebook. 'I'm being interviewed?'

'Just humour me, and try to describe your dreams.'

'I was being interrogated by the committee.'

'What did the committee look like?'

He pulled a face and then sipped his coffee. 'I don't know; I didn't see them. I never see them.'

'Were they hurting you?'

'All I know is it was very unpleasant.'

'And the islands, can you describe them?'

'They're similar to here. Trees, roads, houses, all surrounded by the ocean.' He frowned, and his eyes took on a faraway look. 'It's dim.'

'Dim? As in lacking light?'

Narcifer nodded. He took a sip of his coffee. 'That's exactly what I mean. It isn't bright like it is here. You're writing this down?'

Macy glanced up, sucking the end of the pen. 'I certainly am. Describe the trees. The leaf colour, that sort of thing,' she said, expecting him to describe the rainbow trees he noticed in her magazine.

'Just ordinary trees. They don't have any leaves.' She caught him looking out of the window. She glanced around to see the tree outside. It was a proud oak tree with bare branches reaching for the winter sun. She jotted her observation down in the notebook. Then reached for her coffee.

'Interview over already?' Narcifer asked.

'If there's anything else you can remember, please tell me,' she said, ignoring his snark. She couldn't blame him. He was a victim, just like the entire human race.

'I told James you'd text him when we're ready to meet up,' Narcifer said, as if wary of the conversation. He finished the rest of his coffee, then stood up and put his cup on the bedside table. 'I think we should head to where Calder's car was found.'

'It's a good place to start,' she said and watched him head into the bathroom. He'd barely looked at her, but what did she expect?

He came out a moment later, fully dressed.

FORTY-SIX

Macy checked out of the hotel while Narcifer waited in the car. He was back behind the steering wheel. In silence, he drove them to the car park where they'd parked yesterday. The tide was out, and the little boat lay stranded on the seabed. Squawking seagulls fought over the beached fish.

'We've time to get breakfast,' Narcifer said, and Macy couldn't stop a smile. He was always thinking about his stomach. She looked at him and was about to say something when he pushed open the car door and walked down the coastal path without waiting for her.

She followed him. It was a bright, sunny day. The rain and wind from yesterday might never have been. It was still cold, though, especially as the chill from the ocean rose to blanket them.

'Aren't you waiting for me?' Macy called to him, trying to keep up with his long stride.

He stopped and half turned. 'I didn't think you'd want to be seen with me, considering...'

'Considering what?'

He shrugged. 'That I'm an alien.' He turned and walked away again, but his stride slowed, allowing her to catch up. She walked behind him, glaring at his back. He was being childish.

The little café was open, but they couldn't risk Narcifer going inside, so Macy went in alone, and Narcifer found a bench overlooking the beach. Macy ordered bacon and sausage rolls and two coffees. She took them to Narcifer and sat next to him on the seat, handing him his food. There was a distance between them. It had been there yesterday too, but now it was a vacuum.

They ate in silence—a silence that hurt.

'I'm sorry,' she said at last. 'I've handled this all wrong.'

Narcifer screwed up his rubbish and aimed it at the rubbish bin. The litter dropped in smoothly. He picked up his coffee, his gaze catching hers.

'And I'm not handling it at all,' he admitted. He turned to watch the ocean and sipped his coffee.

'Do you want space?'

'I don't want you to leave my sight,' he said. He reached across to squeeze Macy's hand, which lay limply on her lap, but let go just as quickly.

'I know you think I'm crazy,' she said, 'but can you just believe that *I* believe you came here six years ago?' She watched him close his eyes to his frustration. 'I trusted you all that time ago in the cave, remember? So now I'm asking you to trust *me*.'

Narcifer opened his eyes and looked at her. 'And why can't *you* trust *me* when I tell you I'm not an alien? I've lived on Earth all my life; my *family* have lived on Earth all *their* lives.'

Macy reached into her pocket and brought out her mobile phone. 'Your dream last night... I recorded your words. There's not much to see, but will you listen?'

Narcifer looked from her phone up to her face. 'You recorded me shouting out a few strange words?'

'You admitted you had a bad dream last night, and the words you shouted are a mixture of English and Itor. Or whatever.'

Narcifer grunted, and Macy found the recording and pressed the play button. Then she turned up the volume.

'*Kraovo sa! Kraovo! Mu mizule! Mu!*' Narcifer's voice came from the dark screen. '*Kraovo Macy.*' Macy watched Narcifer's face as her phone continued to spill out words. '*Kraovo, please kraovo. Wake up, for fuck's sake, pounit un! Kraovo us all. Pounit un! Wake un! Pounit un!*'

Narcifer continued to sip his coffee, and Macy turned the phone off. He looked calm when she glanced at him, but her leg was jiggling again. She rested her hand on it to hold it still.

'Yesterday, when I spoke to Courtney, I asked her to repeat "kraovo sa" and "pounit un" to Aldarn. So, hopefully, we'll find out what they mean,' she said when he still hadn't spoken.

'They're just words! Idiotic nonsense—talking in my sleep!' he spat. He was frustrated, angry that the world he loved and wanted was imploding, and hurt that she was the one causing the crash. They fell into silence again.

'I'm sorry,' Macy said when the silence had stretched into agony.

'Play it again,' Narcifer said.

Macy pressed play, then got up and walked away a short distance to give Narcifer space. When the short video ended, she turned around. His eyes were on her.

'You shouted "wake up" in English in your sleep,' she said. 'Even your subconscious is trying to get you to wake up.'

Narcifer gave a hollow laugh.

She came and sat back down, not putting any space between them this time. She took his hand. 'There were ten spaceships—space pods, really; not big enough to be called ships. One was guided in by Johnsen and his team but finally destroyed. The rest, pretty much, is as you remember it. Except James tried to *rescue* the occupants of the tenth spaceship. He isn't the enemy, Narce. Calder and Aldarn aren't either. And I know you don't believe James and me yet, but you will. And when that time comes, I want to be there for you because the truth will hurt. Well, it's hurting already, isn't it?'

He stared intensely at the ocean. 'I feel like everyone is the enemy at the moment,' he said.

'I know.'

Narcifer pulled his hand free from hers and stood up. He began walking down to the shoreline. He tossed his empty coffee cup in the bin on the way.

'Do you want to be alone?' she called.

Narcifer looked back and then shook his head. Feeling relieved, Macy followed him. She threw her litter into the same bin, and a hovering seagull swooped down to investigate.

Hurrying after Narcifer, Macy didn't see the rock hidden beneath the sand. Her toe hit it, and she lost her balance. She didn't have time to make any noise, but Narcifer caught her before she hit the ground. He righted her, his hands resting on her upper arms until he was sure she had her balance.

'You will always be there for me, won't you?' she asked, grabbing his wrists and stopping him from moving away. She searched his eyes. 'My hero.'

'Do you remember last year when we first met?' he said suddenly.

Macy remembered it very well. The summer had been long and hot. They'd walked hand in hand along the coastline, horsed around in the sea, built sandcastles, and made love in a sandy spot sheltered from everyone else. Back then, everything seemed simple. She'd loved Narcifer, and he loved her. It *was* simple.

'I remember,' she said. 'It was magical.'

'It still is magical to me. I could never quite believe that you could have loved someone like me.'

There was a lump in Macy's throat as she acknowledged he'd spoken in the past tense. She couldn't talk. She nodded instead.

Macy *did* love him. She could just never have him. He didn't belong to her; he didn't belong to this world. And however much it hurt, she had to make him believe it.

'Without looking, what colour is the ocean?' she said.

'What?'

'Humour me.'

'I seem to be doing that a lot lately.' He had his back to the sea, but in front of him was a peeling billboard of a brilliant blue ocean, with a grinning surfer riding high on a white wave. Macy had seen it, and now she waited for Narcifer's answer.

'Blue,' he said. 'It's bright blue with white waves.'

The sea behind him was a flat iron grey. He was either describing what he believed or the image on the billboard had settled in his subconscious. The wind buffeted her, and Narcifer pulled up her hood and held it tight around her neck as he stared into her eyes. She looked up at him. His all-black eyes glittered with emotion.

'I'm wrong, aren't I?' he asked.

She nodded.

'It's the committee's technology. It's malfunctioning. People are waking up, and Jelvias' memories are distorting. I'm scared of what's around the corner for us—for *you*.'

Narcifer turned around, and they both looked at the sea. A light wind scattered debris across the path to collect against the beach wall.

'The light in your eyes... it happens a lot. I thought it was passion, emotion or something, but it's not, is it?' She looked at him askance. 'It's the committee talking in your head.'

'Macy, we're not like you. We're Jelvias. We're different... probably too different, after all.'

'You're aliens,' she said, and Narcifer's jaw tightened. He clearly thought she was still delusional, but everything was suddenly clear. Even the clouds seemed brighter.

The sea sparkled, then became blurred as Macy turned to focus on it. She felt her chin tremble.

'Hey,' he said, lifting her chin with his fingers. She looked at him. 'None of this is your fault.'

'I feel like such a bitch,' she said, her eyes filling with tears again.

His mouth quirked in a smile. 'A bitch? That's a dog, right?'

She laughed through her tears, and Narcifer smiled at her. He was trying to make her feel better. He was an alien, but he still loved her.

'You believe what you want. As long as you believe that *I* love you, nothing else matters. I don't even care that you don't love me. And I do trust you, Macy.'

She nodded, tears falling down her face. She stepped forwards and pressed her forehead against his chest. His arms circled her a millisecond later.

'I also remember when we first started to get to know one another,' he said to the top of her head. 'I told you then that you could always walk away. You can still do that if you want. I won't stop you, and I won't hold it against you.'

'I don't *want* to walk away,' she said, looking up at him. 'I love you so much. So much it hurts, and that's why this is all so hard. I don't want to lose you, but it feels like I don't even *have* you to lose.'

A spot of rain fell on her, followed by a few more. She looked up. The sky was mainly blue, apart from a looming grey cloud. Narcifer grabbed her hand as the rain intensified. They ran towards the coastal path and the car park beyond. Macy was out of breath by the time they reached the car. They clambered in.

Inside, they looked at one another.

'You *do* have me,' Narcifer said. 'You have me here.' He touched his chest, where Macy had laid her head so many times to feel his heart beating. 'But what about you? Do I have you?'

'Every time something happens, I say to myself, "Things can't get any worse". First, the hostage situation in the bistro, being pushed from a moving car, you being kidnapped, and now this.' She rubbed her nose with the sleeve of her coat. 'But as long as I have you... as long as we have one another,' she amended, 'I think I could survive anything. Even this.'

She looked down at their hands, clasped together over the handbrake. Narcifer squeezed her hand in his, then raised it to his lips and kissed the back of her hand.

Macy smiled.

They were interrupted by the ringing of Macy's phone.

She checked the screen. 'It's Courtney.' She looked up at Narcifer. 'She might have an answer to the words you shouted in your sleep.'

Narcifer nodded.

Macy answered the phone, and after exchanging greetings, she asked Courtney if she would mind if she put the call on speaker.

'I take it Narcifer is there with you?' Courtney asked.

'I'm here,' Narcifer said, directing his voice towards the phone.

'I still can't forgive you for how you treated me, trying to get Aldarn to speak to you, but I understand why you did it,' she said.

'That's all I can ask for at the moment,' he said. 'But I *am* sorry, Courtney. I did it for the right reasons.'

'You rang to give me an answer to the meaning of those words?' Macy asked.

'When I speak to Aldarn, it's like speaking to a computer glitch. Sometimes his words are English, but sometimes they don't make sense. But anyway, he told me that "kraovo sa" means "help me" and "pounit un" means...' she broke off. But it wasn't theatrical. She sounded like she was struggling. 'It means "wake up".'

It was the confirmation that Macy expected, yet a chill swept over her. She glanced at Narcifer, who looked back at her.

'I also told Aldarn what you told me yesterday,' Courtney continued. 'And... I don't know... I sensed relief from him. The news of the WUMs isn't reaching him, so he doesn't know that the world is waking up. I got the sense that this was a revelation.'

'It sounds like you believe me,' said Macy.

'I haven't woken up, if that's what you're asking. But I have always felt that something odd was happening. And the brats,' she said, referring to her nephews, Harley and Logan, 'have been acting really strange lately. Mel put it down to stress over your accident and probably not wanting to return to school after Christmas, but they keep talking about "the aliens". When Mel questioned them about it, they said the Jelvias were aliens. They aren't upset or anything—they're taking it all in stride. And I suppose Jelvias *have* been here all their lives. But Harley had a history lesson at school where they were learning about the Jelvian involvement in World War Two, and he had to be removed from the lesson. He kept calling the teacher a liar.'

Macy glanced at Narcifer, who was staring out the window. His eyebrows were knitted together, and he looked as if he'd just had terrible news confirmed. Macy reached over and grabbed his hand.

'I think more and more people are going to wake up now,' Courtney continued while Macy and Narcifer stared at one another.

Narcifer smiled, and Macy offered one in return. They were united.

Macy promised Courtney she'd phone again after they spoke to James, then ended the call. She and Narcifer sat in the car, their hands clasped together between the seats, while a fine rain—almost gentle after last night's downpour—obscured their view.

'Whatever happens, I've no regrets,' he said, breaking the silence.

'Me neither. I'm glad we had our time.'

They squeezed one another's hands.

'Look,' Macy said. She pointed to a rainbow. Its colours were bright against the suddenly built-up clouds.

Narcifer peered to look. 'What's that?'

Macy smiled. 'What do you think it is?'

He was silent for a moment. Then he said, 'Hope.'

Don't miss out!

Visit the website below and you can sign up to receive emails whenever T.E Kessler publishes a new book. There's no charge and no obligation.

https://books2read.com/r/B-A-YUTH-UCJRB

BOOKS 2 READ

Connecting independent readers to independent writers.

Also by T.E Kessler

Lightning Source UK Ltd.
Milton Keynes UK
UKHW011846181022
410670UK00004B/207